"SIR, WHAT IS IT YOU WANT FROM ME?"

There was no danger of their being overheard, and yet her whispered voice seemed to boom through Hugo's senses like a cannon.

For once, he was at a loss for words. "I don't know. Everything. Nothing. I know only that for the past five years I have been unable to release you from my imagination. Against your will, without your knowledge or consent, I have held you captive in my mind, Evelyn. I have held you in an embrace you may never feel. I have kissed you—"

"Kiss me now, then," she said so softly he barely heard her. "Or else I shall accuse you of being selfish."

Her lips parted as he lowered his head. He kissed her once, very gently, tentatively, his lips pressing lightly against hers. Then he pulled back from her and stared into her deep blue eyes. He saw in her gaze a startling innocence.

He kissed her again, this time more passionately, and suddenly realized he was kissing a woman who had never been kissed like this before. Evelyn, the Countess of Goreham, was a novice in the ways of seduction.

BOOK YOUR PLACE ON OUR WEBSITE AND MAKE THE READING CONNECTION!

We've created a customized website just for our very special readers, where you can get the inside scoop on everything that's going on with Zebra, Pinnacle and Kensington books.

When you come online, you'll have the exciting opportunity to:

- View covers of upcoming books
- Read sample chapters
- Learn about our future publishing schedule (listed by publication month *and author*)
- Find out when your favorite authors will be visiting a city near you
- Search for and order backlist books from our online catalog
- Check out author bios and background information
- Send e-mail to your favorite authors
- Meet the Kensington staff online
- Join us in weekly chats with authors, readers and other guests
- Get writing guidelines
- AND MUCH MORE!

Visit our website at
http://www.zebrabooks.com

THE BEDEVILED BARRISTER

Bess Willingham

Zebra Books
Kensington Publishing Corp.

http://www.zebrabooks.com

ZEBRA BOOKS are published by

Kensington Publishing Corp.
850 Third Avenue
New York, NY 10022

First Printing: December, 1998
10 9 8 7 6 5 4 3 2 1

Printed in the United States of America

For Frank W. Hunger—I love you.
And for Hugh P. Taylor, my most constant
and bedeviled friend—I love you, too.

Prologue

The third-floor parlor of Widow Letitia Philpott's Georgian town house thrummed with all the excitement of an unlicensed gambling hell. Scrupulously watching the punters at her faro table, the widow wedged herself into the small space between the dealer and Lord Henry Goreham, an elderly rake whom she'd known biblically at a time when powdered wigs were the rage.

Her black bombazine gown boasted an incongruously low neckline. Her vast décolletage resembled mounds of well-aged Stilton cheese. Yet the widow possessed a keen sense of observation.

She scrutinized the lone female at the opposite end of the table, a pretty young blonde playing dangerously deep. Then, her gaze scanned the men fringing the green baize-covered table. Skipping over the half-dozen or so military officers on leave from Spain, her stare was arrested by a handsome man with solemn, grey eyes, a broad forehead, and russet-colored hair.

Widow Philpott noted his clenched jaw, the total concentration that burned behind his eyes. Occasionally, he stole glances at the blond lady across the table. Her mien was equally unfrivolous; she seemed to have nerves of steel, but she bit her bottom lip like a schoolgirl. They were a strange pair, those two, not the usual sort of daring gamester that frequented Letitia's drawing room.

Beside her, the dealer re-shuffled.

The soldiers, enjoying a respite from the intensity of the game, relaxed their posture, clacked ivory chits and drained glasses of contraband Bordeaux. Lord Goreham remained unbending, his hawkish gaze pinned to every movement of the dealer's supple fingers. The russet-haired man, his muscles flexing beneath a snug black cutaway coat, gripped the edge of the table with white knuckles, staring grimly at the depleted mound of chips before him.

As for the young lady, her serious expression repelled any familiarities the men surrounding her might otherwise have risked. Widow Philpott wondered what she was about; she possessed the air of refinement that good breeding bestowed, while lacking the fine clothes of an elegant lady. To top it off, she wagered as recklessly as Georgina, the Duchess of Devonshire.

Having thoroughly shuffled the cards, the dealer fanned them, face down on the table. Then he inserted the deck, face upward, into a small wooden card-box, or shoe. The punters quickly laid their bets, distributing chits and pound notes among the thirteen cards painted on the green baize. A chit laid on a painted card was a bet that card would win, or be left face up in the shoe on *any given turn*. A penny—or copper—laid atop the chit represented a bet that the same card would lose, or be dealt *first and laid on the table*.

Miss Evelyn Waring sent up a silent prayer. Her heart skittered as she reached across the table, placing chits among the various cards emblazoned on the felt. She was well ahead for the evening, but the evening was young. And she hadn't won enough to leave the game. She needed three times her original stake in order to raise enough blunt to send her younger sister Celeste to Bath. She had doubled her original bet. She needed one more winning shoe before she quit the game.

In total, Evelyn laid seven bets on the table, leaving ivory markers on three numbers, coppering her bets on four others. Hers was a risky wager, considering the first turn had yet to be played.

As the dealer discarded the top—or soda—card, sliding it to one side of the table, Evelyn scanned the faces surrounding the faro table. Despite her jangled nerves, one face caught her interest.

He watched the cards intently. Half-listening to the conversation of the men surrounding her, Evelyn learned that he was a barrister from Lincoln's Inn. But there was something about the tall, broad-shouldered gentleman that set him apart from the men encircling the table. Evelyn thought he hadn't taken notice of her at all, so intently was his attention riveted to the cards being played.

Perhaps it was his seriousness that intrigued her. The man's high forehead, accentuated by a hairline slightly thinning at the temples, connoted a deep intellect, perhaps even a brooding nature. And his grey eyes, so mercurial and shrewd as they watched the dealer's nimble fingers, bespoke an introspective nature quite foreign to the rowdy soldiers jostling his granite-hewn shoulders.

Evelyn shifted her attention to the game. The dealer pushed a card through the narrow slit at the top of the shoe, and laid it on the table. Evelyn noted the denomination of the winning card left face up in the box. She reminded herself that she couldn't afford to lose her concentration. Celeste's health depended upon her winning.

As play continued, Evelyn kept track of which cards were played, and which remained in the deck. She recorded the winning and losing cards by penciling O's and X's on the small paper cupped in her hand.

When one turn was left to be played, Evelyn had nearly tripled her original stake. While most at the table had suffered poor luck, she'd enjoyed a lucky streak. She had only to win the last turn to ensure that her sister would spend the cold winter months in Bath.

Unsuppressed excitement buzzed the table as the other men, or at least those who'd been attentive enough to keep track of the cards played, worked out the odds in their head. Quickly scanning her note paper, Evelyn determined that the three cards remaining in the last turn were Queen, Jack and Ace.

"Call the turn!" Widow Philpott cried.

The stakes were high, and most of the men scooped up their wagers, preferring to avoid such a risky bet. But, Evelyn could not afford to lose. Nor could she afford to bet conservatively. She knew how much money she needed, and what she had to do to get that money. In her mind, anything short of the amount it would take to get Celeste to Bath was meaningless. In the past week, the child's racking cough had worsened, and the doctor was adamant that the child's only hope for survival was in taking the curative mineral waters at Bath.

When the dealer's gaze fell on her, Evelyn lifted her chin. "A *paix-paroli* on Ace, Jack, Queen." Her quiet voice belied the anxiety that plagued her stomach.

If the cards came out of the shoe in the order Evelyn predicted, she would win six times her original stake. If they came out in any other order, she would lose everything.

Only three punters remained at the table with bets in play. One was the unsmiling, elderly gentleman at the end of the table. The other was the handsome barrister directly across from Evelyn. Hesitating, he reached into the pocket of his waistcoat, withdrew a small leather pouch, and unfolded a wad of paper currency.

The din in the room faded to a prickly silence. "Jack, Queen, ace to hock," he said, as he methodically placed his money on the table.

Evelyn watched in amazement as he laid enough blunt on the green baize to support a family of four for half a decade. Had she not been so far out on a limb herself, she might have considered counseling him to show some restraint.

He straightened, his money spent. Then, he turned and his gaze locked with Evelyn's. Apprehension wrapped its icy grip around her heart as she recognized the desperation—or was it hunger?—in his eyes.

There were other barristers from Lincoln's Inn at the table. They gathered round their colleague, and urged him to take up his money, to think twice about what he was doing. The frivolity had gone out of their chatter. They stared at their companion with concern and interest; everyone knew they were about to witness either the financial ruin of an up and coming jurist, or the lightning-quick bestowal of tremendous wealth on a daring gamester.

Widow Philpott shoved off from her place between the old man and the dealer. She sauntered toward the young barrister, sidling up beside him.

"Are you quite certain you want to lay such a large bet, Sir Hugo?" she asked.

Evelyn thought it strange that the older woman would question the barrister's bet. Chances were, he would lose. Widow Philpott's faro bank would be engorged by the amount of blunt he lost.

But the widow's actions were soon explained. She made a shelf of her bosom, resting it on Sir Hugo's arm. Then, she ran her fingers through the hair at his temples. Rising on her toes, she whispered something in his ear that drew a flush to his cheeks and a frown to his lips.

Sir Hugo clutched the edge of the table in a white-knuckled death grip. With a grimace, he shook his head, shrugging off the older woman's advances.

Unable to look away, Evelyn was fascinated. But she was embarrassed when the barrister looked at her, and caught her staring. Still, she met his gaze head on, and a tiny explosion of awareness burst inside her. His eyes were so full of hurt and want. His high forehead was well creased, his jaw was carved in stone. Beneath the glow of the chandeliers, the man's hair shone coppery at the sides of his head.

After a beat, he smiled, but not with his lips. Crinkles deepened at the corners of his grey eyes as he held Evelyn's gaze. Something too hallowed for words, something indescribable and magnetic, passed between them. It was an awareness of shared pain—bone deep and heartfelt. A tear came to Evelyn's eye, but she quickly brushed it away. Whatever tragedy the young barrister had suffered, it compared not a whit to the one she lived each day.

The elderly gentleman at the far end of the table cleared his throat. "Ace, Queen and Jack to chase," he said gruffly, tossing a handful of chits on the table.

With a huff, Widow Philpott left the barrister's side and returned to her place beside the older man. It was clear she knew him intimately. "A kiss for luck, Lord Goreham," she said, and he bent so that she could give him a sloppy kiss on his sunken cheek.

Lord Goreham's mouth barely turned up at the corners. But he slanted the woman a lascivious look. "Save your sweet talk for the pigeons, Letitia. I'm too old to think there's more pleasure in the bedroom than in a gambling parlor."

"When you were younger, you weren't afraid to take your chances in my boudoir," she shot back.

"Which only goes to show what a foolhardy gamester I was! Well, at least you can never accuse me of going skinny on my gambling debts—I never ran out on you, did I, Letitia?" The old man let out a harsh bark of laughter, then nudged the woman with his elbow. "Now, let us get on with it."

Hands propped on hips, the widow turned to the dealer. "Deal the cards!"

Tension thickened the air. The young barrister's acquaintances leaned over the table, open-mouthed and mesmerized. Sir Hugo, eyes deepened by purplish bruises, forehead dotted with perspiration, stood rigid. Evelyn's gaze flitted round the table. She was afraid to watch the cards, terrified that they might not emerge from the shoe in the sequence she'd predicted. Of the three remaining punters, only Lord Goreham seemed unperturbed. He grunted his satisfaction as the first card was exposed.

"Ace," the dealer said.

Sir Hugo was out of the game. With one fell swoop, his entire wager was forfeit, his money raked off the table by the croupier.

Evelyn detected only the slightest tightening of the young man's lips as his eyes met hers. The passing of time was suspended while another wave of awareness shimmered between them. Fellow barristers consoled Sir Hugo with claps on the back and condolences.

"Good try, old man," they refrained. And, "Better luck next time." Among them, there seemed to be the attitude that losing such a huge amount of money was regrettable, but something which an out-and-outer learned to cope with.

Amid the din of his companion's voices, Sir Hugo looked at Evelyn, and mouthed the words, "Good luck to you."

Her heart hammered in her chest. She glanced at the old man at the far end of the table, then returned her gaze to the cards.

The dealer dealt the next card. "Queen!"

Her stomach fell to the floor. She was out, and as her bets were scraped off the table, her sister's chances at recovery vanished. Her knees wobbled while a light-headedness overtook her. The elderly gentleman had called the sequence of cards correctly, and, for his wager, earned an obscene return. The croupier's rake pushed mounds of chits toward him as the on-lookers cheered his good fortune.

The room spun wildly beneath Evelyn's feet. Her humiliation was complete. Not only had she lost her entire meager fortune—and meager it was, consisting of her father's pension, paid to him in exchange for losing his life alongside Wellington in Spain—but she'd also ruined her sister's chances for convalescence. What a mess she'd made of things!

A curtain of blackness descended. The last thing Evelyn remembered was a pair of strong arms encircling her waist as her feet left the carpet.

Her senses returned in a cloud of confusion. Slowly, Evelyn struggled back to consciousness, her eyes blinking against the glare of a single taper held aloft. Scanning her surroundings, she self-consciously smoothed the bodice of her plain, dark blue woolen gown. She felt very vulnerable lying on a bed, her head propped on pillows, in what was obviously the Widow Philpott's *boudoir*.

The room faded into view. See-through negligees draped the top of a tole screen in the corner. Animal skin rugs topped the worn Axminster carpets. An oil painting of a Rubenesque nude decorated the wall opposite the bed.

Widow Philpott sat on the edge of the mattress, her pie-shaped face smeared with concern. Lord Goreham and Sir Hugo stood behind the widow.

Evelyn's gaze followed the candle's flame as Widow Philpott passed it to Sir Hugo. The older woman laid her palm on Evelyn's forehead.

"She's all right. Too much excitement, and the disappointment of losing so much blunt, that's all. Perhaps your undergarments are a tad too restrictive as well, eh, girlie?"

Evelyn's cheeks blazed at the impertinence of such a question. And in front of two men, as well! She pushed herself onto her elbows, eager to stand and flee Widow Philpott's faro house as quickly as possible. But, the room tilted when she lifted her head, and all she could do was sink back into the pillows. A sickly moan escaped her lips as a wave of nausea passed over her. Hardly surprising, given that she hadn't eaten in two days. There had been barely enough food for Celeste, and she hadn't wanted to deprive the child of a single crumb of sustenance.

"If you wouldn't mind, Mrs. Philpott," Sir Hugo said,

grasping the woman's elbow. "Perhaps I can be of some assistance."

The widow stood, and allowed the barrister to take her place on the edge of the mattress. Leaning over Evelyn, Sir Hugo grasped her hand and wound his fingers around hers. "I've had some experience in matters such as these, I'm afraid," he said. "You see, I'm the oldest of five, and all my younger siblings were females. Fainting wasn't such an unheard-of experience in our home, I can assure you."

Evelyn's fingers tightened around his, and a surge of warmth flowed through her veins. Sir Hugo's eyes smiled through a veil of weariness. Something about the texture of his skin, the prominence of his nose, appealed to her. His jaw was shadowed by a coppery bristle. Evelyn smiled back at him, strangely relieved to be in his care, if only temporarily.

But, thoughts of her predicament—and that of her sister's—returned with a vengeance. Without warning, Evelyn was reminded of the precariousness of Celeste's health. Uncoiling her fingers from Sir Hugo's, she turned her head to the side, suddenly embarrassed and terrified at having lost every penny she owned. She had no family, no fortune and no protector. In one impulsive, impetuous gamble, she'd lost what paltry funds she had. Now, Celeste would never get to Bath, never partake of the curative waters which might have restored her health. Hot tears threatened to gush from behind her blinking eyelids, but Evelyn bit her lip and staved them off.

"Whatever is the matter?" When Sir Hugo leaned over her, the scent of him—dense and masculine—surrounded Evelyn. "Why, dear child, you look as if you have lost your last friend."

She covered her face with her hands. How could she tell him what she'd done? Why should she, in fact? He would think her actions abominable, and there was very little chance he'd have an ounce of sympathy for her.

He pried her hands from her face and, cupping her

chin, turned her face toward him. His expression held a
depth of emotion, emotion of a sort that Evelyn thought
only women could feel. To see such compassion and poign-
ancy strain Sir Hugo's rugged features was shocking,
indeed.

Perhaps she *could* tell him what she'd done! For a
moment, Evelyn stared into his grey eyes, wondering
whether he might understand her dilemma. Dare she confide in him? Dare she trust him?

From the other side of the room, seated at her vanity
table, Widow Philpott spoke impatiently. "Come on, now,
gel. I cannot have you sacked out in my bed all night. If
you're well enough to stand, I'll see to it that you're put
in a hackney cab and sent on your way. I'll even pay for
it, seeing as how you've gambled so deep and lost so dearly.
'Tis the least I can do."

The old man, silent until now, turned and shot the widow
a withering look. "The least is all you ever do, Letitia. For
God's sake, get the chit a cup of tea, why don't you? Or
something more fortifying, like a glass of brandy . . . yes,
that's what she needs."

As the widow left the room, the elderly lord turned his
gaze on Evelyn's half-prostrate figure. His rheumy eyes slid
over her, from the tips of her bedraggled slippers to the
top of her head, lingering on certain parts in between,
and making Evelyn decidedly nervous.

"Care to tell us why you fainted?" Sir Hugo crossed one
long, booted leg over another, and stared expectantly at
her. "I'm a good listener, believe it or not. And before I
see you put in a cab and sent trundling into the night, I'd
like to assure myself that you're going to be all right."

It was quite easy to see that he'd been the older brother
to a pack of girls. He wore an expression that encouraged
confidences, and lacked totally in condemnation or judgment. Evelyn had the comforting sensation that she could
tell him anything.

It was also quite easy to forget the presence of the tall,

gaunt figure looming at the bedside. Avoiding Lord Goreham's gaze, Evelyn addressed Sir Hugo. "Why, sir, I don't
even know your full name."

He dipped his head. "Sir Hugo Mansfield, at your ser-
vice. Presently of Lincoln's Inn, where I have recently been
called to the bar. And you, ma'am, what is your name?"

"Miss Evelyn Waring." She paused, embarrassed to
admit that she and her sister were residing in temporary
lodgings in a seedy section east of the city proper, much
too close to the docklands to be safe or convenient. Besides,
they wouldn't be there much longer, not since Evelyn had
just lost every penny at the faro table.

Inserted into the silence was the lord's throat-clearing.
Reluctantly, Evelyn and Sir Hugo turned curious looks on
the old man.

"As long as we're making introductions, I am Henry
Dethman, second Earl of Goreham. Pleased to make your
acquaintance, young lady." To Sir Hugo, Lord Goreham
gave the most cursory of nods. Then, the old gentleman
resumed his intent perusal of Evelyn's form and figure.

"You still haven't told me what caused you to faint," Sir
Hugo said.

Evelyn's cheeks burned, and her throat clogged with
emotion. If only that old man weren't staring down at her.
She felt quite certain that she could tell Sir Hugo anything,
just as he promised. *If they were alone, that is.*

And he was a barrister, too. Perhaps Sir Hugo would
know of some way out of her present difficulties. She was
so deep in dun territory that she thought she'd never get
out on her own, but perhaps some clever barrister could
figure out a way to wrangle a larger pension out of the
government. After all, Lieutenant Waring had served quite
bravely in the Peninsular Wars, and received several decorations for saving the lives of his comrades during battle.
Surely, his only surviving heirs were entitled to more than
fifty pounds a year. Why, you could hardly keep a cat alive
on such a small amount. Maybe Sir Hugo could petition the

proper government official for an increase in the stipend Evelyn and Celeste were reduced to living on.

"I suppose it was the excitement of the moment that caused me to faint, sir. Not that I'm the fainting sort. Really, I can't remember when I ever did before. But, losing every penny I owned at a time when my sister—"

"Every penny?" Sir Hugo clasped her hands in his own. "You can't be serious?"

"Surely, you didn't wager every penny you had to your name?" Lord Goreham asked.

She nodded, vigilantly keeping her gaze pinned to Sir Hugo's. His eyes were warm and accepting; Lord Goreham's were watery and sharp. "I am telling the truth. I needed to win, you see, because my sister—"

Her explanation was cut short by Widow Philpott, who appeared at the bedside with a tray in her hands.

"You don't mean to say you lack the funds to pay your debt downstairs, do you?" Setting the tray on the bedside table, the widow shot Evelyn a shrewd look. "You signaled to the croupier that you were betting a *paix-paroli* on the last turn, and therefore you owe the house an additional five thousand pounds. Which must be paid before you leave this establishment, mark my words!"

London Bridge collapsed on Evelyn's chest—or so it seemed to her. "Five thousand pounds! How can that be?"

Widow Philpott had a ready explanation. Had the cards been dealt in the sequence Evelyn predicted, she would have won six times her original stake. Unfortunately, having lost the bet, Evelyn forfeited her original stake, which by the time the last turn was dealt, was nearly triple the amount of money she possessed when she walked into Widow Philpott's. And now the widow demanded she pay her debts to the tune of five thousand pounds. Or else.

"But, madam," Evelyn stammered, sitting up on the side of the bed so that Sir Hugo was obliged to rise to his full height. "I do not have five thousand pounds. 'Struth, I have only the clothes I am wearing on my back, and nothing more.''

Widow Philpott's lips formed a thin, white line. "Well, isn't that fitting and proper? I should have known better, an innocent-looking miss like you! You hadn't any intention of paying your debts if you lost, but you would surely have walked out of here with plump pockets if you won!''

Evelyn leapt to her feet. "That isn't true at all! I had every intention of paying my gambling debts if I lost. It's just that . . . well, I hadn't considered on losing. You see, my sister's very future depends upon—''

Lord Goreham's harsh voice overrode hers. "Well, Miss Waring, it appears to me you have got yourself into something of a bumble broth. However shall you extricate yourself from it?''

The question, rife with suggestion, swept over Evelyn like an arctic blast. However was she going to get out of Widow Philpott's establishment without the blunt to satisfy her debts? And what would the woman do to her if she couldn't pay?

"I'll call the Bow Street runners and tell them you've tried to skip out on a debt. You'll be tossed in Newgate before sun up,'' the widow chortled, as if she could read Evelyn's troubled mind. "And you won't get out until you come up with five thousand pounds to pay me what you owe me.''

Evelyn gasped, her hands flying instinctively to her throat. Sending her to Newgate was tantamount to sentencing her to death. And Celeste, too. Why, the poor child wouldn't have a chance of surviving in this world if Evelyn were sent to debtor's prison.

"Now, wait a minute,'' interjected Sir Hugo. "You've an unlicensed faro house, here, and I seriously doubt you'd expose yourself to the authorities by turning over this green girl for prosecution on a bad debt. 'Twould be suicidal, Mrs. Philpott.''

"Enough of your legal twaddle,'' Lord Goreham said.

"There's a way out of this for the lass, don't you know? She needs five thousand pounds to free herself from the threat of prosecution. Which one of us is going to lend it to her? How 'bout you, Letitia? Care to have the girl about for a couple of years? You can think of some way for her to work off her debt."

"I am not running a house of ill repute," Widow Philpott retorted. "Nor do I want some silly miss underfoot who doesn't know the first thing about wagering—or pretends she doesn't! Thank you, but I intend to leave the rescue of this young damsel to the two of you! And one of you had certainly better rescue her, or else I'll close my doors to you both from this night on."

Lord Goreham's bony chin jutted in Sir Hugo's direction. "How 'bout you, young man? Care to invest five thousand pounds in a risky venture? I daresay, that's a *steal* considering how pretty she is. She'd make a fine wife for the likes of you, if you can cure her of her penchant for gambling."

Evelyn's heart went cold. Her gaze swung to Sir Hugo's, and what she saw behind those steel grey eyes chilled her to the bone. The light behind his eyes had died; his features had hardened in a mask of inscrutable detachment.

She pleaded with her eyes, silently begging him to buy her out of this horrid mess.

The night-crier passed on the street below, his bellow splitting the nervous silence like a fog-horn. But, Evelyn couldn't tear her gaze from Sir Hugo's. She couldn't imagine how a man who'd held her fingers so tenderly, and soothed her with the kindest words spoken in the most velvety tone, could so quickly turn to ice. Had his comforting words been the prelude to a raw seduction? Had he been meaning to rob her of her virtue and then toss her on the streets like a common strumpet?

"Come on, boy, now what will it be?" Lord Goreham's gaze slid from Sir Hugo to Widow Philpott.

The young barrister's cheeks darkened. But he looked

Evelyn straight in the eye when he spoke. "I regret to say that I am unable to assist Miss Waring. It occurs to me that the earl is in a better position to remedy the young lady's situation."

Desperation seized her. "Oh, surely, you can make me a loan, sir. I swear that I will repay it! I can read and write, and I've quite an unusual education for a female—perhaps I could even assist you in your law practice, writing letters, making copies of important documents, that sort of thing!"

"Pshaw!" Widow Philpott shifted her bulk from one foot to the other. "Who ever heard of such a thing? A woman working in a barrister's chambers!"

The Earl of Goreham echoed this sentiment. "The only work you'll do to repay such a loan will be done flat on your back, gel. You've no need for a special education for that sort of drudgery!"

This could not be happening to her! Evelyn's heart beat so rapidly, and her breathing grew so shallow that she thought she might faint again. That prospect only terrified her further. It would leave her even more vulnerable to Widow Philpott's avarice, so she struggled to maintain a modicum of composure while she appealed to the young Sir Hugo. "I'll do anything!"

He swallowed hard, shaking his head curtly. "I cannot help you, miss. I am sorry."

"A man of morals," the widow chuckled.

"Or so broke he can't afford to buy the wench," said Lord Goreham.

Buy the wench? Evelyn's knees wobbled at the earl's grotesque suggestion. "No one is going to buy me, my lord! I would be willing to accept a loan from this gentleman, but I am not for sale, I assure you. I'll have you know, my lord, that I was raised by Christian parents. My father was at Badajoz, beside Wellington, until he took a fatal musket ball to his side. My mother, may she rest in peace, died giving birth to my younger sister, but not before she entrusted our religious education and upbringing to a worthy maiden aunt. I'm no milk maiden with scrubbed knuckles and raw morals, and I'll thank you not to treat me as such!''

"Bravo!" The earl was clearly amused by this disputation. "So, the little chit has some breeding."

"More than you'll ever have," Evelyn shot back.

"Watch your tongue, gel," inserted the widow. "Or the earl might change his mind and decide not to rescue you after all."

"I don't want to be rescued by the earl." Evelyn turned her eyes on Sir Hugo, but he remained silent.

"Then it's off to Newgate for you," pronounced Widow Philpott.

"That's an idle threat, Miss Waring." Sir Hugo's voice was low, throaty. "I can see you safely to the street and perhaps give you accommodations for the night, but after that . . ."

"After that, you're on your own," filled in Lord Goreham. "Whereas, I am offering to pay off your gambling debts entirely."

Evelyn met Sir Hugo's gaze. "Can you guarantee that I will not be apprehended by the runners and tossed in debtor's prison?"

The young barrister hesitated, and when he did, the earl broke in. "Did I hear some mention of a younger sister? Some sort of illness she's afflicted with, is that it?"

Evelyn's pulse bolted. She stared into the older man's craggy face, and immediately saw what he was offering. "Celeste has suffered from diphtheria since she was a child. Her cough has weakened her lungs, and at present, she has barely enough strength to move from the bed to the breakfast table every morning."

"And what have the doctors said?" Lord Goreham asked.

"That she needs constant rest, good food and warm clothes. That she needs a clean, comfortable home in which to live, not the cramped and dirty apartment I have been forced to take. That she needs to take the cure at

Bath, as well, for the restorative spring waters there have been known to cure such maladies in a matter of weeks, even when the patient has been ill for years.''

"And what are you willing to do to save your sister's life?'' the earl asked.

"I will do anything,'' Evelyn said with utter conviction.

"Would you be . . . *my wife?*'' The old man's query sent waves of shock through Evelyn's body. "Are you willing to marry me and be the Countess of Goreham?''

Her heart stopped beating, she was sure of it. Behind the earl's eyes, she glimpsed the very gates of hell. Yet, her dilemma was confounding. Perhaps making a Faustian bargain with the Earl of Goreham would condemn her soul, but if it would save her sister's life, she was willing to consider it.

After all, she had very little choice in the matter. The way Evelyn saw it, she could risk being carted off to Newgate, or she could accept the earl's marriage proposal, saving her sister into the bargain. Inhaling deeply, she summoned every ounce of courage she possessed. But before she answered the nobleman, she turned a measuring gaze on Sir Hugo.

The frankness in her eyes would haunt him forever.

Staring at Miss Evelyn Waring, Sir Hugo watched the machinations of her mind. Her choice was not an easy one; indeed, she was damned if she did, and damned if she didn't. His soul ached for her, pleaded with her to rebuff the earl. But, in his heart, he knew she had little choice. And if he were in her position—destitute, without family or protector, and with a younger sister to support— he'd have done the same thing.

If only he had the blunt to bail her out himself. Had Sir Hugo Mansfield owned five thousand pounds, he would have plunked it down without condition. Moreover, had he owned anything worth five thousand pounds, he would have sold it in a flash, and bailed the poor lass out of her troubles.

But, Sir Hugo was so deep in dun territory that he could hardly keep himself afloat. Creditors visited his doorstep more often than clients. And he had his own demons to wrestle. This was the first night in a fortnight that Sir Hugo had entered Widow Philpott's faro house, but he was well known to her, and notorious among the more prestigious gaming hells for having an absolute obsession with gambling and games of chance.

Sir Hugo, it had oft been said, and well he knew it, would wager on anything, the gender of a child yet to be born, the length of time it would take a young rakehell to seduce a saucy widow, the number of seconds it would take a raindrop to streak a windowpane. Truth be told, Sir Hugo's appetite for gaming was more voracious than Lady Devonshire's.

Unfortunately, his luck was very nearly the same. The difference was, he didn't have a wealthy spouse or indulgent mama to rescue him from his debts each time he ran them up to the heavens. Sir Hugo's fascination with gaming was as strong as his father's before him.

He'd often wondered, in fact, whether he'd inherited his demons from his father. Sir Hugo was barely out of knee pants when his father wagered and lost his entire fortune on the outcome of a three-legged dog race. But, he was old enough to assume the responsibility for stewarding his younger sisters into adulthood. He deeply regretted that his gambling had taken precedence over that obligation. Without the help of his mother's brother, the Mansfield women, sisters and mother included, would have starved.

In fact, Sir Hugo would never have got through school absent Uncle Reginald's patronage. The older man, a barrister himself, paid his bills directly, settling accounts with creditors when necessary, doling out funds to Hugo even though the young man habitually wagered his last farthing. It was Reginald who paid his tuition at Eton, then sponsored him at Lincoln's Inn. It was Reginald who referred cases to the young barrister, keeping Hugo afloat despite his penchant for prowling the gambling hells.

It should have been a fine and lucrative living for Sir Hugo. In the year since he'd been called to the bar, he should have amassed a modest amount of savings. After all, he had only himself to support now that his mother was living with his youngest sister.

But, Sir Hugo's pockets were constantly cleaned out. He'd have been tossed in prison long ago had it not been for his uncle's intervention. The turn of a card, the roll of a dice—these were the pegs on which Sir Hugo's fortunes hinged. His emotions, as well as his accounts, were controlled by happenstance.

In the year following his call to the bar, Sir Hugo had struggled mightily to escape the bonds that tied him to the gaming tables, to free himself from the shackles of his gambling compulsion.

His resolve never lasted. A few weeks—that was the longest Sir Hugo had ever refrained from tossing his money on the table. Despite his good intentions, an idle hour would find him back at Brooks's, Boodle's, Watier's, or even at Widow Philpott's house, a private residence temptingly close to Lincoln's Inn Fields. It was a sickness, an affliction that Hugo could not escape despite the power of his intellect and the strength of his desire to cease gambling.

Now, more than anything, he wanted to help Evelyn Waring. He stared at her plaintive expression, parted lips, the slight tensing of her shoulders. Her eyes beseeched him, yet she maintained her pride, refusing to break down or erupt in feminine sobs while her future hung in the balance.

"I admire a gambler," he lied, his voice thick with sarcasm. "But we must all lose at one time or another. God knows, it wouldn't be *gambling* absent the risk of losing."

Lord Goreham gave another of his mirthless chuckles. "Them who can't afford to lose shouldn't be wagering, then, should they? What's your answer, gel? I can't be waiting here all night, I'm not the young buck I once was."

Evelyn shuddered. Hugging herself, she dropped her gaze to the floor.

The impatient tapping of Widow Philpott's hefty slipper grated on Sir Hugo's nerves. Standing rigidly, fists balled at his sides, his chest ached against the angry pounding of his heart. If only he had the money to save Evelyn Waring! If only he had saved his income, rather than frittering it away in the hells of St. James's Street!

He thought of grasping Evelyn's arms, shaking her and screaming, "Don't do it, Evelyn! I'll marry you and we'll figure it out later!" But he didn't dare, for what had he to offer this woman? What had he to offer someone so clearly in need of deep resources? He'd only bog her down, damn her to a life of ruin. She'd spend an uncertain future worrying whether he'd gamble their fortune away on the most whimsical of wagers.

And so he held his tongue while Evelyn lifted her chin and met the old lordship's beady gaze.

"All right, I will marry you, my lord." Her features were smooth, her eyes hard but limpid with unshed tears. "On one condition: That you take in my sister Celeste as well, and that you agree to send her to Bath where she can take the waters and recuperate from her illness. She'll require a proper coming out, too, when the time comes, and I'll not allow you to be stingy with her wardrobe and education."

"I'll not squawk over fribbles, Miss Waring. You'll see that I can be a generous man."

"You've made a wise decision," added Widow Philpott smugly. Opening her palm, she allowed Lord Goreham to load it with a stack of pound notes. Greedily stuffing them into her cleavage, she gave the nobleman a wink. "So there's two babes in the woods I've given ye. Take care, and treat this one as kindly as the first, won't you, m'lord?"

"I'm a fair man, Letitia. She'll learn that soon enough."

Sir Hugo took a stiff step backward, bowed and extended

his hand to Evelyn Waring. The prospect of her unhappiness sickened him. Just managing to suppress the outburst of emotion that welled up inside him, he squeezed her hand. Looking into her eyes—her confused, entreating eyes—filled him with self-loathing. He hated himself for not having five thousand pounds to give her; that she didn't hate him for failing to give it increased his guilt tenfold.

Wishing above everything not to appear a silly cake before such a courageous woman as Evelyn Waring, Sir Hugo released her hand. Turning on his heel, he felt her gaze follow his retreating form. But though the hair on his nape prickled, he didn't look back. He knew he appeared the veriest jackanapes who'd ever walked the face of the earth; yet, if there was a shred of honor left in him, he had to reject Evelyn's entreaty. Were he to take her into his protection, he would ruin her. Under the protection of a wealthy earl, she would at least live a cloistered, comfortable life. As would the sister she'd made reference to.

But, Sir Hugo walked out of Widow Philpott's establishment a changed man. In the next five years, he never entered another St. James hell or faro house again. When asked to place a wager on a horse race, political campaign, or even the outcome of a battle in the bloody war in Spain, the young barrister would grit his teeth and decline.

His desire to gamble never abated, however. He sat for hours in his chambers, dreaming of setting foot inside Brooks's, imagining himself at the faro table, longing to feel dice in his hands, burning for the smell of playing cards. But he knew that one hour in a gambling den would soon turn into an evening; an evening would cost him a fortune, and that would require another spree to earn back the money he'd lost.

And the vicious cycle would repeat itself. He'd be swallowed up by his urge to wager everything. Because it was impossible for Sir Hugo to engage in even a friendly card

game without betting every tuppence he owned, he had
to refrain completely from any sort of wagering. That was
the only way he could control his urges.

Slowly, he built a rampart of self-esteem to protect himself from the fatal attraction he had toward gambling. Sir
Hugo earned a reputation as a fine barrister. But deep
inside, his soul was gnawed at by an emptiness, and the
ever-present knowledge that he had failed a young woman
named Evelyn Waring. He knew little of what happened
to her after that fateful night when she accepted Lord
Goreham's offer of marriage. He knew that she remained
married to the earl, and he knew where she lived. He
walked in front of her town house each morning, hoping
to catch a glimpse of her. He never sought the company
of other women; in a strange way, it would be an infidelity,
a breach of the secret, unspoken bond he had with Evelyn.

For, despite his having failed her, despite not seeing her
once after he left her in Widow Philpott's boudoir, Sir
Hugo knew he loved her.

But he knew that he would never have the chance to
love Evelyn Waring, now the Countess of Goreham. He'd
let that opportunity slip through his fingers. He didn't
expect he would ever see her again.

Having turned his back on gambling, Sir Hugo thought
that luck had passed him by.

Chapter One

Will I die a virgin?

It was her constant thought, of late. The recently
deceased Earl of Goreham had made his wife a young
widow, but he'd done nothing to change her status as a
virgin.

That thought permeated every corner of her mind as
Lady Evelyn, Dowager Countess of Goreham, stood at the
tall windows overlooking Lincoln's Inn Fields. Tilting her
head, she strained for a glimpse of the broad-shouldered
barrister who made his way across the grassy square each
morning at precisely ten minutes till eight o'clock. As regular as a nun's prayers, he walked with long purposeful
strides and eyes cast slightly downward.

For five years, she'd watched him from that window,
having first seen him crossing the square the week after
she'd moved into the earl's Lincoln's Inn Fields town
house. His prominent nose, solemn gray eyes and receding
hairline had instantly caught her eye; he was the young
barrister she'd met in Widow Philpott's faro house, the
man who'd failed or refused to bail her out of the quagmire

she'd got herself into. The man with the kind eyes. *Had he any notion that she spied upon him each day?*

Would he be amused to know that she watched him every morning? Or would he be slightly terrified to think that the woman he'd rebuffed at Widow Philpott's had studied him so assiduously for the past five years, that she knew every nuance of his facial expressions, every bend and angle of his tall, muscular body? Would her secret obsession repulse him? Would he be incensed by her surreptitious invasion of his private morning ritual?

Evelyn narrowed her eyes as Sir Hugo came into view, heading northeast toward the block of grey buildings that housed the courtrooms where he would begin his workday. Rising on her tiptoes, she searched for a clear view of his face. As she studied his expression, she held her breath, entirely absorbed in interpreting the firm set of his lips, the downward angle of his reddish brows.

Even from a distance, she detected a harshness in the lines of his face. He wasn't happy this morning. A sense of uneasiness rumbled through Evelyn, and she closed the book she'd held in her hands, leaning closer toward the window, her nose nearly touching the glass.

Not that his solemn expression surprised her. There had been many days when Sir Hugo frowned all the way down the street in front of the earl's town house, then turned away from the tall third-floor windows to cross the square with hunched shoulders, tension rippling off his back like the dissonant chord of an untuned pianoforte. There had been days when Evelyn could have sworn Sir Hugo Mansfield was the unhappiest man in the world.

And she'd spent hours wondering what produced the bleak expression on his face. But, she couldn't imagine what would perpetually sadden a man so handsome and intelligent.

She invented reasons for his melancholy. An unrewarding fling with some trollop, she mused, torturing her imagination. In that way, she textured her mental picture of him with some venal weaknesses. It helped her fend off the dangerous delusion that he was a knight in shining armor who would one day rescue her from her hellish existence—and from the isolation which, even though the earl was now dead some eleven months, continued to imprison her.

Sighing, the countess pressed her lips to the cold glass window pane. Sir Hugo had turned toward the court buildings, offering her a view of his retreating back, his broad shoulders and black many-caped coat that swirled around his boot-tops.

Willing herself back to reality, Evelyn reminded herself that the man whose dashing figure she so admired was the same man who had refused to help her the night she accepted the earl's marriage proposal.

True, the bright young barrister had threatened to report the unlicensed faro house to the authorities, but that had been an idle threat; the widow was certainly far more connected in certain circles than the young barrister had been.

And he'd offered to see Evelyn safely into a hackney cab, to provide her shelter for the night, if that was what she needed. But what good would that have done? Even if Evelyn had succeeded in evading the clutches of Widow Philpott and her minions, she still would have been broke.

Penniless, she still would have been unable to provide for her sister, Celeste. She might even have turned to selling her body in order to put food upon the table. In her heart, Evelyn knew she would have done anything to save her sister's life.

The thought—the appalling memory of her desperation—made her shiver. In the end, Evelyn had only to marry a wizened old man to secure her sister a comfortable future and an adequate dowry. Eventually, the earl's chaste kisses and innocuous pats on her behind had ceased to repulse her. Before he died, she even developed an affection of sorts for the grumpy old man.

So what was there to be sorry for? Evelyn and her sister would never again go hungry. In the past five years, they hadn't wanted for anything. Celeste had made a miraculous recovery. She had been on death's doorstep, and now the girl was the picture of radiant health. Next season, she would come out in fine style, with vouchers to Almack's, the prettiest gowns money could buy, and a dowry that was sure to attract a gentleman of suitable background and character.

If Evelyn fulfilled the terms of the earl's will.

Staring absently out the window, her breath frosting the cold pane, Evelyn silently recalled the terms of her husband's will. As long as she remained *unmarried, unattached and untouched* during her mourning period, she would be entitled to a generous pension for the rest of her life. More importantly, a healthy sum would be settled on Celeste, and a dowry would be paid to her future husband.

Unmarried, unattached and untouched. Those were the very words the earl's will had contained. An unusual condition, admitted Sir Cuthbert deLisle, one of her husband's lawyers, as he'd explained to Evelyn the terms of the will. Subject to interpretation, he had murmured, arching his brows.

Evelyn remembered that day as vividly as if it had occurred yesterday. Sir Cuthbert, a flaxen-haired dandy wearing wasp-waisted trousers and an elaborately tied cravat, sat in the front library of the earl's town house, painstakingly reciting each condition of the will, his nervous gaze flitting from Evelyn to her stepson, Percival Dethman.

The earl's son, the third Earl of Goreham, sat beside Evelyn on the sofa, stroking his thin black mustache, working his lips as if he were chewing the words read aloud by Sir Cuthbert, digesting them with relish.

"So, you say my stepmother has to be unmarried, unattached and untouched one year from Father's death?" His voice was as thin and lacking in character as he was. "Or else she forfeits her pension and Celeste's settlement as well?''

"Correct," replied Sir Cuthbert, seemingly embarrassed by his deceased client's bizarre wishes.

"Unmarried is clear enough." Percival paused, while Evelyn's scalp tingled with humiliation. "And *unattached* implies an engagement or some sort of official connection, I suppose. *Untouched,* now there's a fuzzy concept. What do you suppose that means?''

Sir Cuthbert's cheeks had darkened. "It might be difficult to prove, but I interpret the clause to mean that the countess is denied her portion in the event it is proved that she engages in any . . . ah, sexual relationship.''

"Sexual relationship." Percival repeated the words softly, savoring them.

That was eleven months ago, and since then, Evelyn had sequestered herself in the earl's town house, where Percival now lived, watching her every move, monitoring her comings and goings, as if he were waiting for her to commit some sort of egregious indiscretion.

Well, he'd wait till hell froze over, Evelyn thought. After all she'd gone through to provide for Celeste, she had no intention of throwing it away in favor of some silly romance. Notwithstanding her secret obsession with Sir Hugo Mansfield, she was hardly a romantic. She was not the type to cultivate anything so useless as a *romance* even if she weren't constrained by the terms of the earl's will.

Not by any stretch of the imagination was Evelyn a frivolous or impetuous woman. Having been forced to fend for herself and Celeste since their father died in the Peninsular Wars, she'd learned early on to practice caution in everything she did and said. She might be willing to risk her own future for her sister's—she'd proved that, at Widow Philpott's five years ago—but she would never throw away security to chase an impossible dream.

With the palm of her hand, Evelyn polished off the fog on the windowpane. She'd done quite well for herself,

she reflected, enjoying her morning solitude. She had no
regrets, and shouldn't have. Yet as she dried her hands on
the black wool of her widow's gown, and peered at the
diminishing figure crossing the square, she couldn't help
feel a painful squeeze in her chest. She'd given up so
much—her youth, her opportunity for a family, even the
chance to know what true physical passion could feel like.

Her wistfulness deepened. How could that man with the
kind eyes and warm, velvety voice have abandoned her?
How could he have wrapped her up in the protective cloak
of his gaze, then left her in the predatorial clutches of the
Earl of Goreham?

How could he have forgotten about her?

"See something interesting out there, *Mummy?*"

The earl's son, just two years older than she, had crept
up behind Evelyn. He stood disturbingly near, his breath
fanning the tendrils of hair that escaped her upswept coif-
fure. Glancing over her shoulder, Evelyn deftly sidled away
from him, and turned her back to the window. She noticed
the young earl's gaze follow the receding figure of Sir
Hugo Mansfield, and a slender thread of apprehension
slithered up her spine.

"I like to listen to the street vendors sing their ditties."
Clutching her book closer to her bosom, Evelyn lifted her
chin a defiant notch. "I have come here every morning
for five years, you know that. It relaxes me."

"Yes, I have noticed." Percival Dethman turned from
the window, and stared at her. His pencil-thin mustache
twitched as he spoke. "I have made it a practice to notice
your routine, *Mummy*. After all, you are a fascinating
woman, an endless source of amusement and edification
for an uncouth rogue such as myself."

"I have asked you a thousand times not to call me
Mummy." Evelyn kept her voice low, but her tone was indignant. "It is a ridiculous affectation on your part, when
you so obviously dislike me."

His eyebrows squirmed. "On the contrary, dear. I am

rooting for you. Less than a month to go, and you'll be a rich woman, thanks to my father."

"Let us not pretend, Percival. You have done nought but hold me in cold disdain since the day your father married me. You would love to see me fail to satisfy the conditions of Lord Goreham's will."

Percival clucked his tongue. "Perish the thought."

"You are the outside of enough." Evelyn started toward the far end of the drawing room, where the breakfast table was set and where she habitually enjoyed her morning repast in exquisite privacy. "Now if you will excuse me, I should like to enjoy my meal."

"But I have two rather pressing matters I wish to discuss with you, Mum— excuse me, my lady."

Something in the earl's voice compelled Evelyn to halt in her tracks. Slowly pivoting on her kid half-boot, she stared into her stepson's cold, beady eyes.

His gaze fell to the volume held snugly against her bodice. "Rumor has it that you are nearing completion of your manuscript. Soon it will be your own book that you hold so near your heart."

She glanced self-consciously at the biography of Henry VIII she'd spent the night devouring. A tawdry Tory rendition of the 16th-century monarch's reign, it had caused her to laugh out loud on several occasions. "Had you attended last month's meeting of the Society, you would have heard it from my own lips, Percival. Yes, I have but a few more weeks of editing my work, and then I shall turn the manuscript over to Mr. Murray for publication. I think, my lord, that you will find the results of my research most interesting."

"I want to read your book," he said stiffly. "Before publication."

"No."

"You have used materials from the family archives in conducting your research." Clearly, Percival had rehearsed his argument. His color heightened as he spoke, and his voice was strained. "You had no right to rifle through the family papers at Goreham Castle. As such, I demand to be allowed to review your manuscript before its publication."

Evelyn rankled. "I had every right, Percival, and you know it."

"You did not have my permission to quote from the Dethman diaries, or to use them as the basis for your research. Never mind that Father gave you his permission on his deathbed. Hell, he was rarely lucid the last six months of his life—"

"Wasn't he?" Evelyn cocked her head. "Was he crazy when he wrote his last will, then?"

The third earl's eyes narrowed, and his breath came out in a hiss. "I am the rightful heir to the Goreham title and all that goes with it. Father would never have allowed you access to those papers if he'd understood you intended to refer to them in some ridiculous revisionist biography of Henry VIII's life! What is it that you've discovered in those papers, anyway? And what connection does the Dethman family have with the Tudor king? I demand to know!"

Ignoring Percival's pointed questions, Evelyn said, "Good heavens, Celeste and I were banished to that drafty old castle in Kent every summer for nearly five years! What else was I to do but take advantage of the library there? The fact that I stumbled across your ancestor's diaries annoys you because I realized their historical value before you did. You could have studied them yourself, had you been so inclined. But no, you were too busy chasing strumpets and drinking yourself into oblivion every night with your dandified friends."

"Be that as it may, the diaries belong to the Dethman family."

"Dr. Peeps was in the sickroom when your father granted me permission to take the diaries into my sole custody, Percival. I protected my rights by seeking a witness to your father's words, I'll admit. But if you attempt to argue that your father was in no mental state to grant me that permission, then I shall be forced to make the same argument as regards his will."

"Where are the diaries now, Evelyn?" Lord Goreham's voice fell to a sibilant whisper.

"They are in a safe place. When the manuscript is published, I will return them to the Dethman library at Goreham Castle. That is where I found them, and that is where I shall replace them, properly encased in glass this time so that your posterity might enjoy them as well."

The earl's face twisted into a nasty scowl as he took a step toward Evelyn. "I will not allow this. I was a member of the London Society for the Study of the Tudor Monarchy before you ever heard of it. To think that upon Father's request, I actually sponsored the induction of the first female member of the Society!"

"I am grateful to you," Evelyn whispered, inching backward.

Fists clenched at his sides, the earl's son swiftly closed the distance between them. His face was mere inches from Evelyn's, so close she could smell the brandy on his morning breath, a fetid combination of odors that wrinkled her nose and soured her stomach.

She reared back, but refused to retreat further. She'd come this far; she wouldn't let this inebriated little rooster spoil the success she'd worked for so arduously—even if he was, technically speaking, the rightful owner of the Dethman diaries.

"I shall ask you again! Precisely what is it that you found in the Dethman diaries that you believe will set the Society on its head?"

Without hesitation, Evelyn replied, "Read my book when it becomes available and you will find out at the same time everyone else does. I daresay, the revelation will do nought but endorse the notoriety of the Dethman reputation."

"What the hell does that mean?" The earl's hands hovered in the air, his fingers coiling and uncoiling perilously close to Evelyn's slender neck.

"Evelyn? Are you all right?" Celeste's voice sounded from beneath the scalloped velvet panels that separated the breakfast room from the front drawing room.

Whirling, Evelyn fled toward her younger sister, a rosy cheeked girl with huge, blinking blue eyes and straw colored hair arranged in ringlets on either side of her head. Celeste shot Percival a disdainful frown.

As usual, the young man lost his starch in the face of unbeatable opposition. Sulkily, he headed toward the doorway.

"Before you go, Percival," Evelyn said to his retreating back, "What was the other matter you wished to speak with me about?"

For an instant, he froze. At length, his body slowly rotated, and a smug smile quirked at his lips. "I almost forgot! You and I are having a country house party, my lady. In a sennight, as a matter of fact. Sorry that I couldn't give you earlier notice of it, but I hadn't yet decided on the guest list."

Evelyn laughed. "I have no intention of attending a country house party, Percival, much less hostessing one with you. Surely, you didn't think I would be interested in such a frivolity. After all, I am in mourning. It wouldn't be proper."

"It wouldn't be proper for Celeste to attend without you," Percival replied. "She is not in mourning."

"She is too young! She isn't out, yet!"

Celeste nearly hopped into the center of the room, already flushed with excitement. "A party! What kind of party, Percival! Oh, Sister, we must go, we simply must. I won't attend the dancing and suppers. I'll stay in my room the entire time. Well, except for nuncheon and tea, and, whenever it might be proper for me to be seen."

Evelyn turned on Percival with a look of disgust. "How dare you mention such a thing in front of her? Now she'll be disappointed that she cannot attend. I am sorry, Celeste."

The young girl's face fell like a landslide.

Percival chuckled. "I strongly advise you to attend this party, dear. 'Tis to be in honor of your departed husband. A sort of going-away party, if you will."

"He went away nearly a year ago, Percival. Your wake is a trifle belated, don't you think?"

Evelyn's dry response apparently struck Percival as hilariously funny. When he was able to speak between gasps, he said, "Father always did love a good party. The Dethman men are famous for their parties."

"I can not deny that," Evelyn replied.

"Then a party is only appropriate. Eleven months have passed and the mourning period is nearly over, as you pointed out. What better way to end that period of mourning than to throw a party? A party in honor of dear old dad. You'd be dishonoring him if you refused to attend, *Mummy.*"

"Couldn't we go, Evie?" Celeste stood beside her sister, clutching her arm, looking up at her with large, liquid eyes. "You could wear black the entire time. What harm would it do?"

Evelyn bit her lip. She was sick and tired of being cooped up in the earl's town house with nothing to do but measure time, and wait for Sir Hugo to cross Lincoln's Inn Field every morning.

And her preoccupation with the barrister was becoming somewhat of an unhealthy obsession.

Perhaps it would do her good to spend some time in the country. Even if it was unbearably cold at this time of year in that big old castle. She loved it anyway, with its imposing medieval turrets and parapets, its crumbling, crenellated walls. And the library . . . oh, that was heaven to her.

Against her better judgment, she relented. "All right."

Something in Percival's pleased look told her she'd made the wrong decision, but Celeste's excitement quickly vanquished any doubts she had.

"What shall I wear?" the younger girl cried. "Oh, Evelyn, we've only two weeks to figure it out. We'll have to see Madame Racine right away, before the other ladies descend upon her with a crush of orders. May I be excused now, my lord? Please?"

Celeste fled the room. As she pounded up the steps, her voice could be heard calling out to her abigail for assistance in dressing for a visit to town. Within minutes, news of the impending party spread among the maids and lady's servants; it would require two weeks of non-stop sewing and washing and pressing and embroidering to get Celeste ready for such an important event.

"Would you like to assist me with the guest list?" Percival asked. "I am afraid I have taken the liberty of having the invitations engraved already. With your name as hostess, of course."

Evelyn detested being alone with the earl; he made her skin crawl. Giving him a wide berth, she crossed the room, passed him, and headed for the stairs. At the threshold, she said over her shoulder, "I am much too busy revising my manuscript to concern myself with your guest list. I am quite relieved to leave the entire matter up to you. Just be sure you invite my friends, Miss Freemantle and Lady Ramsbottom, will you?"

"Of course, my lady." Percival watched her go, a smile splitting his cadaverous face.

Sir Hugo Mansfield sat behind a battered partner's desk in the small sitting and reception room just off his bed-chamber. His were cramped quarters to be sure, two rooms with sparse furniture, and a single threadbare rug to cover the worst of the gaping holes in the plank floor.

Still, a barrister could hardly expect to make a living if he strayed too far from Lincoln's Inn. His Parker Street address, within walking distance of the law courts, was ample compensation for the Spartan conditions of his accomodations. As an added bonus, Sir Hugo had to walk past the Goreham town house each morning in order to cross the grassy field that bordered the law buildings.

Of course, he knew where the Countess of Goreham lived. He'd casually asked about her years ago, and discovered where she resided. And he'd seen the earl's death announcement in the Morning Times a year earlier. He knew, also, that the countess sometimes stood before the third floor window, her body angled toward the glass, her face half hidden behind the folds of the heavy drapery. On rare occasions, when he couldn't restrain himself, Sir Hugo turned and glanced upward, hoping to lock gazes with her, imagining that she might lift her hand in greeting, and smile.

But that was the stuff of fantasies, he reminded himself, shaking the cobwebs from his mind, turning his attention elsewhere. It was late afternoon, and Sir Hugo had just ushered his last client of the day out his door. He was tidying up his desk, penning letters and reviewing the pleadings presented to him by opposing counsel in a particularly complex case. With herculean effort, he pushed all thoughts of Evelyn Waring, now the Dowager Countess of Goreham, from his mind. After all, it was futile and puerile wool-gathering to think that there was a chance he'd ever exchange a word with the lady.

She was now far above his station in life, cloistered in an elite world of servants, balls and country outings. She'd made her decision that night in Widow Philpott's faro house, a decision that had propelled her into wealth, luxury and a carefree life of ease. Why would she want to speak with the likes of Sir Hugo Mansfield? Why would she waste one moment of her day fraternizing with a man who had failed her five years ago?

"Why, indeed," Sir Hugo said aloud. Cursing, he realized that he'd allowed the nub of his pen to pierce the lengthy letter he was composing to one of his clients. He violently crumpled the paper in his hands, and tossed it into a rubbish basket beside his desk. He'd just dipped his pen into the inkwell, and touched the tip to a fresh sheet of foolscap, when a knock at the door sounded.

Sir Hugo was surprised to find on his landing a liveried footman, resplendent in olive coat and gold epaulets. With military bearing, the servant nodded deferentially, then presented to Sir Hugo a vellum envelope sealed with scarlet wax.

Sir Hugo placed a coin in the young man's hand and kicked shut the door. He wondered who had sent him such an elegant, distinctive missive. It wasn't as if he had a wide circle of friends; since he'd ceased frequenting the gaming halls and faro houses, he'd concentrated on nothing but his work. In fact, he'd forced himself to think of nothing but his law career. He often wondered if he'd simply traded one obsession for another.

At any rate, the only correspondence he'd received in the last year—other than that strictly related to his business—had been from his youngest sister informing him that their dear mother had expired. And since the good old woman had been dead nearly three months before his sister saw fit to write him, he hadn't even journeyed north to see his mother's grave.

Why take that much time from his work, he'd rationalized, when there was nothing he could do for his mother? He preferred work over everything. Or so he tried to convince himself. At least, his compulsion to fill his waking hours with useful industry had kept him out of the gambling establishments for nigh on five years.

An amazing accomplishment, he thought, lowering himself into his straight-backed chair. He'd done what his father could not have.

Ripping open the thick vellum envelope, Sir Hugo chided himself for his smug self-satisfaction. So ill-placed it was, for after all, there were still many nights when he sat on the edge of his bed, sweat pouring from his brow, head cradled in his hands, wishing with all his heart that he might spend just one hour at White's or Watier's or one of the smaller, less elegant gaming establishments. Many a night, he'd put on his breeches and boots and shrugged into his coat, actually intending to leave his quarters and head toward St. James's.

But somehow, he'd managed the past five years to control his impulses, and return to his bed before the urge to gamble overwhelmed him. It required every bit of strength he possessed. Staying away from the card tables and gaming hells was the hardest thing he'd ever done.

Only the memory of his failure to help Evelyn Waring five years ago gave him the strength to avoid temptation. That had been the very worst moment of his life, and he vowed that if he ever met Lady Goreham again, he would not be penniless or powerless to help her. No, he would be something entirely different, a man she could respect, *a man that he could respect.*

And, that is what he had become. But what did that signify to a countess who had probably forgotten all about him?

But, she did watch him from her window every morning, did she not?

Or was it purely coincidence that she appeared there to gaze down at Lincoln's Inn Fields every morning at precisely the same time Sir Hugo crossed the grassy square and headed toward the inn for his breakfast?

And was he fantasizing when he looked down at the thick vellum card, engraved in gold, and saw Evelyn's name inscribed there?

He turned the folded vellum paper over in his hands, disbelievingly. The invitation was elegantly worded, a simple request that he attend a country house party hosted by Percival Dethman, third Earl of Goreham, and, Evelyn, the Dowager Countess of Goreham, at Goreham Castle, near Kent, on the Friday evening two weeks from now.

An invitation to an elaborate weekend party? Given by a man whom he'd never met, and a woman whom he'd only met once, five years ago, under less than respectable circumstances? Delivered a mere sennight in advance? That was exceedingly odd, even to Sir Hugo's unsophisticated sense of party-going etiquette. Which convinced him that there was some sort of mistake involved in his receiving the invitation.

Or was this Evelyn's way of summoning him? Did she share his strange obsession? Did she need him, want him, suffer from an irrepressible desire to talk to him? God forbid, was she in trouble now, with no one else to call upon?

Sitting bolt upright in his chair, Sir Hugo studied the verso side of the letter, confirming with not a little surprise that it was indeed addressed to Sir Hugo Mansfield, Esquire. For a long moment, he merely stared at the flowing penmanship of the address. Then he re-read the party invitation and ran his fingers over the lettering. Had Evelyn herself penned those words? Had she held this very sheet of vellum in her fingers, pressed it to her lips, sealed it with her own hands?

Or was this some perverse joke?

What did he know of this Percival, third Earl of Goreham? He recalled some talk of the Dethman propensity for throwing scandalous, almost orgiastic parties, but of the third earl's character, Sir Hugo knew nothing.

A cold tremor ran through his body. He felt suddenly as if his entire world had been knocked off its axis. What ulterior motive could the countess or the young earl have in inviting him to the Goreham castle in Kent for a country house party? What sort of intrigue surrounded this invitation?

The blood coursing through his veins was deafening. Lowering his aching head to his hands, elbows propped on his cluttered desk, Sir Hugo squeezed shut his eyes and pictured Evelyn that night five years ago when she accepted the earl's invitation of marriage. The quiet resolve, the steely determination that had shone in her eyes had inspired him many times to stay away from the gaming hells. It was as if her strength had somehow galvanized his own.

And now, the Countess of Goreham was inviting him to a house party. Not only would he encounter the woman who had occupied every waking and sleeping moment of his imagination for the past five years, he would do so beneath the scrutiny of her husband's son and heir.

If he chose to attend the party, that is.

He'd spent five years schooling himself to stay away from gaming hells. But Sir Hugo Mansfield lacked the strength to stay away from Evelyn Waring Dethman if she wanted to see him. Truth was, he didn't even care to try.

He quickly penned a response announcing that he would attend the party. His chest ached in anticipation of the moment when he would see Evelyn, lift her knuckles to his lips, and once again breathe the scent of her.

Chapter Two

The next two weeks passed in a blur of shopping and fittings for Evelyn. Though she intended to wear widow's weeds the entire weekend, she did concede to having a few new gowns sewn, some with rows of tiny black silk roses or ribbons as trim along the neckline and hem.

Celeste was absolutely overcome with excitement that she would be allowed to attend the house party, if not the actual dinners and dances. Once assured that there would be plenty of activities to keep her busy, and many opportunities to meet the handsome lords and ladies who would be in attendance, the younger sister gave her unalloyed approval of the gala. By the time she climbed in Lord Goreham's gleaming equipage, Celeste was positively giddy with delight.

Easy to please, was Evelyn's silent remark as she turned her eyes from the bleak countryside, and regarded her sister's bright, eager expression. Given that Percival had chosen to go ahead of the ladies to Goreham Castle, and had been gone from London a week, the trip was actually a welcome respite for both Celeste and Evelyn.

For her younger sister's sake, Evelyn was looking forward to the house party and the swarm of people that would congregate in the Goreham mansion. The Dethman men were famous for their devilishly extravagant parties, and for once Evelyn—probably because Celeste's excitement was infectious—anticipated a jolly time.

The roads were treacherous, slick with ice in many places, slowing Goreham's four roans to an unseemly gait and doubling the normal time it took to get from London to Kent. After three days, having spent one uncomfortable night in the coldest and dirtiest of roadside inns, Celeste and Evelyn arrived at the castle. They crossed the old-fashioned moat that surrounded the compound, relieved that their arduous journey was near an end.

And even though she was so tired she nearly fell out of the carriage into the arms of a waiting footman, Evelyn never failed to be awed by the imposing structure that rose up above her, all grey stone and crumbling masonry, crenellated ramparts and glazed windows. Goreham Castle was a magnificent Tudor masterpiece set on a raised island that originally afforded it the greatest protection possible from hostile forces who might storm the walls.

Stumbling out of the carriage behind Evelyn, Celeste stared up at the darkening skies beyond the castle's parapets. "Do you think there is another storm brewing?"

Icy wind whipped at Evelyn's ankles, plastering her woolen gown to the backs of her legs. Mindful of Celeste's delicate health, she grasped her younger sister by the arm and propelled her up the stone steps. A gust of wind swept them through the huge wooden doors which were held open by a footman.

Stamping their frozen feet, and rubbing their gloved hands, the ladies stood in the huge hall, once the main room of the house where the lord of the manor dined and his knights and servants slept. A fire blazed at the far end of the room, lending some warmth to the raftered chamber. Evelyn and Celeste instinctively walked toward the fire, eager to warm their cold, stiff bones.

From a high-backed wing chair, Percival stood and emerged from the shadows. Evelyn and Celeste, startled at his appearance, gasped as if they seen a ghost. Indeed, with the room filled with old suits of armor worm by previous Dethman warriors and jousting champions, the sudden materialization of Percival's sinister face was startling.

He stood apart from them as they ripped off their gloves and warmed their fingers before the crackling fire. "You're late, Evelyn. Most of our guests have already arrived, and are safely ensconced in their rooms above stairs before cozy little fires."

"The trip was difficult, to be sure," she replied, more tartly than she'd intended. But her shivering teeth lent a crispness to her voice that couldn't be helped.

"You'll be pleased to know that nearly everyone responded to our invitations, *Mother*. Truly, I do not expect a little inclement weather to keep the others away. After all, this promises to be the house party of the year. You should have taken a peek at the invitations, dear. You would know what I mean."

Evelyn scoffed. "This promises to be the coldest house party of the year. Why, the entire notion of throwing such a last-minute affair in the dead of winter is ludicrous!"

The great double doors burst inward, seemingly from the impact of an arctic blast. Servants scurried forward, prepared to help the arriving guest with his *portmanteau* and his greatcoat. As the single man tossed off his beaver hat, he looked up and nodded toward the three people standing at the fireplace. Then his gaze scanned their faces more closely, and he stiffened, his coat half-shrugged from his broad shoulders while a maid servant plucked at his woolen scarf.

Evelyn's breath caught. The warmth she'd been seeking from the fire suddenly rushed through her veins like bubbling lava. As the visitor strode across the huge hall, she experienced a terrifying rush of emotions. Clasping her hands together, acutely aware of Percival's scrutiny, she forced her features to assume a mask of polite gentility.

Sir Hugo's eyes locked with hers. Evelyn had never felt such utter confusion roil through her bones. *What in the devil was Sir Hugo Mansfield doing at Goreham Castle?*

The earl broke the thick silence. "I presume you are Sir Hugo Mansfield, the famous barrister? Allow me to introduce myself, my stepmother and her sister."

Sir Hugo extended his hand to Celeste, and shook it gently. But when he reached for Evelyn's hand, she hesitated. Her mind was still reeling. How could she possibly allow this creature—this figment of her wildest imagination—to touch her?

The moment lengthened, until at last, Evelyn slipped her fingers in Sir Hugo's big hand. His flesh was surprisingly warm, considering that he'd just come inside. And when his fingers closed around hers, Evelyn felt a rush of awareness spread through her. Her heart hammered as he lifted her knuckles to his lips. Beneath her skirts, her limbs, encased in warm woolen stockings, trembled like saplings in a storm.

Releasing her hand, Sir Hugo straightened. Had his gaze raked over her, or had it been her prurient imagination? Evelyn's cheeks burned hot at the thought of Sir Hugo appraising her figure and her face after these five years. Suddenly self-conscious, she was relieved when Percival began his usual inane chatter.

The third earl launched an interrogation that concerned everything from the barrister's trip to Kent to the success of his law practice. From the conversation, which rang unpleasantly in Evelyn's ears, she learned that Sir Hugo was making a name for himself in London, and enjoying much financial success.

His eyes cut to hers once or twice, but he made no show

of having known Evelyn previously. Certainly, Celeste, who, with a yawn, excused herself and retired to her room, showed no sign of being aware of any subliminal message exchanged between the barrister and Evelyn. Evelyn was grateful for that.

But, did Percival know that she'd met this man before? How did Sir Hugo's name get on the guest list? *And, why hadn't she examined the invitations before they were sent out?* What a paperscull she'd been, allowing herself to be surprised like this! Why, Lord Goreham must be silently laughing his head off.

Another great commotion at the double doors announced the arrival of more guests. This time, two couples who'd traveled together in a rented coach stumbled into the great hall. Spying Percival, they called out their greetings and, as the two ladies in the party were weakened by their long journey, announced they would immediately adjourn to their chambers.

"If you will excuse me," Percival said to Evelyn and Sir Hugo. "I must see to my guests."

She could have sworn she detected a slight smirk on her step-son's face. But with his pencil-thin mustache, an adornment that gave him the appearance of having a permanent sneer, it was difficult to tell.

Sir Hugo stood facing the fire, while Evelyn turned her back to it. They stood alone at the end of the hall, the tension between them as palpable as the heat leaping from the flames. For a long while, neither said a word. When the foursome was escorted up the great staircase by Percival and a bevy of servants, the hall fell quiet except for the occasional crash of a log, and the wind pounding the glazed, colored glass in the arched windows.

"You looked surprised to see me, Evelyn. Or should I call you Lady Goreham?"

She swallowed over a lump in her throat, barely able to frame a response. Something between anger and indignation clawed at her gut. "Are you mocking me, Sir Hugo? The truth is, I am *shocked* to see you."

His gaze swung to hers; she could see from the corners of her eyes that his expression was one of incredulity. He started to say something, swore instead, then apologized for his rude speech. At length, he took a sidestep nearer to her, and said in a harsh whisper, "Then, why did you invite me here? What mischief are you about? Did you expect me not to come, is that it?"

Gasping, Evelyn put some distance between her and Sir Hugo. His very presence put her on edge, filled her with strange yearnings that she did not want to feel. "Why did you come to Goreham Castle, if not to torment me?"

"I received an invitation, my lady," he said softly. "Naturally, I assumed you wanted me to come here."

"I did not invite you here. Indeed, I had no idea you would be here," Evelyn said through clenched teeth.

Their eyes met for an instant, and Evelyn was amazed to see a genuine look of bewilderment on the barrister's face. "If you didn't invite me, then how did my name get on the guest list?"

"Percival, of course. Is he a business acquaintance of yours?" But, Evelyn quickly recalled that Percival had traced her gaze as she watched the barrister cross Lincoln's Inn Fields. The young earl knew, or suspected that she was attracted to Sir Hugo Mansfield. Perhaps, he'd even heard some vague gossip about what had taken place at Widow Philpott's five years earlier.

"Does he know?" Sir Hugo asked. "Does Percival know how you met your husband?"

"If you are asking me whether my husband told anyone the circumstances of our meeting, no. I can assure you, he wanted no one to know that he had *bought* me. It was given out that we were a love match, if you can believe that."

"A man with a high opinion of himself wouldn't want

the *ton* to believe his wife had no affection for him," Sir Hugo remarked.

"If Percival knows anything of what occurred that night, he did not learn it from his father. Perhaps Widow Philpott has loose lips, as well as loose—"

"Doubtful. In her business, discretion is paramount." Sir Hugo sighed.

After a length, Evelyn said, "You thought I had summoned you. Then, you came here . . . to see me?"

"Of course. Why else would I have come to this god-forsaken castle in the middle of nowhere, in the dead of winter?"

"Dashed if I know."

"Because I received an invitation from the third earl, and the Dowager Countess of Goreham, to attend a house party. 'Twas not unnatural for me to assume that you had a hand in putting my name on the guest list." Sir Hugo shook his head, frowning. "I see that I was mistaken. There is something very havey-cavey about this set-up. I should call for my carriage and return to London. 'Twas foolish of me to come. I have no business here, except to gaze at you and wonder what might have been."

His words ran through Evelyn like a sword. The realization that he harbored some regret over his actions five years ago pained her. Yet that same realization somehow buoyed her spirits. So he still thought of her. He cared what had become of her. She wondered if he was as haunted by the memory of that night as she was.

"Yes, you should go." Steeling herself for Sir Hugo's agreement, Evelyn stood as rigid as a board. He *should* go, if he knew what was best for both of them. He should go, and release them both from this torturous encounter.

He nodded, his eyes full of sadness. Reaching out, the barrister took her hand, squeezing her fingers, running his thumb over the delicate skin of her wrist. Evelyn studied his face, five years older than before. Beneath his eyes, faint shadows of purple darkened his skin. He worked too much. An almost indiscernible widening of his waistline convinced her that he wasn't eating properly, or that he was eating too much out of boredom or depression. His old-fashioned breeches, snug against his muscular legs, connoted a distinct disregard for fashion. Indeed, Sir Hugo had all the earmarks of an unmarried man. And for some reason, Evelyn took a scant amount of comfort in that.

Bowing low over her hand, he said, "Goodbye," then turned and stalked across the hall.

Evelyn watched his back, his broad shoulders, the movement of his muscles beneath those snug-fitting breeches. Her heart pummeled her ribs, and her mouth went dry. God, how she wanted to run after the man, throw herself at him and beg him to stay!

But, she couldn't. *Unmarried, unattached and untouched.* The words rang in her head like a dirge. Her stepson was above stairs, nursing his grudge against her, and hoping against hope that she'd compromise her virtue and forfeit her inheritance by engaging in an affair before the month was up.

But, even if she died a virgin, Evelyn would never risk Celeste's future by failing to fulfill the conditions of the old earl's will.

Something inside her cracked as she watched Sir Hugo speak quietly with the footman at the door. She'd made a bad bargain, her heart told her. She'd bartered her soul for financial security and a life of ease and contentment.

As tears streamed down her face, Evelyn stared at Sir Hugo. He turned and met her gaze, unleashing a wave of unbearable yearning inside her. Covering her face with her hands, Evelyn whirled and faced the fire, unable to countenance another moment of the man's disturbing presence. When she heard the slam of the great double doors, she was relieved that her tormentor was gone from Goreham Castle, and gone from her life. It had been so much safer to encounter him only in her imagination.

* * *

Snow fell steadily, and stuck to the thick, opaque panes of glass in the window in Evelyn's bedchamber. After calmly ascending the steps to her rooms, she'd closed the door behind her, and thrown herself on the huge four-poster bed where she cried until her eyes were nearly swollen shut. An insistent tapping at her door roused her, and, in a voice congested with spent emotion, she called out for the servant to enter.

With her head buried in her arms, stomach flat on the bed, she said, "I'll have my bath later, if you don't mind. But, would you bring me some tea, please?"

The voice that answered her, however, was that of her dearest friend in the world, Miss Louisa Freemantle. "I've not come this far in a blizzard to fetch you tea, dear."

Lifting her head, Evelyn rolled to her side. "When did you get here? For heaven's sake, you're shivering uncontrollably. Climb in and get under this coverlet before you freeze to death!"

Before the two young women scrambled beneath the thick, down blankets, Evelyn pulled a bell-cord and summoned a tray of tea and biscuits. By the time the maid arrived and placed the tray on the bed between them, they had kicked off their boots, piled bolsters behind their heads and settled themselves beneath mounds of counterpanes and covers. Crumbs scattered everywhere as they crunched cook's crispy biscuits, and sipped the steaming tea.

As usual, Louisa Freemantle did not beat around the bush. "Why on earth have you been crying? Your face looks like a pin cushion, dear."

Completely confident of her friend's discretion, Evelyn said, "There was a man who came here, but he has gone now. At any rate, I was quite overset to see him downstairs. Thank the good Lord he had the decency to remove himself from the house when he met me."

"Who is he?" Louisa snuggled deeper into her pillows, obviously relishing this girlish talk.

"His name is Sir Hugo Mansfield and I met him five years ago." Evelyn hesitated. She'd never told anyone the details of her meeting with the Earl of Goreham. No one had ever asked, for that matter, not even Miss Louisa Freemantle. Despite the old earl's attempts to persuade the *ton* theirs had been a love match, Evelyn knew that it was taken for granted that a young female married to a crusty old man had married for money—which, Evelyn supposed, was true enough in her case. But it was a grossly simplistic explanation of her predicament. And an unflattering depiction of why she'd agreed to marry Henry Dethman, Lord Goreham.

"Louisa, if I told you a secret, would you swear never to tell anyone else? Even upon pain of death?"

"Stick a needle in my eye," the young woman replied.

Evelyn studied her carefully; in looks, her friend was her opposite in every way. Where Evelyn had pale blond hair, Louisa's was jet black. Where Evelyn was slight in stature, Louisa was big-boned and lanky. But one thing the girls shared was their love of books and music and opera and plays. They'd whiled away many hours discussing their various interests, and Louisa had provided invaluable help in editing part of Evelyn's manuscript on Henry VIII, the Tudor king.

"All right, then, I shall tell you how I met my husband." Without varnishing the story one whit, Evelyn described her desperation the night she had wagered all her funds at Widow Philpott's faro house. She told Louisa about her fateful loss, and the earl's offer to marry her. She also told her friend about Sir Hugo's presence, and his advice to flee the house and let the law deal with Widow Philpott in its own inevitable way.

"You mean he didn't offer to bail you out of your troubles?" Louisa asked.

"He didn't offer to loan me the blunt, if that's what you

mean," Evelyn said. "Although he made it quite clear that in his legal opinion, I had been rooked at an illegal gambling establishment. The widow didn't even have a license, you see. So, perhaps she wouldn't have had the nerve to contact the Bow Street Runners and turn me in to the authorities."

"But what if she did? Or what if she sent some bludgeon-men after you to beat you up, or do something terrible to your sister? She might have, just to make an example of you. A woman like that can't afford to let it get around that her customers are allowed to leave her establishment owing her money. A reputation like that would have put the old tabby out of business straightaway."

Evelyn shrugged. "Yes, and the earl assured me that Widow Philpott was very tightly connected with the London authorities. Given the smug look on that widow's face the entire time I was in her trap, I'd say old Goreham was correct in all that he said. I daresay, I feared I'd be rounded up the very next day—assuming the Runners could find me—and tossed into Newgate. And where would that have left Celeste?"

"You mean you did it all for your younger sister?" Louisa's dark eyes rounded in astonishment.

"She was quite sick at the time." Evelyn shuddered at the memory of her little sister in bed in that awful flop-house room they'd shared. Celeste had lain for days, sweating and shivering, hot one moment, cold the next. Her brow burned with fever, and her teeth rattled with chills. Indeed, Evelyn had thought she was going to die.

"Well, what's done is done," Evelyn finally said, with a sigh. "The point is, I thought Sir Hugo a noble man, despite his being unable to help me."

"Was he unable, dear . . . or was he *unwilling*?"

Evelyn paused. "That, I cannot answer. I trust he gave me the best advice he could think of. 'Twas a lawyer's bit of gammon, that was for sure. But, I quite believe he believed it himself."

"Perhaps." Louisa looked reluctant to voice her opinion. Nevertheless, in short order, she haltingly said, "Perhaps he didn't have the money to bail you out."

"How could that be? I heard Percival say today that Sir Hugo has made himself a small fortune as a barrister! He has earned a fine reputation, which of course, does not surprise me. You should see, him, Louisa." Evelyn turned on her side and clutched her friend's arm. Closing her eyes, she pictured Sir Hugo and tried to describe the intelligent, compassionate man she'd spent five years dreaming about.

"Sounds like an Adonis," Louisa said, her voice edged with faint sarcasm. "Though if he did have the money to help you, and he refused, I would call him a heartless cad. And, are your forgetting, dear, that you are still in mourning?"

"Only for another month. And wouldn't Percival love it if I failed to live out my year of mourning as a true spinster? But, I will not allow that to happen!" For the first time, Evelyn's bitterness bubbled to the surface. For years, she'd hidden, perhaps even from herself, the true extent of her unhappiness. But, with the arrival of Sir Hugo at Goreham Castle, her emotions were whipped up like a cyclone, and she was powerless to control them.

"You mean, you're still a virgin?" Louisa squeaked.

"As pure as the driven snow," Evelyn said flatly.

Though no one could have heard them above the roar of the wind buffeting the castle walls, Louisa's voice fell to a conspiratorial whisper. "I am beginning to understand why you are so disturbed by the presence of this Sir Hugo. La, your eyes lit up like a bonfire when you described him to me. Have you got a notion to allow the man to seduce you, dear—after your year of mourning is up, I mean?"

"Heavens, no! I would never—"

A violent gust rattled the glass panes so hard that both women started, and grabbed each other's hands. Teacups and saucers fell from the bed to the floor with a clash and clang. Nestled deep beneath the warm security of their blankets, the two young women giggled to cover their fright. They were still laughing when the maid entered the room and swept up the debris of cakes and teacups on the carpet.

"I'll bring more tea later," Mrs. Shipton said.

When she'd gone, the two young women resumed their whispered conversation.

"I would never have an assignation of the type you referred to, even if the earl's will did not forbid it," Evelyn repeated.

"How very virtuous of you," Louisa answered, but her tone contradicted her words, sending the girls into peals of laughter.

Gasping for breath, tears running down her cheeks, Evelyn rolled on her back and stared at the lacy canopy above her head. It felt good to confide in a friend, and she was glad she'd told Louisa her secret.

"Didn't you ever feel sorry for yourself, trapped in a loveless marriage?" Louisa asked.

"On the contrary." Evelyn faced her friend and added, "Except for a moment, today, downstairs, when I encountered Sir Hugo again. I did feel sorry for myself, then. Because I thought how much I had given up, how much I would have liked to know a man like that . . . I mean, really *know* him."

"When your period of mourning is up—"

Evelyn shook her head. "No, even when the month is gone, there will still be something inside me that has made it impossible for me to truly give myself to a man. I mean give myself *completely*, Lou. I can't explain it, but something died in me when I agreed to marry the earl. I made a bargain with the devil, and he took part of my soul in return. I have sacrificed so much for personal comfort that I daresay I'll never fall in love the way people do in novels."

"Don't say that! Of course you'll fall in love."

"One has to be able to believe in love before she falls in it." Evelyn wiped a tear from her cheek. "I forced myself to think there was no such think as romantic love; that is how I got through the past five years. I turned off my feelings, Lou. I can't just turn them back on again. I'm afraid I have buried that part of my heart that could have believed love—true, selfless love, unmotivated by personal gain—is possible.''

"How very sad. Then you'll die a virgin.''

Evelyn cut her friend a sly look. ''I didn't say I had cut off *those* feelings, dear. Sex has nothing to do with love.''

"Oh, dear, you really are a greenie,'' Louisa said, chuckling. ''At any rate, you may be confronting temptation sooner than you think.''

"What do you mean, Lou?''

"The roads are closed. If your friend Sir Hugo attempted to return to London in the past few hours, he was turned back, I assure you. My coach barely arrived before the snows started in, and I heard the servants say that anyone who hadn't made it to the castle by this afternoon wasn't going to get here at all. Not for the next week, at least.''

Evelyn sat up, her spine as rigid as a board. ''You mean that Sir Hugo wasn't able to return to London?''

"My guess is that he is safely interred in one of these guest rooms, perhaps even next door!''

"Oh, Lou!'' Evelyn fell back on her pillow, burying her face in it, and pounding the bed with her fists. ''I cannot bear to see him, again. You must help me avoid Sir Hugo! You must!''

Lou stretched like a cat and yawned. ''I will help you, dear. Don't fret about that. I'll do whatever I can to make my little friend happy.''

Evelyn cried until she fell asleep, then dreamed of Sir Hugo kissing her, holding her hands, gazing into her eyes. When she awoke, her skin was feverish with suppressed desire. Her room was pitch dark, and Louisa was no longer in her bed.

* * *

Below stairs, Sir Hugo Mansfield stood at the far end of the Great Hall, where a small party of guests had congregated. A grouping of wing-back chairs and small sofas had been drawn near the fire, which, with the wind lashing at the windows and snow piling up against the castle walls, served as a warm beacon. Shadows leapt on the walls and off the rafters. The ancient shields and coats of armor glinted in the firelight. Only the Axminster carpets and Georgian furniture detracted from the medieval ambience.

Conversation centered around the severe weather, and the prospects of returning to London when the weekend was over. Sir Hugo, decidedly glum after being forced to turn back less than a mile from the castle, sipped a fortifying brandy and gazed at the fire.

His attention was caught by the sound of a familiar voice.

"Has anyone ventured toward the rear of this sprawling stone elephant?" A dandified young man with wispy blond hair and the most elaborately tied cravat Sir Hugo had seen in years, gestured demonstratively as he strode toward the half-dozen or so guests lounging in the hall. "If you haven't, you should! The parlor is done up in a fantastic motif that only a Dethman would have dared hoist on his unsuspecting company!"

"Cubby! What are you doing here?" Sir Hugo pumped the solicitor's hand enthusiastically.

"I might ask you the same thing," Sir Cuthbert deLisle replied, grinning. "Are you a friend of Percival's? Why didn't I know it, if you are?"

Hugo moved to a claw-footed sideboard, and poured Sir Cuthbert a glass of brandy. Though he considered Sir Cuthbert a friend, he'd never socialized with him, and knew precious little about the solicitor's clientele or his circle of friends. But, then, he didn't socialize with anyone. These days, a man couldn't go out for dinner without being forced into a friendly game of wagering over something, even if it was how long it would take the barmaid to plunk a round of tankards on the table. Hugo's isolation helped him avoid his gambling demons.

"I am not a friend of Percival's," Sir Hugo told Cuthbert. "How are you acquainted with him?"

Sir Cuthbert shot him a curious look. "I've done some law work for his father. In addition, Percival and I are fellow members of the London Society for the Study of the Tudor Monarchy. An interesting group, Hugo. You should consider joining us sometime. Rumor has it that you spend all your time closeted in your office, or with your nose buried in some dusty tome in the law library. Have you read everything Coke has written by now?"

"Just about it." Sir Hugo frowned, perplexed as ever at why he'd been invited to this party. "Are all the people at this party members of the Society?"

"Oh, no!" Sir Cuthbert looked around at the group gathered near the fire. "But the countess is. Have you had the pleasure of meeting her yet, Hugo? I daresay, she is one of the most attractive females I have ever met. And smart as a whip, too."

An older woman with grey hair and ample bosom turned in her chair, and lifted a finger to interject. "I couldn't help overhearing, sir. My name is Lady Adelaide Ramsbottom, and I couldn't agree more with you on that score. Evelyn has been a dear friend of mine now ever since I met her at some dreadful hot-house crush several years ago. My daughters love her! But, where is she, I wonder? I haven't seen hide nor hair of her all afternoon."

A dark-haired young woman with a retroussé nose and impertinent smile, spoke up from the chair opposite Lady Ramsbottom. "Evelyn is bone-tired from her journey, poor dear. I left her above stairs where she is napping. I'm sure she'll be at the party tonight."

"Wait till you see the parlor!" Sir Cuthbert crowed.

Sir Hugo was hardly interested in the decor of the parlor. He wanted to take his friend aside, and interrogate him about this strange fellow, Percival Dethman. But, of course, that would have been conspicuous and unseemly. Biding his time, Sir Hugo drained his brandy glass, and moved closer to the fire.

Sir Cuthbert, as luck would have it, followed him. When the two men were out of earshot, the solicitor said, "So if you're not a friend of Percival's, what the devil are you doing here?"

"Damned if I know."

"Friend of the old man's, were you? Perhaps you did some work for the wizened old codger? After all, this party is to honor the old rogue, and end the official period of mourning."

"I barely knew the man."

Sir Cuthbert scratched his chin. "Well, then, perhaps you know the countess. A mysterious creature, that one. But, I would stay away from her, if I were you."

"Why?"

"I'm not at liberty to say, old man. But she is in mourning, you know, at least for another month. Until then, I think it would be ungentleman-like to get too friendly with her."

"I don't think you need worry on that score. I was introduced to her when I arrived earlier this afternoon. She gave me the cold shoulder."

Chuckling, Sir Cuthbert ambled back to the sideboard, and grabbed a crystal decanter of brandy. After splashing a healthy dose in his glass, and Hugo's, he leaned against the rough stone wall of the Great Hall, one bootheel wedged in a chink caused by the uneven quality of the medieval building materials. "I'm not surprised to hear that. Wait till her mourning's over. I suspect she'll be as hot as a fire poker by then. God knows, she couldn't have been carnally satisfied in her marriage to the old earl.''

''I'll thank you not to speak of the countess in such disrespectful tones.''

''Are you sure you're not her lover? Or about to be?''

''Don't be ridiculous!''

Sir Cuthbert arched his flaxen brows. ''It seems to me, kind sir, that thou dost protest too much. Forgive me, Hugo, but why else would you be invited to this party if you're not friends with Percival or his deceased father, and you're not a lover of the Countess of Goreham?''

The barrister inhaled deeply, unable to furnish the solicitor an answer. Evelyn had adamantly denied inviting Sir Hugo to the castle. He could hardly believe that she would lie about such a thing—unless she'd invited him on an impulse then regretted having done so.

''Ah, here's our host, now,'' said Sir Cuthbert.

Hugo looked up to see Percival, third Earl of Goreham, enter the Hall. He crossed the long room like a strutting cock, his lips twitching beneath his carefully groomed mustache. Without having adequate cause, Sir Hugo felt a niggling distrust of the man. Not because he was slightly effeminate or showy, but because the earl wore a sly smirk on his face, like someone who knows a scandalous secret and is dying to tell it.

After greeting his other guests, including the dark-haired girl who was introduced as Miss Louisa Freemantle, Lord Goreham sidled up to Sir Cuthbert and slapped him heartily on the back.

''Well, I see my old friend has met my new one. Cubby, I hope you're not regaling Sir Hugo with any of those salacious tales you like to invent about my escapades at Cambridge.''

''On the contrary,'' Sir Cuthbert said, grinning. ''I've never had to invent a thing. You were the naughtiest boy I ever went to school with.''

Lord Goreham appeared pleased with this recommendation of his character. Twisting the corner of his mustache, he turned to Sir Hugo. "Have you had the pleasure of viewing the back parlor yet, sir?"

Sir Hugo shook his head. He wished he could simply ask the earl why he'd been invited to the castle. But to do so would cast suspicion on Evelyn, something his instinctive urge to protect her wouldn't allow him to do. And, it would be supremely rude. Forcing a pleasant expression on his face, Sir Hugo, said, "No sir, I've spent the last hour here, meeting your other guests, and renewing my acquaintance with Cubby."

"Splendid." The earl clapped his hands, then stepped aside and gestured toward an opening in the north side of the stone wall.

Lady Ramsbottom and Miss Freemantle stood and, with the other guests who had been loitering in the Hall, proceeded toward the opening and through the narrow passageway that led off it. Sir Hugo followed Sir Cuthbert and the earl through the damp, low-ceilinged corridor. As he walked, he noticed through the windows a courtyard at the center of the castle compound.

From what little he'd seen of the castle, Hugo surmised it was a series of old and new buildings surrounding a square courtyard. Large halls were connected to family rooms and 18th-century bedchambers by narrow passages. The effect was a medieval castle updated to Georgian standards and tastes.

Cold, dark and depressing, furnished with heavy furniture made to scale for Henry VIII's bulk, the castle was a forbidding, Gothic chamber of antiquities. Icy air whistled through cracks in the stone walls. Cobwebs draped the fifty-feet-long passageway leading from the hall to the parlor.

Sir Hugo had just brushed past a full coat of mail, complete with helmet and jousting tabard, when he stepped into the room that Lord Goreham was so eager to show him.

"The parlor, of course, is the most recent addition to

the castle." Percival stood with his hands clasped behind his back, staring expectantly at Sir Hugo. "As you can see, the room has a Nash-like feel to it. I insisted on the French doors, so that the courtyard is visible from here. And the patterned carpet was personally selected by me. As well as the pale blue and gold color scheme and pianoforte there in the corner."

"Egad, what a room!" Cubby strode toward the center of it, gazing at the huge paintings that covered the walls. "And, look what you've done with it! How clever, Percival. Really, the Dethmans are notorious for throwing grand parties, but this is over the top. You've outdone yourself."

"I'll say," murmured Lady Ramsbottom, peering at the contents of the room with a quizzing glass.

Miss Freemantle, her dark eyes glowing with inquisitiveness, appeared at Sir Hugo's elbow. "Are you all right, sir?" she asked, touching his arm lightly.

Nodding, he cleared his throat. But, he was not all right. For it wasn't the grandeur of the room's furnishings that overwhelmed him, or the richness of the artwork crowding the silk-paneled walls that gave him a start.

It was the faro table set up in the center of the room.

Still, that was insignificant compared to the shock delivered to his system an instant later.

Footsteps pounded down the passageway leading from the hall to the parlor. Turning, Sir Hugo stared as a tall, wan-looking man dressed in butler's uniform burst into the room.

Percival, clearly annoyed at this rude interruption, rounded on the man. "Good God, Grumby, what's the matter?"

For a moment, Sir Hugo breathed a sigh of relief. Any distraction that might avert him from the temptation of the gaming tables was welcome.

But the servant's message was not. Panting, the man clutched at his throat. After a few deep wheezes and labored gasps, he managed to deliver his fateful news.

"Lord Goreham, 'tis the countess. I'm afraid ... I'm afraid ..."

"Out with it!" shouted Percival Dethman.

"She is terribly sick—possibly dying!" And with that, the servant collapsed into the earl's arms.

Chapter Three

Or rather, Mr. Grumby fell against the earl.

Dethman violently shrugged the unconscious man off him, then bolted for the door. Sir Hugo and Sir Cuthbert ran behind their host. The remaining guests swarmed around Mr. Grumby's prostrate form.

The men raced through the narrow passageway that opened into the Great Hall; then, they pounded through that long room and up the magnificent stone staircase.

Turning right, they strode the carpeted corridor abreast. Divided into sleeping chambers, this section of the castle, situated directly atop the Great Hall, was obviously an 18th-century renovation. Aubusson carpets ran the length of the corridor; wrought-iron wall sconces filled with glowing candles cast an eerie glow on the plastered walls. And door after door opened off the hallway, a warren of rooms unlike anything a medieval builder could have envisioned.

The countess's bedchamber was at the end of the hall, two doors down from the room in which Sir Hugo had deposited his own baggage, and where he'd spent an hour that afternoon contemplating his unfortunate luck. In the threshold stood a pasty-faced maid servant. At the sight of Percival Dethman, her expression grew even more pinched.

Dethman brushed past the servant. Sir Hugo and Sir Cuthbert followed him to Evelyn's bedside.

She lay beneath the counterpane and coverlet, her blond hair spilling on the pillow. Her skin was alabaster, her lips bloodless.

Without thinking, Sir Hugo shouldered Lord Goreham out of the way. Bending over the bed, he was assailed by memories of the first time he'd seen Evelyn lying prostrate on a bed, the night she had fainted in Widow Philpott's faro house. Clasping her delicate hand, he stared anxiously at her fluttering eyelashes.

Her voice was weak, barely audible. "What—what happened?"

The maid spoke from the foot of the bed. "You almost died, that's what! If I hadn't come into the room when I did, child, you'd be dead as a doornail right now!"

Sir Hugo seized control of the moment. "Exactly what happened?"

"She was choking when I came in! Couldn't breathe and was green as a fish gone bad! First I screamed so loud that Grumby came running. Then, I pounded her on the back to clear her throat, and Mr. Grumby—bless his heart—blew air into her mouth till she started breathin' again. Never seen nothin' like it, but Grumby says he learned it in the army!"

Lord Goreham wore an expression of shock. "Good God. 'Twas sheer luck you looked in on the countess when you did!"

Inflated with importance, the maid took her time in relating the rest of her story. "I came in once't earlier with a pot of fresh tea for the lady. But she was sleepin' so I merely left the tea on the table beside the bed."

"What time was that?" It was in Sir Hugo's nature to ask questions, after all. And there was something darkly sinister about the whole affair. An impromptu end-of-mourning celebration in a drafty old castle in the middle of winter. An invitation from a woman he hadn't seen in five years, and who denied having invited him to the house party. A parlor converted into a gambling hell, the very worst sort of temptation Sir Hugo could imagine. And, now, a near fatal incident of vomiting and choking. Hugo's pulse raced as he realized someone was stirring up trouble for him—or for Evelyn. Or, perhaps for both of them.

Lord Goreham practically shouted at the maid. "Mrs. Shipton, you were asked a question. What bloody time was it when you entered with the tea tray?"

The old woman started. "Dear me, I don't know precisely. I suppose it was around four o'clock. Oh, it could have been a half hour later. Or earlier. I don't know, really."

"You're no help!" the earl expostulated.

"You're making her nervous," Sir Hugo said softly. "Mrs. Shipton, did you by chance look at the countess when you came in at four? Was she sleeping peacefully, I mean?"

Evelyn moaned, but said nothing during this interrogation.

"She was a trifle hot, sir. I didn't think it that unusual, though. The fire had been going for quite some time and the room had gotten stuffy. She was under mounds of blankets, too."

"Did she appear sick to you at that time?" Sir Hugo persisted.

Mrs. Shipton hesitated. "I bent over her and laid my hand on her forehead. Oh, dear, me! She was warm to the touch, but I didn't think she was sick. I pulled back the quilt before I left the room. I'd have never left her if I thought she was sick!"

"I'm sure you wouldn't have," Sir Hugo said.

Extracting a crumpled handkerchief from her apron

pocket, Mrs. Shipton began a series of explosive nose-blowings.

"When did you return to this room?" Sir Hugo asked between blasts.

"Just minutes before I sounded the alarm, I'm afraid. 'Twas just after five o'clock, and I thought the countess might want a bite of something before she dressed for dinner. I opened the door and the poor child was sitting on the edge of the bed, her head between her knees . . ."

Mrs. Shipton proceeded with a graphic description of Evelyn's illness. Several damp towels on the floor attested to the violence of the countess's ordeal. To Sir Hugo's learned ears, it was obvious the countess's stomach had reacted violently to something she'd ingested.

Celeste Waring suddenly appeared at the threshold. Spying Evelyn prostrate and pale as a ghost, the girl flew to the bedside. "What has happened to my sister?"

Sir Hugo was forced to release Evelyn's hand and step back to allow the young girl to sit on the edge of the mattress.

"I'm all right," Evelyn whispered, unconvincingly.

Mrs. Shipton spoke soothingly. "She must have eaten something that made her ill. She'll be fine, Celeste."

Lord Goreham interjected. "Didn't you say you ate some mutton at that wretched inn you spent the night at?"

The young girl turned, and stared at the men. Her face was streaked with tears, and her eyes were round with fright. "We I ate the same thing. Why am I not sick, too?"

"She must have eaten more than you."

"No!" Celeste looked at her sister's ashen face. "She looks like a corpse, for heaven's sake!"

A slight smile wavered at the corner of Evelyn's pale lips. "Thank you, Sister. Remind me to return the compliment."

"Come now, Miss Celeste." Mrs. Shipton moved forward to clutch the younger girl's shoulders. "You will overset your sister. She needs some rest now. She has just pitched up her dinner, that is all."

"She'll be fine," repeated Lord Goreham.

Sir Hugo bent down and laid his hand on Evelyn's forehead. He felt the scrutiny of Lord Goreham's and Sir Cuthbert's gaze. He also felt the normal temperature of a healthy young woman. Assured that Evelyn had indeed passed any point of critical danger, he straightened.

Sir Cuthbert spoke at last. "I'm afraid that means the countess will not be down for dinner, much less for the gala you've planned for the night. How unfortunate, Percival."

Percival nodded. "The party will go on, though. I'm sure Evelyn wants it to, don't you, old girl?"

Evelyn nodded weakly. Her lashes fluttered, and her lids lowered. She looked drained, as if she could hardly hold her eyes open.

Sir Hugo experienced a heady, spine-tingling surge of apprehension. Something was terribly wrong with Mrs. Shipton's explanation of what had happened to Evelyn. He looked around the room, his gaze lighting on the table next to the bed. "Is that the teapot which you brought into the countess's room?" he asked the maid.

She glanced at it. "Aye, 'tis the same. I'll remove it straightaway." After tucking the covers around Evelyn and arranging the pillows to make her more comfortable, Mrs. Shipton picked up the tray on the bedside table.

"Mind if I look in it?" Without waiting for the maid's assent, Sir Hugo lifted the top of the tea pot. He wasn't surprised to see that the interior of the pot was empty— and wiped perfectly clean. Replacing the lid, he shot the earl and Sir Cuthbert an uncommunicative smile. "Everything appears in order."

The maid left the room on Sir Cuthbert's heels.

The Countess of Goreham was already asleep when Lord Goreham doused the candles. Sir Hugo watched the third earl's every move, then followed him from the room.

*   *   *

Evelyn slept fitfully, tossing from side to side. Her stomach ached, but the awful nausea had subsided. Her head ached, too, but the burning fever abated. Now, she was exhausted and grateful for the darkness of her bedchamber, and the comfort of her soft, feather mattress.

Someone entered her room. The door closed with a soft click, then heavy footsteps slowly crossed the carpet. Evelyn's eyes blinked, and her pulse quickened as Sir Hugo's face faded into view. But, she wasn't certain whether she was dreaming, or whether the barrister had actually materialized at her bedside.

He placed his single candle-holder on the bedside table, then perched on the edge of her mattress. In the flickering golden light of the burning taper, his expression was hauntingly sad.

Shadows played across his face, accentuating the angle of his firm jaw, deepening his charcoal eyes. He leaned forward, and his hand found hers atop the covers.

Evelyn stared, consumed by the heat of Sir Hugo's gaze.

The stubble along his jaw—the mere sight of it—raised gooseflesh along the sensitive skin of her shoulders and arms. Her lips moved, but Evelyn was unable to voice her thoughts. Floating in half-sleep, she watched the barrister. He smiled; the tiny wrinkles bracketing his eyes deepened as he scanned her face.

"Don't speak." He pressed a finger to her lips.

She tasted his flesh, felt the blood pulsing beneath his skin.

He rubbed the pad of his thumb along her lower lip. His features tightened, as if a spasm of pain were shimmering through his body. His eyes squeezed shut, and a moment later, a tear sparkled on his lashes.

When Evelyn tried to speak, nothing but a kittenish moan escaped her lips. Even the effort of staring at Sir Hugo exhausted her.

"Don't say a word." His voice was hoarse with suppressed emotion. "I shouldn't have come here, Evelyn. It was a mistake."

She wanted to tell him it wasn't a mistake. She wanted to tell him she needed him. But her eyelids grew heavier by the moment.

"Sleep, my lady," he whispered in her ear.

She felt his warm breath on her neck, smelled his musky, masculine aroma, and shivered at the scrape of his beard against her skin.

Sir Hugo pushed off the bed and picked up his candle.

Evelyn heard the click of the door as darkness overwhelmed her.

With the morning came a fresh onslaught of snow, quashing any chance the earl's visitors might have had of returning to London. Sir Hugo had spent most of the night in his room, two doors down from Evelyn's, consumed with desire. His need to descend to the back parlor and take his place at the faro table was nearly as compelling as his need to see Evelyn.

Somehow, he managed to remain above stairs, though in all truth, he doubted if he could have were it not for Evelyn. The allure of the gaming tables was strong; the magnetic pull that the countess had on him was even stronger.

In the end, he hadn't been able to resist her. Sometime in the middle of the night, Sir Hugo had risen from bed. Fully dressed—for he'd never taken his clothes off—he crept down the hall. He'd been as stealthy as a panther, letting himself into Evelyn's room without making so much as a floorboard creak.

But when he'd returned to his room, as luck would have it, he encountered another person.

"Fancy meeting you here," whispered Sir Cuthbert, holding his taper aloft. He was just entering his own room, directly across from Sir Hugo's. With his shirttail out, and his hair disheveled, it was evident he'd been visiting some willing lady.

"What the devil are you doing up at this hour?" Sir Hugo asked, as if he didn't know.

"I should ask you the same question, particularly since you just came out of the countess's room. How is she, by the way? Fever abated? Nausea gone?"

"She's asleep," Sir Hugo answered tersely.

"Yes." Sir Cuthbert seemed to mull this over. A knowing smirk played at his lips. "I shouldn't let the young earl see you coming out of Lady Goreham's room if I were you, Hugo. Take my word for it, it would be a most unpleasant business for everyone involved."

"I would never do anything to invite scandal on Evelyn's head—"

"Oh, are you on a first name basis with the countess?"

"Don't be an idiot! Have you forgotten that awful business of this afternoon? The woman was deathly ill, and I was only looking in on her to see that she was breathing."

Sir Cuthbert gave a low chuckle. "So you're a doctor as well as a lawyer. How convenient. At any rate, you'll stay away from her if you know what's good for you. Or don't— it's of no consequence to me."

With that, Hugo entered his room, closing the door softly behind him. He threw himself on his bed, miserable and feeling like a fool for having visited Evelyn in the first place.

He marveled at the tricks his own mind played on him. Had he thought he would sneak into Evelyn's room, take her in his arms, and tell her he loved her? Had he thought he could erase from her mind the fact he'd failed her five years ago?

More importantly, had he thought he was capable of promising his love to any woman, much less Evelyn, who deserved so much more than he could offer her?

Unable to sleep, he rose from his bed, grabbed an iron

poker and tongs from the hearth, and set about reviving the fire. As the embers glowed orange, and flames crackled among the logs, he leaned against the mantelpiece. Warmth suffused his face, but his heart was cold as stone. He had to keep a safe distance from Evelyn; she was as dangerous and as tempting as a pair of Fulham dice. If he allowed himself to succumb to her charms, he would be forced to confront his weakness, his inability to form a lasting connection with her, to love and marry her, and to provide for her.

After all, an incurable gambler could never promise marriage to a woman like Evelyn. Hugo never knew when he might fall prey to his urge to wager every penny he owned. Any woman who married him would have to know that her future was built on the shakiest of foundations. She would have to recognize, as Hugo had done long ago, that he was incorrigible, irredeemable and incapable of change.

But, he loved her. As he scraped a clod of mud from his boot with the brass poker, Hugo despaired that he would ever be fit to court any woman. He was too truthful to promise he'd never enter another gambling hell, and too honorable to marry a woman whom he might betray, disappoint, or even render destitute. Truth be known, he wasn't certain whether he could stay away from faro tables and hazard tables the rest of his life. He only knew that it required nearly every drop of energy he possessed—every waking hour of every day—to keep his gambling demons at bay.

Returning to bed, he lay on his back and stared at the shadows flitting across the ceiling. Hours later, his eyes felt as if he'd been in a sandstorm. He watched the sun rise, and stared out his window at the falling snow. It had piled up deep, halfway up a man's shinbone. It was a certainty that Hugo wouldn't get back to London before the middle of next week.

Still, he'd survived another night without succumbing to the temptation to gamble.

And he'd survived another night without taking Evelyn into his arms and possessing her.

Standing at the window in his bedchamber, his breath frosting the cold pane, Sir Hugo felt renewed strength surging through his veins. *He could resist the faro table.*

But, his strength was tempered by a throbbing desire. The real question was, could he resist Evelyn, the Dowager Countess of Goreham?

Evelyn looked up as her bedroom door creaked open. Celeste peeked around the frame, her blue eyes hopeful. Miss Louisa Freemantle's nimbus of dark hair appeared above Celeste's head. The two women hung in the threshold, staring at Evelyn as she handed her cup of tea to the maid.

"Come in, you two. Mrs. Shipton is just leaving." Her voice was stronger. Patting the bed, she said, "Celeste, climb on up. Louisa, pull up that chair, will you? I've been wondering when the two of you would make an appearance."

"We've waited all morning!" Celeste stretched out beside her sister. Taking Evelyn's hand in her own, she said, "Shipton wouldn't let us near you until you'd had your bath and tea. Are you feeling better now?"

"A trifle weak," Evelyn admitted. "But much better."

Louisa Freemantle leaned forward to pat her friend's hand. "You gave us quite a scare. Do you know what you ate that made you so ill?"

Evelyn, truly perplexed, shook her head.

Celeste said, "We ate all the same things, Sister. Unless you had something here at the castle after we arrived. Did you?"

"Nothing but tea," Evelyn answered.

"And I drank the same tea as you," Louisa said. "It didn't make me ill."

Evelyn chewed her lower lip. "Whatever it was, I am well now. Thank goodness Shipton entered the room when she did. It was dreadfully embarrassing, but I'd have choked if she hadn't tended to me."

Celeste snuggled closer to her sister. "You missed a great party last night."

"You weren't there, I hope!" Evelyn's eyes flashed.

"She might as well have been," Louisa said. "She made me tell her everything that happened. Celeste was waiting for me in my room when I came up from the party, as a matter of fact. I spent more time telling her what it was like than I did at the party."

"I thought you'd never come to bed," Celeste cried. "It was near three o'clock when you stumbled in."

"And now you shall have to tell me, too. Poor Lou," Evelyn said.

"I don't mind." But Louisa shot Celeste a sharp look, clearly embarrassed by the younger girl's disclosure of her scandalous bedtime. After describing the parlor decor, with its faro table, card tables and glittering chandeliers, she began a painstaking description of the dress Lady Ramsbottom's daughter wore.

Celeste burst out laughing. "It must have been hideous! Whoever told her that an orange crepe gown with a green Elizabethan ruff would complement her rather generous figure?"

Even Evelyn risked a hearty chuckle, though it precipitated a coughing spell. At last, after Louisa had given scathing fashion critiques of every woman attending last night's celebration, Evelyn turned the conversation to her real interest.

"Was Sir Hugo in attendance?" She was careful to keep her tone casual.

Louisa tapped her chin in a pensive gesture. "Come to think of it, I don't remember seeing him."

"He must have been sick or something," Celeste said. "Why would anyone stay away from the party, unless they had to, or unless they were too young to attend?"

"Just so," Louisa added. "Perhaps someone should inquire whether the barrister is ill. Would you like me to pen a note, Evie, and have Grumby slip it under his door?"

"No." Evelyn was firm. "I was just curious, that's all. Tell me more about Lady Ramsbottom's daughter. Does Hermione still have that loud, cackling laugh?"

"I could hear it from the hall," Celeste blurted.

"The hall? What were you doing there?" her sister asked.

The younger girl's face reddened. "I—I had gone down looking for hot chocolate, and I just wandered into the hall to find a maidservant. They were scarce, given the bustle going on in the parlor."

"Celeste! I won't countenance such behavior. You are forbidden to loiter in the hall while gambling is going on in the parlor! From now on, I'll keep a better watch over you. I daresay, last evening, I wasn't up to supervising anyone."

Louisa stood from her chair, leaned down and squeezed Evelyn's hand. "No harm done, dear. She's of an age, after all."

Evelyn sighed. Her agitation over Celeste's provocative behavior was fueled by her curiosity over Sir Hugo's absence from the party. She would have expected him to make an appearance at the faro table. She could picture him, in fact, as he was five years ago, his eyes trained on the card box at the end of the table, his lips set in firm lines, the muscles beneath his jaw flinching.

Something about that image sent chills up her spine. Sir Hugo's expression had been so dark, so brooding and anguished. Unlike many of the men she'd seen wagering in gaming hells, he looked miserable. Clearly, he wasn't the sort who gambled purely for sport. He took the game seriously, as he did everything.

Evelyn clucked her tongue, drawing Celeste's and Louisa's attention.

"What is it?" Celeste disembarked the bed, and smoothed her woolen gown. At Goreham Castle, the women dressed for warmth, not fashion—when they weren't in the gaming parlor, anyway.

"Are you sure you're all right?" Louisa queried, her brow furrowed.

"I am fine," Evelyn lied.

But, she was not fine. The image she'd conjured of Sir Hugo, standing at the faro table, with his hooded eyes and clenched jaw, filled her with foreboding. She suddenly realized she knew nothing about this man who'd been the object of her fantasies for five years.

How foolish of her to think she knew anything about him! Why, he could be the cruelest man on earth, or the most loathsome cad to ever cast his eye on a woman. For all she knew, he was precisely what Louisa suggested he was yesterday—a heartless rake who hadn't cared a whit whether Widow Philpott had Evelyn tossed in Newgate.

But he'd come to her room last night—or had she dreamed that, too? And the way he'd looked at her, instilling in her a warm, liquid heat that gushed through her limbs like a fever—had that been real, or was she living in a world of fantasy—*still*?

Sir Hugo had spent the morning pacing the length of his room, brooding over the significance of Sir Cuthbert's having spied him exiting Evelyn's bedchamber. A few minutes after ten o'clock, he heard a knock on the solicitor's door. But, he never heard the door open and shut again, so he wasn't certain whether Cuthbert remained alone.

Just before nuncheon, when he couldn't contain his impatience any longer, Sir Hugo crossed the hallway and rapped on Sir Cuthbert's door.

There was no answer. After a moment's hesitation, and

a guilty glance over his shoulder, Hugo turned the knob and entered Sir Cuthbert's bedchamber.

As he suspected, he found the blond-headed man sprawled on the bed, counterpanes tangled around a splay of limbs. Sir Cuthbert snored loudly, obviously sleeping off the effects of a long, drunken evening.

"Wake up!" Hugo gave the man's shoulder a firm shake, which failed to rouse him. Only when Hugo grasped Cuthbert's shoulders and rattled him violently did the solicitor wake.

When Hugo released him, Cuthbert slumped to the bed, his eyes blinking convulsively. Rising on his elbows, he cried, "What the devil? I've just crawled into bed, Hugo! Can't it wait till morning?"

"It is morning, you sapscull! In fact, it is nearly noon. You've slept half the day away."

Scratching his scalp, the solicitor yawned. "Ring the bell-cord and get me some tea or coffee, would you, old boy?"

Sir Hugo complied, and within minutes, a maid appeared with a tray of tea, scones, and hard, crunchy biscuits. When she'd left, Hugo dragged a chair to the side of the bed.

"So, tell me," he said, eyeing Cuthbert over the rim of his cup, "how was the party last night?"

Sir Cuthbert, his nakedness covered only by a strategically placed counterpane, leaned against the pillows and popped a biscuit in his mouth. "Splendid. You should have been there. Why in hell weren't you, by the way?"

"Had a bad case of the megrims. Must have something to do with this nasty weather."

"Are you certain you didn't spend the evening with a certain young woman . . . our hostess, perhaps?"

Sir Hugo lowered his cup, clanging it angrily on the saucer. "I should pack you a facer if you were anyone else, Cubby! That kind of talk can get a man in trouble, so I'd advise you to keep your mouth shut."

"I might have been foxed last night, but I was sober

enough to know what I saw. And I don't believe that gammon about checking on her just to make sure she was breathing."

"Then you aren't much of a gentleman," Sir Hugo replied stiffly. "After all, everyone else had adjourned to the parlor to gamble. There was no one above stairs to keep a watch over her. It was only right that I peek in, and make certain that she was sleeping peacefully."

"With logic like that, I'm surprised you have ever won a case." Sir Cuthbert smiled, sipped his tea and arched one brow behind his teacup. "Look, old man, no use in pretending with me. She's a beautiful woman, and much too young to be a widow. She needs some cheering up, if you ask me. It might as well be you who does the cheering up."

"Didn't you tell me just last night to stay away from that woman? Why the sudden reversal in your advice? As a solicitor, you should know the importance of sticking with your convictions."

Cuthbert laughed. "My advice to you as a friend would not necessarily be the same advice I would give as your solicitor."

"What the devil does that mean? Is there something about this woman that you're not telling me, Cubby?"

"As you know, her deceased husband was my client, Hugo. You know that I cannot reveal to you anything that would breach my duty of confidentiality to him."

"But he's dead."

"Yes, but in many ways, his will continues to live on."

"Don't be so bloody cryptic," Sir Hugo said, his voice seething with suppressed fury. "You might as well know that she denies inviting me here! Which means that my name was put on the list by her stepson, Lord Goreham, whom I have never laid eyes on previous to arriving at Goreham Castle. It's a mystery to me why I'm here, and I would like very much to return to London, but I cannot because the roads are closed."

A light sparkled in Sir Cuthbert's eyes, a light that made Sir Hugo most uncomfortable. "Are you saying that you came to Goreham Castle because you thought Evelyn had invited you?"

The solicitor's question was met with silence.

"That does put a new face on it," drawled Sir Cuthbert. "But you're a big boy, quite able to take care of yourself, I suppose. This should be an interesting weekend."

Sir Hugo stood, his spine ramrod straight. He glared angrily at Sir Cuthbert, wondering with some trepidation whether he'd been wrong to consider this man his friend. The fact that Cuthbert had seen him emerge from Evelyn's room was a major irritant; somehow, Cubby seemed to think of this bit of information as a powerful tool, but Sir Hugo couldn't figure out why.

Even if the worst interpretation of the scene were proved true—even if Sir Hugo had kept an assignation with Evelyn—she was an unmarried woman. Scandal might rain down on her head—or it might not, depending on whether Cubby's story were believed. And, given that the countess was deathly ill just hours before Sir Hugo was seen exiting her room, it was very likely that even the most rabid gossip-monger would be reluctant to depict this particular indiscretion in too portentous a light.

Turning on his heel, Sir Hugo stalked toward the door. When his hand was on the knob, Sir Cuthbert said, "Wait! There is one more thing. Just out of curiosity, old man, how long do you think it will be before the countess becomes engaged to be married?"

Sir Cuthbert spoke in an icy voice. "How the hell should I know?"

"Odds have been laid on it, old man. At Watier's, they're saying she'll be engaged by March. The earl himself has wagered a hundred pounds that she'll form a connection before the season begins. I, for one, have put money on her eloping to Gretna Green before her period of mourning is up. Truly, she is a saucy girl and she can't be expected to live like a nun now that old Dad has turned up his toes."

Slowly, deliberately, with every muscle in his body tensed, Sir Hugo turned. He glared at Sir Cuthbert, with enough anger in his gaze to cause the tow-headed man's cup and saucer to rattle in his hands.

"Why are you goading me like this, Cubby? Why the change of heart since last night, when you were practically begging me to leave Evelyn alone?"

"Don't you want to lay a bet on it, old man? Come on, now, what do you think? Will she be married before the spring? How much money are you willing to place on your bet, Hugo?"

Through clenched teeth, Hugo said softly, "I am not a gambling man, Cubby."

"What? Why not? Every man gambles, Hugo. Have you some moral objection to gaming? When did that come about? This is the first I've heard of it."

"I have no moral objection to it as long as it does not obsess or consume a man or cause harm to his loved ones. As for betting on whether Lady Goreham will remarry— and when—I find that a cruel, demeaning bit of chicanery. A gentleman should have more regard for a lady's reputation."

Sir Cuthbert gulped. "You've got a nasty gleam in your eyes, Hugo. I'm sorry that I offended you."

After a long, tense silence, Sir Hugo nodded brusquely, and left Cubby's bedchamber. He would have pulled the door shut with a violent bang, but for his consideration of Evelyn's nerves. Glancing at her door, he hoped she was sleeping peacefully. He hoped she was stronger today, after her unpleasant illness the afternoon before. He wished, more than anything, that he could go to her again, hold her hand, and comfort her.

With a growing sense of unease, he went below stairs and entered the Great Hall where a sideboard was laden with leftover breakfast buns and cold sausages. Taking a charger, he helped himself to the food, but when he sat down at the long medieval banquet table, found himself unable to eat. His attraction toward Evelyn bedeviled him. He was consumed by thoughts of her. He only hoped his obsession wouldn't prove injurious to the one he loved—*her*.

"You can come out, now." Sir Cuthbert stood, tossing the crumpled counterpane on the bed behind him.

Percival emerged from behind a tole screen.

"For God's sake!" Sir Cuthbert donned his unmentionables, then stepped into his breeches. "This weekend is turning out to be a horrid affair. Why don't you just leave it alone, Percival? Let the chips fall where they may. You can't control everything!"

"No, but I don't intend to stand by idly while that conniving little wench ruins my family name and breaks the bank, to boot!"

"I don't like it. And I don't like being part of it."

"Don't be self-righteous with me, Cubby! You want the fee I've promised you—you'd sell your mother if the price were right. And believe me, you'll get well paid if Evelyn fails to live up to the conditions of Father's will."

"Even that won't stop her from publishing her manuscript, Percival," the solicitor replied, using a long-handled shoehorn to pry his feet into his knee-boots. "She had every right to use the Dethman diaries. Dr. Peeps and I were present when your Father gave her his permission, you know. And if you deprive her of her inheritance, she'll be even more motivated to publish her book. She'll need the money, then. Have you considered that you might be cutting off your nose to spite your face?"

Percival's face twisted in an ugly sneer. "There won't be any manuscript published, I assure you."

For a long moment, Sir Cuthbert stared at his client. At last, choosing his words carefully, he said, "I don't want you to make any incriminating admissions to me, Percival, but that business yesterday was most imprudent."

"What the hell are you babbling about?"

"Evelyn's stomach upset. She nearly choked to death. Had she done so, there would have been an official inquiry. I couldn't have protected you, Percival, if you'd been found in possession of—"

"Of what?" The spindly man exploded, his hands flying wildly in the air. "Do you take me for a fool?"

Sir Cuthbert averted his eyes as he laced up his breeches.

"She ate something that disagreed with her, and she threw it up," Percival said, as if rehearsing his defense. " 'Twas most opportune that Mrs. Shipton found her when she did. Otherwise, there might have been a terrible, fatal accident. That is what happened, Cubby. And that is all that happened!"

"If you say so," the lawyer answered quietly.

"You owe to me a duty of secrecy." The earl's voice was a low, venomous hiss. "And if you help me, you stand to make a great deal of money. Given that you are deep in dun territory because of your gambling debts, I suggest that you do not refuse this opportunity, Cubby. You need me."

Sir Cuthbert glared at him in icy disdain, but said nothing as Percival crossed the room and perched on the side of his bed.

It was a bargain with the devil. Percival's voice was like a potato peeler shredding Cubby's nerves. But he kept his counsel, remaining silent while the earl talked. Lord Goreham was wrong in thinking that Sir Cuthbert needed him. The solicitor merely needed the other man's money. To what lengths he would go to get it, even he was unaware.

Chapter Four

Evelyn remained confined to her bedchamber. The afternoon passed slowly, tediously, except for the moments when she succumbed to the powerful daydreams that haunted her.

Aching and irritable from the boredom of lying in bed all day, she tossed off her covers, and scampered across the room for her woolen night-wrap. With a pull of the bell cord, Evelyn summoned a maid who brought her a pot of hot chocolate.

Waiting for her abigail to come and assist her in dressing, Evelyn sat in a wing-back chair beside the fire. Feet tucked beneath her, she drank her chocolate and stared absently at the leaping flames. Why had the earl made her inheritance contingent on remaining "unmarried, unattached, and untouched" a year after his death? What kind of perverse joke was that?

It was so unlike old Henry Dethman. Despite the man's rude handling of her the night he offered her marriage, he eventually proved himself a decent man. Crusty on the outside, soft on the inside, he had in his youth, been an incorrigible rogue. Evelyn had heard the servants whisper that his first wife, who died from consumption, was a veritable saint for tolerating his escapades.

Evelyn had married a controversial figure, as it turned out. There were many among the *ton* who despised Henry Dethman, the second Earl of Goreham. He was considered by them as uncouth, arrogant, a ruthless user of women. But, Evelyn had seen glimpses of a very different sort of man, isolated and lonely. Convinced that no one loved him, he went out of his way to reject others before they rejected him.

Shivering, she drew her knees to her chest and hugged herself. She hadn't loved him, not as a wife should love a husband. Certainly not with the breathless passion that Sir Hugo, by comparison a stranger, instilled in her. But, she had respected her deceased husband. And the gratitude she'd felt toward him for saving her and Celeste from a life of poverty was powerful, indeed.

There had been a bond between them, and the old earl's death had robbed her of something—her optimism, perhaps—or, her sense of security. Now, she was on her own again, very much the same as when she first met the earl. And she had the inescapable feeling that her future welfare—and Celeste's—was once more hanging in the balance.

Her fear that destitution was only a heartbeat away came rushing back to her.

Why had her husband changed his will?

And why had Sir Hugo, the man of her fantasies, the man who'd all but propelled her into the earl's arms five years earlier, reappeared?

Her hot chocolate left her cold inside. Sir Hugo might very well topple everything Evelyn had built in her life. If he didn't leave her alone, he might ruin everything she'd worked for, dreamed for, hoped for. If she couldn't harness her feelings, she and Celeste might once again be on the streets and penniless. Unless of course, her book proved a success.

The abigail entered with a freshly laundered gown. Tossing aside her woolen wrap, Evelyn stepped into the dark blue woolen dress. She knew what she must do: she must avoid Sir Hugo at all costs, and she must concentrate her efforts on the publication of her book. If she'd learned one thing in the past five years, it was that no one would look after a woman who couldn't look after herself.

Romance, sexual attraction, the selfish exploration of physical passion . . . those dalliances were not for Evelyn, the Countess of Goreham. She had to stay focused on remaining chaste and avoiding scandal. She wouldn't allow Percival to gain the ammunition he needed to cut her out of the old earl's will.

For Celeste's sake, and for her own, she fully intended to live up to the conditions of the old earl's will.

"At least it isn't black." Celeste eyed her sister from head to toe.

Having crossed the length of the Great Hall, Evelyn lurched her last steps toward an empty wing chair. She grabbed the arm of the chair, then lowered herself into it while clutching her stomach.

Her sister jumped to her feet, and rushed to her side. "You're pale as a ghost, Evie. You should have stayed in bed!"

Lady Ramsbottom, comfortably tucked in the cushions of a sofa, her ample lap covered by a woolen blanket, spoke over the clucking of the younger sister. "She was quite right to descend from her bedchamber, if only for a little while. It does a body good to dress and get about, especially when one has lain in bed all night and day."

Louisa Freemantle rushed to Evelyn's side, also. She pressed her hand to her friend's forehead, then shouted for tea at a servant who happened to emerge from the corridor that led to the parlor.

Evelyn flinched at the volume of Louisa's voice. "For heaven's sake, Lou, you yelled in my ear!"

"Sorry, dear," murmured the dark-haired girl, returning to her place beside Lady Ramsbottom.

Though the fire crackled and leapt in the hearth, the hall remained drafty and dark. Outside the lead glass windows, snow was piled up practically to the sills. As it had for the past two days, the wind keened like a lonely wolf and added to the feeling of gloom and isolation that pervaded the castle.

"What a dreary weekend this has turned out to be," Lady Ramsbottom said, marking Evelyn with a maternally critical eye.

The countess bravely gave her guests a wan smile. "But, I heard from Celeste and Louisa that the parlor was decorated like a gaming hell, and that everyone had the time of their lives playing cards and faro last night."

"Not everyone, dear." Lady Ramsbottom slanted a knowing look at Evelyn. "I, for one, remained in my room. It is directly across the corridor from yours, child."

It took a moment for that information to sink into Evelyn's cottony brain. So, the old lady had seen or heard Sir Hugo enter her room last night, was that it? The ramifications were portentous; if Percival got wind of such an indiscretion, he might very well use it to disqualify her as an heir in his father's estate.

The tea tray arrived at an opportune moment, deflecting attention from Evelyn's fretful expression. After the maid had distributed cups and departed, Louisa Freemantle spoke up.

"Do you contemplate further revisions on your manuscript, Evelyn? Would you like me to proof any part of the book for spelling or grammatical errors? Not that you aren't more capable than I at such things, but I do so delight in assisting you with your work."

"And you'll be remembered for your diligence, in my dedication," Evelyn promised. Sipping the hot tea imbued her with renewed strength. Her stomach settled, also, and her thinking slowly sharpened.

When Lady Ramsbottom spoke, a spray of crumbs from the scone she had in her mouth dusted her lap blanket. "You haven't yet explained to me precisely what your manuscript is about. Given that you are a member of that Tudor salon—whatever it is called—I must assume that you have written something pertaining to King Henry VIII's tenure as king."

"Quite right." Evelyn nibbled at a dry cracker, relieved to find that her appetite was returning. "But, I cannot say much more than that. My publisher has warned against disclosing my findings before the book is published."

"Even to your friends?" Louisa Freemantle asked. "You only allowed me to read the first third of your book, dear. Even I—who have long assisted you in the editing of every scholarly paper you presented to the Society—do not know the ultimate outcome of your research into Henry's connection with the Dethman family. Pray, tell us! I am most interested!"

"That does sound exceedingly interesting," Lady Ramsbottom said.

"It is!" Celeste entered the conversation with unmitigated pride in her sister's accomplishments. "Sister and I spent every summer in this big old castle for nearly five years. And while I whiled away my days romping in the gardens and sleeping well past noon—"

"The rest did you a world of good." Watching her sister, Evelyn was filled with contentment.

It truly had all been worth it. The marriage to the old earl, the lonely hours spent in that dusty old library, the years she spent suppressing her own desires . . . If all of that had bought Celeste the health and happiness she now enjoyed, every minute of Evelyn's sacrifice had been repaid.

Celeste's girlish voice echoed off the breast plates of the

ancient coats of armor. "She found a bunch of old diaries! They were so musty and full of mildew, she refused to let me turn the pages!"

"They would have started you on a coughing spell, for sure," Evelyn said.

"Whose diaries were they?" Lady Ramsbottom asked.

"Some old Dethman man," Celeste said, hardly concerned with the historical precision of her explanation. "He was a friend of that horrible cad, Henry VIII, the one who had his portrait painted with a duck leg clutched in his fat fist."

"Celeste, that is hardly an apt summary of Henry's reign." But, Evelyn couldn't help laughing along with Lady Ramsbottom and Miss Freemantle.

"And the Dethman man—was he an earl of Goreham, Sister?"

"No."

"At any rate," Celeste continued, excitedly, "he was a cad, too, according to Evelyn, though she refuses to tell me the entire story. Too racy for my innocent ears, I s'pose."

"That is quite enough!" Evelyn summoned the strength to talk above her sister's indiscreet chatter.

Bootsteps on the stone floor of the hall quelled the casual tone of the ladies' conversation.

"I see you are having a jolly time at the expense of the Dethman family's good reputation," Percival said, leveling an accusing gaze at Evelyn as he approached. He stood at the edge of the small congregation, hands clasped behind his back.

"No one has said anything intended to damage your reputation," Evelyn replied, more icily than she meant to.

"No?" He rose on his tiptoes. "Are you implying that your scandalous little manuscript can add no more tarnish to an already blackened reputation?"

Wisely choosing to hold her tongue, Evelyn merely slanted a frosty stare at her stepson.

Lady Ramsbottom said, "Whatever on earth is the matter

with you, boy? What could Lady Goreham possibly write about a sixteenth-century king that would sully your reputation?''

"I don't take slander lightly," the third earl said.

"What does that mean?" Evelyn asked. "Are you planning to sue me?"

Louisa Freemantle, who had remained quiet throughout this unpleasant exchange, stood. "I think I shall retire to my bedchamber and take a nap," she said.

Watching Louisa cross the hall, Evelyn felt a twinge of guilt for her bad manners as a hostess.

"Percival, we're making our guests uncomfortable," she said. "Let us call a truce."

"All right." The mustachioed man nodded deferentially at Lady Ramsbottom, then turned and stalked toward the passageway leading to the back parlor.

Sighing her relief, Evelyn replaced her cup and saucer on the low table before her. "I do apologize, Adelaide. How rude of us to put on such a show!"

The older woman clucked her tongue. "Posh! I thought the little set-to was exciting! He is a dreadful bore, isn't he?"

Celeste burst out laughing, but Evelyn only lifted her brows. Yes, he was a dreadful bore, but there was something about his avid interest in her manuscript that troubled her. Was he truly worried that her book might ruin his family's reputation?

He should be. Evelyn's book would raise eyebrows in the academic world. And her ability to authenticate her findings would establish her as a respected scholar in the field of Tudor history. But, was it fair to publish a manuscript that would damage her deceased husband's reputation?

It was a disturbing dilemma that she'd often brooded over. But she'd told the old earl in general terms what her studies had unearthed. He'd given her his blessings, then advised her to jealously guard her findings until the book was published. He'd chuckled when she suggested the book might bring scandal on the heads of the surviving Dethmans.

She recalled their bedside conversation just days before he died.

"I am descended from a long line of rogues and rakes, dear," he'd said, his voice wispy. "You can do nothing to hurt me, because I'm about to draw my last breath. As for Percival, he has much to learn about his background that may surprise him one day. Now, don't bore me with the precise details of my ancestors' peccadillos! Unburden your conscience, girl, and make a name for yourself! I will be proud when I am looking down on you from heaven. If I happen to be elsewhere . . . well, we won't discuss that, will we?"

"Your son will hate me," Evelyn whispered, holding the man's hand in her own. His skin was papery thin, so delicate that she had to be careful her gentle grasp did not bruise him.

"Dear, he does already. You're brighter than he, and he has long resented the affection I have for you. I am sorry, Evelyn, that I treated you like a child. I should have released you from the bonds of this marriage long ago— I wouldn't have been bitter had you taken a lover. But, you never did, did you?"

"No, my lord." She'd almost made the mistake of saying, *Father.*

"You'll blossom soon enough, after I'm gone. Just mind that you don't marry some reckless cad like me . . ." The earl's voice was eclipsed by a burst of coughing.

Not until after his death did Evelyn learn of the conditions her husband had placed on her inheritance. Perhaps Percival had persuaded his father to make the revisions. But it didn't matter. The rude shock of knowing the old earl had betrayed her in that way only deepened Evelyn's belief that romantic love was a figment of the collective feminine imagination. It just didn't exist for her, and she never expected that it would.

Lady Ramsbottom's voice interrupted her thoughts. "Dear, shouldn't you return to bed, also? I hate to say it, but you're looking a trifle green around the gills again."

Evelyn stood, grateful for her sister's protective embrace around her shoulders. After saying good-bye to Lady Ramsbottom, the two sisters made their way across the hall and up the stairs. It was a slow, halting process due to Evelyn's weakness, and the dizziness that assaulted her at the landing.

Celeste's room was the first one on the right as they turned down the corridor. Evelyn gamely squeezed her sister's hands, then released them.

"I can make it the rest of the way, Sister. Why don't you go and take a nap, yourself?"

Reluctantly, Celeste opened the door to her room. She stood on the threshold and watched her sister until Evelyn made it to her own room. The sisters traded smiles, then entered their respective chambers.

Exhausted from her brief foray below stairs, Evelyn fell onto her bed, and dozed off the instant her head hit the pillows. She never heard her sister's muffled screams or the crash of Celeste's half-boots on the door at the end of the corridor.

Sir Hugo trudged up the stairs, frustrated, angry and exhausted. The lure of the back parlor, with its card tables and faro table, was so strong that his limbs ached to take him there. He'd only avoided crossing the Great Hall and striding down the long passageway by concentrating his obsession on Evelyn, the Countess of Goreham.

Though she didn't even know that he battled constantly with his gambling demons, Hugo convinced himself that Evelyn would be dreadfully disappointed if he succumbed to his addiction. It was a trick he played in his own mind—

putting Evelyn's face on his conscience—but it worked. So far, every time, he'd suffered the urge to visit the parlor, her sweet imaginary voice had talked him out of it.

With dust in his hair and nostrils, Hugo stood for a moment at the end of the passageway. Evelyn's room was at the far end on the left, two doors down from Sir Hugo's. On the right-hand side of the corridor, Sir Cuthbert's room was directly opposite Hugo's. Lady Ramsbottom was opposite Evelyn, at the end of the hall. And Percival, the third Earl of Goreham was in the first door on the left.

A cozy arrangement, thought Sir Hugo, bitterly. The entire situation was beyond figuring out.

First, he'd been invited to a house party, either by a woman who denied inviting him, or a man he'd never met. Then, he'd been furnished a room two doors down from the most seductive, alluring woman he'd ever known. He'd been warned not to go near her by his friend, Sir Cuthbert, and less than twelve hours later, that same friend had suggested he take advantage of her charms.

To top it off, there was a gambling hell set up in the rear of the castle, a den of vice that called his name like a siren luring sailors onto the shoals. The effort required to avoid going near the parlor was wearing him down. Pinching the bridge of his nose, Hugo realized he was bone-tired. Thinking that a nap was called for, he headed for his room.

A faint mewling brought all his masculine senses to full alert. The hair on his nape bristled as his gaze swung to the first door on his right. Quietly, he stepped toward the heavy mahogany panel, and pressed his ear to it. The sound of a feminine cry propelled him into action.

Shoving open the unlocked door, he burst into the room. The sight of Celeste lying on the bed, her arms and ankles bound with rope, filled him with anger and indignation. A white linen necktie was stuffed in her mouth, gagging her, and another was tied around her head, covering her eyes completely.

Quick as a lightning bolt, Hugo leapt to the side of the bed and untied the ropes restraining her. He gently pulled the cravat from her mouth, and she gasped, her muffled cries now giving way to loud, gulping sobs. He untied the strip of linen that covered her eyes, and stared into her wide, blinking, terrified gaze.

"Are you hurt anywhere?" Sir Hugo asked, rubbing her wrists where they were bruised by the rough hemp ropes.

Celeste shook her head from side to side, unable to speak between her sobs.

Realizing the need for a female in the room, Sir Hugo pulled the bell cord. While awaiting a maidservant, he asked Celeste, "Who did this terrible thing to you?"

"I do not know! I could not see his face, sir. He tied that strip of cloth around my head so that I could not see." Her hysterics were fading; Celeste was evidently a girl of good common sense, far sturdier than her delicate blond looks indicated.

"Can you describe any of his physical characteristics?" Sir Hugo was familiar with the contemporary police methods employed by the Bow Street Runners; he'd had enough opportunity to review the results of their interrogations.

"Taller than I am," she said, between hiccoughs. "Quite strong, even though he had the advantage of surprise. I had just stepped into the room, and when I closed the door, he jumped out from behind it. He clamped his hand over my mouth—"

"Could you see anything of his clothing, his hair color, anything at all which might identify the man?" Sir Hugo asked.

"He wore black leather gloves." Celeste frowned, attempting to recall any detail that might assist Sir Hugo. "I was immediately blinded by the cloth he tied around my head, sir. I saw nothing else."

A gasp at the threshold interrupted Sir Hugo's questioning. Shipton let out a scream and rushed to Celeste's bedside.

"Whatever has happened to you, child?" Shipton stared in horror at the ropes and cravats strewn across the mattress.

Seconds later, a door slammed down the corridor and heavy steps sounded on the carpet in the hallway. Sir Hugo reached for the perpetrator's tools just as Sir Cuthbert appeared in the doorway.

"I heard a scream," the solicitor said, his eyes rounding at the scene confronting him. "What in the dev- . . . what happened?"

Percival, the third Earl of Goreham, materialized behind Sir Cuthbert, and both men entered the room. They stood behind Mrs. Shipton, staring alternately at Celeste's prostrate figure, and Sir Hugo.

Ever vigilant about decorum, Mrs. Shipton quickly covered Celeste with a blanket. She rang the bell cord, summoned tea, then pulled a cane-bottomed chair next to the bedside, where she sat and held Celeste's hand.

Sir Hugo briefly explained what had happened, as far as he knew it. Turning back to Celeste, he asked her, "Are you quite positive this man didn't harm you in any other way?"

"How does she know it was a man?" Percival interjected.

"I felt his . . . *body* . . . against my back." Celeste's straightforward reply drew a blush to Shipton's cheek.

Sir Hugo arched a brow in Percival's direction. "That answers that. Any more questions, gentlemen?"

Sir Cuthbert cleared his throat. "Miss Waring, did the man who did this to you say anything? Would you recognize his voice if you heard him again?"

"No, he said nothing."

"After he put the blindfold on you, what did he do?" The question came from Percival, whose expression bore the look of a concerned brother.

Celeste did not hesitate. "He thrust that horrid necktie in my mouth. I stumbled once, and fell on my knees. He pulled at my arms, and directed me onto the bed. I was too frightened to struggle, and the cloth in my mouth made me feel as if I were going to suffocate.''

"Is that when he bound your wrists and ankles with the rope?'' Sir Hugo asked.

"Yes.'' She faltered, her eyes glazing with unshed tears. "Perhaps, if I had fought harder, I might have escaped the dreadful man. I should have kicked him, or—''

"You needn't feel guilty,'' Sir Hugo said. "You did all that you could do. It must have been a shocking experience for a girl your age. It would have been for any woman, for that matter.''

The young girl gazed up at Sir Hugo with gratitude in her eyes.

Sir Cuthbert said, "What happened next, Miss Waring?''

"After he tied my hands and feet, he made a lot of noise. Going about the room, I think, opening drawers, picking up items and putting them down. I heard my portmanteau click open and snap shut. I think the beast even crawled on the floor, perhaps looking beneath the bed. I felt the mattress move, and thought I heard the scrape of his shoes along the carpet. I could be wrong about that, though. I could not see a thing.''

Sir Hugo was impressed with the girl's astuteness, though. She'd had the good sense to listen and stay reasonably calm. Though she didn't realize it, she'd given him several clues upon which to base a discreet investigation, which he planned to conduct immediately. His outrage at having seen Celeste bound and gagged was growing by the moment.

"Do you have any notion who might have done this?'' he asked her. "Has anyone behaved oddly or threateningly toward you?''

She shook her head.

Rising on his tiptoes, hands clasped behind his back, Percival released a sigh. "Well, there is no more to be done here. I shall return to the parlor, then, and prepare for my guests this evening. Sir Hugo, I do so hope you will join us at faro tonight? You will, won't you?''

Anger coursed through Hugo's veins, but he was careful to modulate his voice. ''It is doubtful, Percival. I try to stay away from the gaming tables these days. Too much temptation to wager my entire year's earnings, and I work too hard to toss it all away.''

Percival chuckled. ''Then keep your bets low, sir. What harm is there in a friendly rubber of whist, or a round of faro? Miss Freemantle and some of the other ladies were inquiring about your absence last night. You are a bachelor, aren't you? Why, then, you should kick up your heels a little. This is a house-party, after all.''

Sir Hugo thought of another question not yet asked. ''Is anything missing in your room, Celeste?''

She shrugged. ''I have not had the opportunity to examine the room, sir.''

''Of course you haven't. Well, when you do, please let me know if there is anything missing.'' With that, he bade Mrs. Shipton stay with the girl to monitor her condition, and alert him if Celeste remembered anything else about the intruder who handled her so rudely.

''Sir Hugo,'' Celeste said, as he was taking his leave. He turned at the threshold and looked at her. ''Thank you for being so kind.''

His chest squeezed painfully. He would have liked to sit with the child and hold her hand, but decorum demanded that he leave her to Shipton's care. Moreover, he had much work to do if he expected to find out what fiend had done this to her—and why.

He ushered Sir Cuthbert and Lord Goreham out the door, closing it gently behind him. The three men stood in the corridor, conversing in hushed tones.

''Who in the devil would have done such a dastardly thing?'' Sir Cuthbert was visibly shaken.

''Who indeed? And what in the world was the creature

looking for in Celeste's room?" Percival stroked his mustache, apparently perplexed by the situation.

"I intend to find out, gentlemen. If you will excuse me." Sir Hugo nodded to the men, then turned and headed for his room. Once inside, he stood and listened until he heard two sets of footsteps descend the staircase and fade below stairs. Opening the door a crack, he perceived that no one was in the hallway. Stealthily, he slipped down the passageway and tapped lightly on Evelyn's door.

It was a dangerous thing to do, and his heart hammered as he stood there, waiting for her reply. Silence met his insistent tapping, however. After a moment, he heard the click of a door opening at the opposite end of the hallway. Someone was about to emerge into the corridor, and he would be seen standing at the countess's door. His presence there would be a damning indictment of his romantic interest in the woman; her reputation would be damaged.

Unthinkingly, Sir Hugo pushed open Evelyn's door and stepped inside. Thank goodness, it hadn't been locked, he thought, and in the same instant, he marveled at the woman's trusting nature. Considering the goings-on in this castle of late, he fully intended to warn her about leaving her bedchamber door unlatched.

He stood in the darkened room, noting the drawn curtains and the crackling fire in the hearth. The chamber was warm, the air heavy and still. With one hand behind his back, he turned the latch and locked the door.

Evelyn lay on the bed, her blond hair in disarray upon the pillow. She slept on her back, a counterpane and blanket tucked beneath her arms. Exposed were her shoulders and neck, a creamy expanse of flesh against the crisp white linens. She wore a muslin nightrail with thin lacy straps across the shoulders. Sir Hugo's hungry gaze drank in the sight of her. As he walked to her bedside, he felt an irresistible urge to touch her.

Carefully, he lowered himself onto the bed, sitting sideways beside her. He leaned over her, his body aching. Her breathing was gentle and steady, as soothing as a kitten's purr. And the expression on her face, one of deep contentment, mesmerized him. He could have watched her sleep for hours.

Her eyes flickered open. Evelyn awoke, her mouth forming a small O as her gaze locked with Sir Hugo's.

"Don't be frightened," he whispered. He wondered if she knew he'd entered her room the night before. Guilt stormed his conscience; a gentleman wouldn't creep into a lady's room, not without her express consent.

But he couldn't leave without telling her about Celeste's misadventure. Her expression, one of bewildered terror, prompted him to soften the blow of the story by assuring her constantly that Celeste was none the worse for having been gagged and bound while some wicked interloper searched her room.

"Are you certain that Celeste is unharmed? I should go to her! Perhaps because you are a man she didn't tell you all that took place!"

Evelyn struggled to her elbows, but Sir Hugo gently pressed her back against the pillows.

"Mrs. Shipton is with her. You may go to her soon, but please talk with me a while. I should like to know what Celeste might have had that would tempt a man to do that to her. Is there something in her room, a cache of precious jewels, for example, that someone might have been looking for?"

Evelyn's forehead creased. "No."

"Who would have done such a thing, Evelyn? Surely, you must have a notion what this is all about."

She sighed. "Unless it has something to do with my manuscript and the Dethman diaries. But . . . no . . . even Percival wouldn't be that wicked."

Sir Hugo wasn't so easily convinced. "Tell me, Evelyn, what did you eat that made you so ill?"

"Honestly, I don't know."

"Do you remember smelling any odd aroma when you drank the tea Mrs. Shipton brought you?"

"Shipton doesn't always brew the most wonderful tea in the world. 'Struth, I have often accused her of re-using the tea grounds twice over to make a fresh pot. I did think the tea a bit bitter, and bad-tasting. That's why I didn't drink very much of it. I didn't want to hurt Shipton's feelings, though, so I—I—"

Sir Hugo urged her to confide in him.

"I poured most of the tea into that vase on the mantelpiece. Over there. Dear me, the hothouse flowers have quite gone past their prime, haven't they? I don't suppose Mr. Davenport, our nearest neighbor eight miles down the road, will be bringing more any time soon. Not until the snows melt."

Sir Hugo stared at the wilted flowers with great interest. "No one has replaced the water in that vase since you poured the tea in it, have they?"

"No, I'm certain not. Shipton has been much too busy with so many guests in the house. And the chambermaids are equally overworked. The Dethmans may throw wonderful parties, but they tend to be a bit cheap when it comes to hiring sufficient numbers of house-cleaning staff. They prefer to work the few unfortunates in their employ till they're near dead."

Sir Hugo's gaze swung from the vase to Evelyn. He'd discovered all that he could. There was no further legitimate reason for him to remain in the countess's room.

He started to rise. "I should leave. If I am discovered here, your reputation will be damaged. 'Tis rude for me to impose on you in such a matter."

"No, don't go."

Her words surprised him. Staring at her, Hugo sat as still as a statue, afraid to shatter the precious stillness hovering between them. At length, he said quietly, "I was here last night. I came in to assure myself that you had recovered from your illness. Please forgive my selfishness. I cannot seem to stay away from you."

Her gaze never strayed from his. The directness of it, the way it roved over his face, filled him with an uneasy yearning. She seemed to peer into his soul. Her scrutiny made him uncomfortable, because he didn't want her to see his black heart or his wicked addiction, or the feeble manner in which he struggled against his own demons, his own desires.

She withdrew her hand from beneath the covers, and reached for him. Sir Hugo clasped her fingers, feeling the warmth of her flesh seep into his own. He leaned closer to her, daring to breathe in her scent, aching to press his lips to hers.

"Sir, what is it that you want from me?" There was no danger of their being overheard, and yet her whispered voice seemed to boom through Hugo's senses like a canon.

For once, he was at a loss for words. "I do not know. Everything. Nothing. I know only that for the past five years, I have been unable to release you from my imagination. Against your will, without your knowledge or consent, I have held you captive in my mind, Evelyn. I have held conversations with you that you'll never be privy to. I have held you in an embrace you may never feel. I have kissed you—"

"Kiss me, now, then," she said so softly he barely heard her. He thought for an instant that he had dreamed the words. "Or else I shall accuse you of being selfish."

Her lips parted as he lowered his head. He kissed her once, very gently, tentatively, his lips pressing lightly against hers. Then, he pulled back from her, and stared into her deep blue eyes. He saw in her gaze a startling innocence, the look of a woman who was herself startled by the physical reactions she was experiencing. A flush darkened her cheeks. She inhaled deeply, and her gaze fell to his lips again.

Answering her silent request, Hugo kissed her again,

this time more deeply, more passionately. Evelyn's arms wound around his neck, and she clutched his shoulders. A more experienced woman would not have reacted to a simple kiss with such excitement, he knew. He realized that he was kissing a woman who'd never been kissed like this before. Her ragged breathing, the desperation in her lips as they met his, the surprise in her blue gaze, all told him that Evelyn, the Countess of Goreham, was a novice in the ways of seduction.

He didn't know what to make of that. Grasping her shoulders, he pulled himself away from her. Heart pounding, he spoke over a lump in his throat. "Evelyn, I want you, but—"

"I want you, too, Hugo." Her eyes burned with desire. "I have never experienced physical pleasure with a man. Are you shocked that I would confess such a thing?"

He was, but somehow he managed to shake his head. "I suppose it is to be expected. After all, your husband was quite old when you married him."

Some emotion he couldn't identify played across her features like a shadow.

"Evelyn, why did you marry the earl?" He wondered if his question was impertinent, but he felt an intimacy with her that suggested she wouldn't be offended.

She answered matter-of-factly. "Because my sister was ill, and our father had recently died, so that there was no one we could go to or depend on to provide for us. Celeste needed rest, and medical treatment, nourishing food and a clean bed to sleep in. I'd gone to Widow Philpott's with my last pound, prepared to lose it all, or win enough to take Celeste somewhere where she could recuperate and grow strong. I almost won enough, Hugo. I came so close. But, when I lost it all, I was desperate, not for myself, but for Celeste. I hated what I did, but there you have it. Hate me if you will."

Evelyn sank into her pillows, and closed her eyes. "Why didn't you stop me, Hugo? A word from you . . . a single sign of disapproval . . . would have been enough to stop me.''

How could he answer that question? How could he tell the countess that he had nothing to offer her five years ago? Sir Hugo stared at her lovely face, the pale lashes that fanned her cheeks, the sweet pink lips slightly bruised from his kiss. A spasm of regret, dizzying in its intensity, stalled his speech. Searching for words, he released Evelyn's hand, and turned his head from her.

He felt her eyes open, her gaze light on him.

Not daring to look at her, he said in a hoarse voice, ''I did not want to be married at the time.''

''Were you in love with someone else?''

He hesitated. ''Yes.'' The lie seemed preferable to admitting he was penniless five years ago because he'd gambled all his money away. He couldn't bear to have Evelyn think of him as a spendthrift rakehell. Her opinion of him meant so much; if her regard for him was shattered, his self-esteem would be, too.

Facing her, he watched a single tear slide down her cheek.

Sir Hugo touched her face, brushed the tear away with the pad of his thumb.

Footsteps sounding in the corridor caused his heart to stop. As his eyes locked with Evelyn's, the steps neared the end of the hallway. They stopped outside Evelyn's bedchamber, then a booming knock assaulted the door.

Wide-eyed, Evelyn whispered, ''You must not be found here.''

The doorknob rattled. Thankfully, Sir Hugo had turned the latch, but whoever wanted into Evelyn's room appeared eager to gain entry.

''Who is it?'' Evelyn called.

Sir Hugo's gaze scanned the room. The bed was too low to accommodate his girth; he couldn't hide beneath it. But, there was a painted tole screen in the corner, behind which he could crouch without being observed.

As Evelyn threw off her covers and sat up, he stole to the screen. Behind it was a large bathtub, and a small chair over which various towels and linens were hung. Seeing no alternative, he climbed into the tub, pulled his knees to his chest and prayed desperately that Evelyn's visitor wasn't a maid come to pour buckets of hot water into her bath.

The knock at the door sounded again, this time more insistently.

"Who is it? I am not decent!" Evelyn evidently tossed a wrap over her muslin nightrail; Sir Hugo could hear the rustle of her gown, and the delicate padding of her slippers across the carpet.

Percival Dethman's voice answered from the other side of the door. "Let me in, right now! I demand to know who is in your chambers! Open this door!"

Sir Hugo's pulse galloped, and every muscle in his body tightened with dread. If he were found in the Dowager Countess's bedroom, her reputation would be ruined. That was the very last thing he wanted to do to Evelyn.

If word got round Evelyn's London set that she'd been found in such a compromising situation, she would be justified in demanding that he marry her. And that was an equally untenable solution, as far as Sir Hugo saw it. Because, after five years of avoiding the gambling hells and saving his money, he still wasn't a fit husband for a woman of Evelyn's caliber.

She was a person capable of great strength and selflessness; she had proven that when she married the earl. By sacrificing herself and her youth for the benefit of her sister, she'd shown she was a woman of the highest moral standards.

He, on the other hand, was a tormented soul who struggled each day to stay away from the faro houses and St. James's hells. The fact that he'd succeeded in staying out of them for five years was a small accomplishment compared to the almost overwhelming desire he had to return there. No, he wasn't cured of his addiction, and he never would be. One day, he might very well succumb to his weakness and lose every penny he owned. He lived in fear that that would happen.

And so, there was no possibility, in his mind, that he would ever be suitable marriage material—not for the likes of Evelyn, Dowager Countess of Goreham.

"Open the door, Evelyn," screamed Percival. "Or I shall knock it down!"

Chapter Five

Evelyn's heart pounded fiercely. If she opened the door, the third earl would barge into the room, and search every inch of it. It wouldn't take him long to find Sir Hugo hiding behind the screen.

A second voice sounded on the other side of the door.

"Whatever is going on there?" Miss Louisa Freemantle asked.

"Lou! Is that you? Oh, do tell Percival to go away! I am not dressed!"

Holding her breath, Evelyn listened to the angry exchange outside her bedchamber.

"She has someone in there with her," Percival hissed. "As her stepson, I demand to be allowed entry into this room."

Louisa scoffed. "Since when do stepsons enjoy the privilege of barging into a lady's bedchamber? I beg your pardon, but you are the rudest, most offensive—"

"How dare you speak to me in such a manner?"

A third voice, that of Lady Ramsbottom, joined the fray. "What is all this about? Has Evelyn taken ill again?"

"She's taken leave of her senses, that's what!" Percival rejoined. "And she has someone in her room, an affront to my dead father, if there ever was one. Why, I demand to be let inside her bedchamber, if only to see the cad who would dare insult the memory of the second Earl of Goreham!"

"Pish-posh!" returned Lady Ramsbottom. Evelyn would have thrown her arms about the matron if there wasn't a door separating them. "I've know Evelyn since she was a bride, and I don't believe a word of what you're saying. Evelyn! Open up the door, dear, and satisfy this silly boy that you are all alone."

Her heart dropped like a stone. *Oh, Lady Ramsbottom, how could you?*

"Open up, dear," Louisa called. "I don't think Lord Goreham is going to leave until you do."

"I am not dressed," repeated Evelyn feebly.

"Then hide yourself," suggested Louisa. "I will assist Percival in his search so that he does not offend you."

"I intend to search every inch of that room," Percival threatened.

"I'll not have you ogling the young countess," Lady Ramsbottom chided him.

Evelyn reluctantly turned the latch. Then, as the door opened, she tore off her wrap and leapt behind the screen, her legs pressed against the side of the tub. She dared not look at Sir Hugo, but saw from the corner of her eye that he was sitting uncomfortably in the tub, holding her discarded wrap in his hands as if it were the Holy Grail, or a snake about to bite him.

Grasping the edge of the screen, she peered around it, allowing her bare shoulder to show. "Don't come back here," she warned Percival as he stalked into the center of the room and looked around him. "I am not decent, I told you."

"I shall see what is behind that screen," he replied, his voice full of malicious promise.

Louisa Freemantle shouldered him aside. Bustling across the room, she rounded the screen and made a great exhibition of looking behind it. Propping her fists on her hips, she stared Sir Hugo straight in the eye. Then, she turned to Percival, and said, "There is nothing back here except a bathtub, my lord. And a half-naked woman. Sorry to disappoint you."

"You should be ashamed of yourself, Percival," Lady Ramsbottom said with an indignant huff.

The earl was defeated. If he insisted on viewing what was behind the screen, he would be guilty of an egregious insult to his stepmother, who was huddling behind it, undressed and humiliated.

Turning on his heel, he shot out of the room without another word.

Lady Ramsbottom watched him go, then said to Evelyn, "You can come out now, dear. What a wretched little weasel he is! How you must have suffered at the bite of his tongue these past five years."

Evelyn's cheeks suffused with heat. Louisa's arms wrapped protectively about her shoulders. Evelyn started to speak, but her friend cut in with admirable finesse.

"My lady, would you excuse us? Evelyn is embarrassed to tears, are you not, dear? I'd like to assist her in getting back to her bed, before she catches a chill. It is drafty back here, you know."

The older woman clucked her tongue. "Oh, I quite understand! You young girls these days are so modest. But, your friendship is commendable, and I understand your not wanting an old windbag like me in here. I'll take my leave, but I hope to see you tonight at dinner, Evelyn. If you're up to coming below stairs again, that is."

Evelyn forced a smile to her lips. "I will try, my lady. And thank you for defending me against Percival's accusations. 'Twas most kind."

The old woman waddled out the door, drawing it shut behind her.

For a moment, stillness hung tenuously in the room. Then, Evelyn sighed, and Miss Louisa Freemantle doubled over in a fit of laughter. Sir Hugo let out a groan of relief. When he did exit the bedchamber minutes later, after Miss Freemantle had assured him of the vacancy of the corridor, he took the vase of wilted flowers with him.

"I can not tolerate the sight of wilted flowers," he told the ladies as he pulled the door closed behind him.

Miss Freemantle's eyes still twinkled at the dinner table two hours later.

Lady Goreham looked up from her plate of roast beef, met Louisa's gaze directly across the table, and shook her head. She had to look away to keep from laughing herself, but she knew how absolutely vital it was to remain steadfast in her assertion that no one—no man, particularly—had been in her bedchamber when Lord Goreham demanded entry.

Candles lit the Great Hall, bathing it in a warm glow that flattered the ladies' complexions. The long dining table in the center of the room sparkled with silver plate, sterling candlesticks and highly polished epergnes. On either side of the main table, smaller tables had been set up to accommodate all of Lord and Lady Goreham's guests.

"It's like a medieval banquet," breathed Celeste, who, in a brand new gown of white muslin with dark blue satin bodice, sat on Evelyn's left. "I've never seen so much roasted fowl and game!"

Evelyn stared at her younger sister. A wave of protectiveness toward Celeste nearly produced a fresh torrent of tears. After Sir Hugo had left the room, Evelyn and Miss Freemantle had rushed to Celeste's chambers. Though Celeste assured them she was unharmed, Evelyn still shivered at the thought of her baby sister overpowered and at the mercy of some madman.

Across the table, seated on Louisa's right, Sir Cuthbert deLisle lifted his glass, drank deeply, and sighed. "Nor have I ever seen so much fine French wine poured since old Boney began his parade across the Continent!"

"I don't think I should enjoy eating dinner at such a late hour every evening," Evelyn responded. "But since the cooks were unable to have the meal ready at the usual six o'clock hour, I was quite content to get an extra hour's rest."

"Are you recovered from yesterday's illness?" The low, velvety, masculine voice sent shivers up Evelyn's spine. She turned her head, nodding at the man who sat on Louisa's left side. The candlelight highlighted his broad, intelligent forehead.

His question, one to which he knew the answer, was obviously for the benefit of the other guests. "I am much the better for my day's rest," Evelyn managed to eke out. "Thank you, sir, for inquiring toward my health."

Thank God that Percival, the third Earl of Goreham, was seated at the opposite end of the long table. Evelyn thought she wouldn't have withstood that odious little man's scrutiny.

"I had hoped you would make it downstairs for dinner," the barrister continued in a friendly, conversational, almost teasing, tone. There was nothing impertinent or rude in his speech, but the man's interest in the woman seated across the table would have been obvious to anyone. "Lady Ramsbottom has been bruiting it about that you are the most intelligent young woman in all of London. I should like to hear more of your scholarly accomplishments. I'm quite an amateur historian myself."

Evelyn's spine straightened. She loved discussing academic topics, and was delighted to find that Sir Hugo shared her interest in books and history.

She told him of the Society, and its purpose, which was the study of the Tudor monarchy. Sir Hugo was surprisingly well-versed in Henry VIII's exploits. Seemingly indifferent to the presence of the other guests, Evelyn and Hugo carried on a long and colorful conversation about the six wives of Henry VIII.

Evelyn had never been happier. She thought Sir Hugo the most intelligent man she'd ever met—and the easiest to converse with. When he looked at her, it was as if no one else existed. She found herself voicing thoughts she'd never told anyone else. He laughed at her jokes, and she at his. If he'd been the ugliest man on earth, she'd have still admired his jocularity, his insight, his attitudes.

But, he was not the ugliest man on earth. Her gaze was drawn inexorably to his lips, full and well-shaped. The subtle cleft in his chin, the strength of his jaw, brought to her the memory of his kiss, warm and promising. To her, he was the most handsome man in all of England. Her response to him was physical, visceral and quite unexpected. Allowing her imagination to wander, she yearned for the scrape of his beard against her face, the heat of his breath against her neck.

The tingling clutch that gripped her insides caught her off guard. Evelyn reached for her wineglass, hoping that in the golden candlelight, her blushing arousal was not obvious.

It must have been, for Sir Cuthbert interrupted the conversation abruptly. "Lady Goreham, tell me, what have you gleaned from your study of the soon-to-be famous Dethman diaries?"

Afloat in the golden glow of Sir Hugo's warm gaze, Evelyn was almost too content to feel wary. "When my manuscript is published, sir, you will find out for yourself. I do hope you will read the book. After all, you are a member of the Society, as well, and share my passion for the study of old King Henry."

"How long have you been a member of this Society?" Sir Hugo asked, leaning forward to look past Louisa at his tow-headed friend.

Sir Cuthbert shrugged. "Oh, a couple of years, not long."

"Has it been that long?" Evelyn spoke freely, the wine and the companionable presence of Sir Hugo loosening her tongue. "I should have thought it was less than that."

"I became a member about the time the old Earl of Goreham passed on," said Sir Cuthbert, with a definite tightening of his expression.

"Yes, but I don't want to talk about anything unpleasant," Evelyn said.

Celeste turned to her. "You certainly are in a jolly frame of mind, Sister. Perhaps you will consider allowing me to attend the parlor games tonight."

"No, indeed!" The suggestion brought peals of laughter from both Evelyn and Louisa. " 'Twas a noble attempt, dear, but I am not in such a reckless mood."

Sir Cuthbert spoke again. "Come on, Lady Goreham, why not tell us something about your manuscript? Something no one else knows about the reign of King Henry VIII. We're your guests, after all, and we've come all the way from London to hear a preview of your explosive new book."

"It is not a scandal sheet, sir," Evelyn replied, smiling. "Trust me when I tell you that it is a scholarly work. I doubt the country will be stood on its head by my revelations."

"But you've said yourself that the academic world will be surprised," argued Sir Cuthbert.

"Only we scholars who are fascinated by the minutiae of the Tudor king's machinations," Evelyn said. "The significance of the Dethman diaries is merely that they offer a contemporary, firsthand account of how King Henry manipulated his friends, and exploited his wives. It is the document which is amazing, not what the writings reveal. King Henry was quite a woman-hater, but everyone knows that. His hostility toward Catherine Howard, particularly, is evidenced by the writings in the diaries. Henry didn't like it when his wives played as deeply at love as he did."

"What man does, dear? There is nothing new about the double standard." This remark came from Lady Ramsbottom, who sat at Evelyn's right elbow, drinking in every word of the conversation.

Sir Cuthbert chuckled, and Sir Hugo gave the older woman a conspiratorial wink. Miss Louisa Freemantle rolled her eyes at Evelyn, and shrugged.

"Can you tell us something about who wrote the Dethman diaries?" Sir Cuthbert asked.

Miss Louisa Freemantle turned a hard look on the solicitor. "Cubby, for heaven's sake, let her alone. She has promised her publisher that she will not reveal anything about the manuscript, and she must keep her promise! Even I was not allowed to proofread the entire book."

"But you have read some of it?" he asked her.

"A little. Nothing that I read set my ears to burning."

Celeste giggled. "I know where the diaries are hidden."

Evelyn's gaiety vanished. Leaning toward her sister, she whispered harshly, "If you tell a soul where those diaries are hidden, young lady, you shall spend the rest of your lifetime in your room!"

The fair-haired girl's mischievous expression altered to one of embarrassed fear. "I—I'm sorry, Sister!"

Tension rippled across the table, vanquishing the cheerful talk and easy laughter that had heretofore prevailed. Evelyn's skin prickled beneath the curious gazes of her guests, and she regretted her outburst, but she simply couldn't allow Celeste to reveal the location of the diaries.

Percival, the third Earl of Goreham, would have them in no time, and he would either demand that publication of her book be halted, or would destroy the diaries before her manuscript was published, thus ruining any chance she had of authenticating her work. Her book would be laughed at if she could not document her sources, and show the Society precisely where she'd obtained her information.

Lady Ramsbottom rescued the sagging conversation. "Is

everyone going to the gaming parlor tonight? Everyone except young Celeste, that is?"

Miss Louisa Freemantle nodded. "I wouldn't miss it for the world."

Sir Cuthbert said, "I must admit, the Dethman men have always known how to throw a grand party. I've almost forgotten about the snows outside."

Sir Hugo hadn't forgotten that he was trapped in this castle, so near to a faro table that he could feel the chips in his fingers, and taste the metallic residue of the copper coins used to mark his bets. There was a smell to a gaming hall, a smell of playing cards and baize-topped tables, and spilled liquor. There was a sound, too, a musical blend of laughter and groans, clicking roulette wheels, snapping cards and clicking markers. It was a sound that rang in Hugo's ears, deafening him to his conscience.

"Will you be there?" Miss Louisa Freemantle repeated, staring at Sir Hugo.

He hesitated.

"Oh, do come to the parlor," Evelyn urged.

He looked at her face, so pale and pretty. Her eyes sparkled like sapphires in the candlelight, and her skin, against the black bombazine of her gown, was as flawless as a white diamond. His gaze fell to her lips, bow-shaped and pink. God, how he wanted to kiss her, drink her in, possess her wholly and fully.

But, she was such an innocent! She'd never known a man before, much less a man as debauched and debased as he. If she only knew what demons lived in his heart, what impulses roared in his head . . . she'd be frightened out of her mind!

Another drink of wine fortified him. Or perhaps it weakened him, Hugo wasn't certain. His blood grew hot and coursed through his veins. Misery clawed at his stomach and tightened every fiber of his body. He wanted to go to the gaming parlor, wanted to feel the chips in his fingers, the pulsing excitement of the place. He wanted Evelyn in his arms, wanted to taste her lips and feel her racing heart against his naked chest.

He wanted release. Release from the torture of his addiction, physical release from the irrepressible desire he felt for a woman.

And his agony was nearly unbearable.

"You haven't answered us, Hugo." Sir Cuthbert slanted his friend a quizzical look. "Are you going to gamble tonight or not?"

Sir Hugo drew a deep breath. Staring at Evelyn, he said, in a voice that sounded alarmingly like his father's, "I am feeling a surge of recklessness, Cubby. Very likely, I will see you at the faro table."

The countess stared at him, her cheeks darkening. He thought he sensed his restlessness. She felt it, too. Something wild inside the barrister struggled to be unleashed. Something inside Lady Goreham—something wild and harshly suppressed—begged for release.

Her lips parted slightly. Her eyelids flickered, and she gulped in a deep breath, turning her face from him. She had felt it, too, that wave of awareness that shimmered between them. Though they sat apart from one another, not touching, not daring to whisper their innermost thoughts to one another, their pulses raced together, their imaginations soared side by side. Sir Hugo had never desired a woman so desperately.

That night, wherever she was going to be, he would be there, too. Even if it meant venturing forth into the gambling hell the Earl of Goreham had set up in the parlor. Even if it meant losing every farthing he'd earned in the past five years. He simply couldn't stay away from Evelyn, the Dowager Countess of Goreham, one second longer.

Evelyn pushed back her chair, and stood. Percival watched her like a hawk. She felt his gaze track her as the dinner party disassembled, and the guests wandered through the Great Hall, admiring the coats of armor, the ancient swords and maces, and other artifacts of the Dethman family history.

Hugging Celeste, Evelyn gave the girl strict instructions to go to her bedchamber. She had arranged for Mrs. Shipton to keep a vigil over the girl tonight. There would be no leaving Celeste alone the rest of the holiday.

Releasing her sister, she glanced surreptitiously at Sir Hugo.

He stared back at her intensely, as he'd done the last half hour.

A shiver raced up her spine. Something dangerous had crept into Evelyn's heart. *Something wild.*

She allowed Lady Ramsbottom to take her arm. The party slowly made its way through the passageway toward the parlor, a few guests remaining behind to enjoy another glass of sherry or port before the stone hearth.

Entering the parlor, Evelyn gasped. She hadn't expected Percival's decorations to be so elaborate, but he had successfully transformed a pleasant, almost feminine room, into a gaudy, decadent gambling hell. Swags of velvet covered the damask curtains, while glittering chandeliers illuminated the shining brass roulette wheel. A small orchestra at the far end of the room played bawdy dance-hall music, rather than the Haydn most often heard on the pianoforte in that parlor.

"Would you care to join the ladies for a rubber of whist?" Lady Ramsbottom loosened her grasp on Evelyn's arm, and headed toward a card table.

Another hand clasped the arm that Lady Ramsbottom released. "Care to play a shoe or two of faro, my lady?"

His gaze was positively frightening in its intensity. Evelyn caught her breath sharply, her heart inexplicably skipping a beat. A frisson of fear skittered along her nerve-endings, and she found herself recoiling if only to draw away and stare at the barrister whose countenance had so darkened, so transformed itself, in the last half hour.

"Are you sure you are all right?" Her voice trembled.

He walked her across the room, his eyes gleaming and fixed hypnotically on the faro table. "No, I am not all right."

"Then why won't you look at me? You're hurting my arm, sir! Do tell me why you look so angry! I refuse to play beside you if you do not don a more pleasant expression!"

All at once, the barrister came to a complete standstill. Around him, the guests milled, their finest muslin and satin skirts rustling, their voices lifted in gay disregard of the swirling snow outside. But Sir Hugo stood, as if in the eye of a storm, unmoved by the frivolity around him.

He ran a hand over his brow. Beneath the bright light of the candles overhead, his hair glowed as copper as the coins that marked bets on the faro table. A deep furrow formed in his forehead as he faced Evelyn.

"I must leave," he said simply, turning on his heel.

Shocked, she watched him stalk the length of the parlor, then exit through the passageway.

Miss Louisa Freemantle materialized beside her. "Whatever is the matter with that man?"

Sir Cuthbert sidled up to the ladies. "No sense of humor, I'll say that for him. Did you see how quiet and tense he became at dinner tonight?"

"Well, you shouldn't have harassed Evelyn so about her manuscript," Louisa replied, batting the solicitor on his arm with her ivory fan.

For the first time, Evelyn noticed the familiarity between the two. Well, they were a good match, those two, he with his acerbic, often irreverent wit, and she with her outspoken pragmatism. Though Sir Cuthbert had represented the deceased earl in the composing and revising of his last will, Evelyn didn't hold him responsible for its contents. For that, she credited the third earl, her stepson.

Percival sauntered among the small group, and rising on his tiptoes, cast them a smug, knowing look. "Where did our friend the barrister disappear to, um? Could it be possible that he does not have a fancy for gambling? Egad, what kind of man is he?"

Louisa and Evelyn exchanged a quick, knowing look. Of course, the barrister gambled. Every man in London did. Sir Hugo had been doing just that five years ago when Evelyn met him. In fact, he'd played just as deeply as she had that night, though he hadn't lost so grandly.

She said archly, "Perhaps he wasn't feeling well. Don't concern yourself, Percival."

"Come on, Lou," Sir Cuthbert said, "Let's find a game of whist, shall we?"

That left Evelyn standing alone with her stepson. A chill rippled over her shoulders when he smiled at her. "My dear, would you care to indulge in some faro?"

She made a concentrated effort not to stare at the aperture through which Sir Hugo had vanished. Her impulse to run after him was tempered by her need to remain aloof from the man. She couldn't afford any of Percival's scurrilous accusations. Even if they weren't true, the appearance of an impropriety might be sufficient to deny her inheritance, and retract Celeste's dowry.

"Why don't you go after him?" Percival said.

Evelyn shot him a quelling look. "Don't be mad. I hardly know the man. What business is it of mine whether he gambles, or whether he sits in his room and twirls his thumbs?"

Smirking, Percival withdrew a small silver snuffbox from his waist coat pocket. He took a pinch, inhaled it, then snapped the lid shut. There was something sexual, something disturbing about the manner in which he stared at Evelyn. His eyes dilated, as if the snuff had produced a mind-numbing alteration of his mood.

"I am no fool, Evelyn," he drawled. "I know that you were hiding the barrister in your bedchamber today. I know it as well as I know the back of my hand."

"Then why didn't you insist on searching the room?"

"Because Lady Ramsbottom looked as if she might

squash me beneath her heaving bosom, dear! Dear me, I don't think I've ever seen such a mountainous woman in my life. You have a great defender in her, Evelyn. You should be pleased with yourself."

"I am not pleased at all over the events of the past few days. I should like to know what happened to Celeste, for one thing. Surely, you know something about that distasteful incident."

Percival's brows rose, giving very much the same effect as when he bobbed on his tiptoes. "Are you accusing me of attacking my dear little stepsister? That is the most outrageous accusation I have ever heard. Father must be rolling in his grave."

"If he is, it's nothing to do with my behavior, Percival. Your father loved you, but even he was aware of your petty nature and your foolish greed."

His eyes narrowed. "You turned Father against me! I shall never forgive you that!"

"I did no such thing. I never spoke an unkind word against you! I didn't have to. The earl knew what you were about, always fretting that one farthing of your inheritance would be diverted, always worried that your father might spend a pound of your future inheritance while he was yet alive!"

Percival's voice was a malevolent whisper. "I hated you, Evelyn. Hated you because you were young enough to be my sister, by God. You never loved Father, you couldn't have!"

"Perhaps not in the conventional sense, Percival. But, I had great respect for your father. He was kind and generous to me, and I was a good and devoted wife to him."

He chuckled. "You must have been so happy the day he turned up his toes."

"On the contrary, it pains me still to know how he suffered. But he is gone, Percival, and I intend to live my life as I please from here on out."

The third earl opened his mouth, then clamped it shut.

Whatever he had thought to say, he chose to censor. At length, he said, "I promise you Evelyn, I shall not allow you to ruin the Dethmans' good name. Nor shall I allow you to squander Father's money on some enterprising bounder who—"

Lady Ramsbottom appeared out of nowhere. "Now, what is all this heated talk about? The two of you look much too serious! Come, Evelyn, I have reserved a chair at the card table in the corner for you. If you don't take it soon, I shall have to face that pig-faced Mrs. Smythson who cheats, but says she doesn't."

Relieved, Evelyn allowed herself to be pulled from Percival's malignant presence. She cast him a backward glance as Lady Ramsbottom took her arm. The look her stepson gave her was full of loathing. Trembling, she clutched her friend's arm, and turned her head. She forced herself to smile at the pleasant faces which greeted her at the card table.

Chapter Six

Sir Hugo strode through the Great Hall, his head throbbing. His fists coiled and uncoiled at his sides as he strode past the stairway leading to the above-stairs bedchambers. Belatedly, he remembered there was no light in the library. Grabbing a candelabra from a commode beside the staircase, he proceeded to the door behind the wide stone steps.

The western corridor, bordering the middle courtyard, was dark and cold. Stalking through it, Sir Hugo felt his ears ring with the noise of the gaming tables he'd left behind, the laughter, the clink of chips, the rustle of pound notes.

He crossed the threshold, entering the library; candlelight splashed over the bindings of the books, many of them gilt-edged and ancient.

It was a spectacular room, with nooks and crannies, refectory tables of polished deal, and huge oaken work tables. Despite the library's solitary ambience, its strewn chairs and longues gave it a chaotic look. Apparently, there had been at least a few Dethman men interested in books and learning. Shaking his head, Sir Hugo reflected wryly that Percival, the third earl of Goreham, was undoubtedly not among them.

If he were, he would have found the Dethman diaries before his stepmother Evelyn did. Wandering about the library, Sir Hugo marveled that she found anything in this disorganized clutter of books, maps, folios, and papers. Tabletops were invisible beneath oversized ledgers and books. On the floor beside chairs were stacks of books, some old, some with newer sturdier bindings. Wall shelves contained all manner of books and ledgers. Pulling open a desk drawer, Sir Hugo saw that it, too, was stuffed with stray papers and smaller ledgers, diaries, perhaps.

Evelyn must have spent days, perhaps weeks or months, prowling this library. Setting down his branch of candles, Sir Hugo imagined her, poking in corners, climbing on ladders to reach some dusty old tome on the top shelf. He knew enough about her to know how persistent she could be. Not for the first time, the words "amazing woman" flashed in his mind.

The adrenaline rush that propelled Hugo out of the parlor, across the hall, and into the library, receded abruptly. Energy drained from his veins, leaving him melancholy and exhausted. Avoiding the temptation of the faro table had required a herculean effort. As always, the aftermath of such an exertion left him depressed and brooding. Slowly, he lowered himself into a chair and propped his elbows on a deal table.

His head fell into his hands, fingers threading his hair. For a long time, Sir Hugo sat, his silence accompanied only by the wailing of the wind. Even in this isolated chamber, where neither light of day, nor brightest star could penetrate, the snowstorm raged audibly, crashing at the castle like a battering ram.

Hugo felt old, tired, cut off from the rest of humanity. Most of all, he felt cut off from Evelyn.

Recalling her expression when he left the library, his stomach clenched. She hadn't understood. *How could she?*

She had to think him crazed, or horridly rude. But, that was preferable to her knowing the truth. Sir Hugo's chest squeezed, and he closed his eyes against the veil of hot tears that threatened to escape him. He didn't cry; he never had in his life. But, in that bitter, desolate moment, he felt nothing but pain and heartache, and there was no escape from it.

He slammed his fists on the table until his hand and every muscle in his body hurt.

He was weak. Bedeviled by his attraction to the faro table. It was a sickness, an affliction that had robbed his father of good sense and dignity. Now, it would rob him of the same qualities.

His mind reeled back in time, to the day when his father had stumbled into the drawing room of his family's modest Belgravia town house. It was a respectable house in a respectable neighborhood, but inside, the furnishings were sparse and more often than not, the cupboard was practically bare.

Sir Hugo's mother had inherited the house from her parents, and had done her best to hang onto the small cash inheritance they'd left her. But, Mr. Charles Mansfield had other ideas about how his wife's inheritance should be spent. And he'd gone about spending his wife's money, without regard for his wife's feelings or opinions. The law, being what it was, gave Mathilda Mansfield no recourse against her husband's spendthrift ways.

Not that he was buying luxury items for the family. He wasn't buying food, expensive cuts of meat or even cases of liquor or French wine. Mr. Charles Mansfield had no taste for well-cut clothes, and so his family had none. Sir Hugo remembered vividly the shame his sisters suffered at having to wear cast-off clothes furnished by sympathetic relatives, dresses with frayed hems and sleeves, out-of-date bonnets with drooping brims and lace collars riven with moth-holes.

No, Mr. Charles Mansfield spent his wife's money at the gambling hells of St. James's. He lost his job as a lord's clerk when Sir Hugo was a young boy. Afterwards, the elder Mansfield took to sleeping half the day, rising in time for nuncheon, then departing abruptly for the gambling halls.

Cards had been Mr. Mansfield's particular vice. Sir Hugo had only seen his father in action once, and that was just before the elder man's death. His mother, distraught because there was no food in the house and not a farthing to buy faggots for a fire, beseeched her son to go and find his father. Hugo had done so; it wasn't difficult to locate Mr. Mansfield. And his father, furious at having his whist game interrupted by a tap on his shoulder, and at a pathetic request from his son to come home, stood up from the table, knocking it over and sending every man's chits and cards flying.

Then, like an enraged bull, Mr. Mansfield had turned and slapped his son full on the face.

Even now, sitting in that dark, damp library, Sir Hugo felt the cold, bracing sting on his cheek. Even now, he hated his father for humiliating him. Even worse, he hated his father for what he—the son—had become.

The scene that night in the gambling hell had been ferocious. The establishment's managers had rushed forward to right the table, and soothe the ruffled feathers of the other card players. Had Mr. Mansfield not been such a well-known patron of the house, he would have been tossed into the street. But, since he wagered deeply there almost every night, and invariably lost more than he won, he was encouraged to have another drink of sherry and becalm himself.

Somewhere in the melee, Mr. Mansfield expressed a modicum of regret at having slapped his son. Barely out of knee-pants, Hugo had been tall for his age and muscular. He could easily have felled his father with one blow. The thought and the impulse had crossed his mind; but he had no intention of injuring his father, a man whom he pitied and loathed, a man of such profound weakness Sir Hugo was ashamed to call him Father.

He had wanted nothing more in that moment than to flee. But some perverse fascination with the game his father had played held him pinned to the spot.

The gambling had resumed. The excitement of a quick flaring of tempers had died down. Mr. Mansfield, seated, looked over his shoulder, and expressed surprise that his son was still present.

"Here, son, have a go at the faro table. No skill involved there, just luck. Watch a few minutes, and you'll know what to do." Mr. Charles Mansfield had crushed a wad of pound notes in his son's hand, before returning his attention to the cards in his hand.

Hugo wandered to the faro table. As his father had predicted, he learned the game quickly. The five pounds in his fist became twenty, then fifty. He didn't stop playing till his father cuffed his neck, and propelled him from the gambling hell.

"Time to go home. I've lost it all, damme! Your mother will be in a state, no doubt!"

Elated, giddy with delight, Hugo had opened his palms and displayed the blunt he'd won.

Drunk, glassy-eyed, his father grabbed at the pound notes and stuffed them in his pockets. "Don't ever tell your ma I let you play at the tables. She'd kill me, sure as the world."

And so, when the two Mansfield men greeted Mathilda later that night, the father produced the money and claimed he'd won it playing whist.

Mathilda Mansfield had wiped a tear from her eye, and embraced her son. "Don't become your father," she whispered, holding him in a tight embrace.

It had been a portentous warning. For, Sir Hugo couldn't forget the excitement of turning his money into more.

The fever was in him, just as quickly as that. And from that day forward, whenever he had a guinea or a pound, he would steal to a gambling hell and stand at the faro table. Often he won, and left with a pocketful of money. More often, he lost, returning home penniless.

After Charles Mansfield died—from drinking, the doctor said—Hugo's uncle took the family in. Hugo obtained an education, but even while he was at the Inn, living on the allowance his Uncle Reginald generously furnished, he spent every spare moment in Brooks's or Watier's, and later Widow Philpott's faro house. He couldn't stay away; the legacy of his father was firmly imprinted on his heart and soul. It was the blackest tattoo any man could have, and it was indelible.

There was simply no way Sir Hugo would allow Evelyn to see into his soul, no way that he would expose that ugly part of himself to her. Despite the fact he hadn't been in a gambling hell in five years, he still had the urge, the need, the desire to play—and play deep. Sir Hugo knew that if he ever did bet a farthing, he wouldn't be able to stop. He'd wind up losing every bit of money he'd saved in five years if he wagered so much as a tuppence.

So, it was better that Evelyn think him rude or crazed.

Sighing, Hugo clutched his head. The candlelight flickered, sending shadows dancing across the book-laden tables. The muscles in his neck and back ached, and he stretched, arching his back and straightening his sore legs. Yawning, his hands fell to the table. His gaze fell to a thick, leather-bound ledger at the bottom of a stack of books just in front of him.

The ledger was smaller and newer than the others, its binding tight. On its side were written, in black ink, the words *My Life, 1773–1783, Dethman, Henry, Earl of Goreham.* There was another volume that chronicled Dethman's life up to ten years ago. Sir Hugo recognized the sort of ledgers that one bought in a printing shop, or bookstore, its pages blank. He was surprised that the old man had kept an account of his life; he hadn't thought anyone but Samuel Pepys had had enough time to do so.

Curiosity overwhelmed him. Shoving the top books off the stack, he drew the earliest diary toward him. He half-stood and moved the candelabra closer, spilling his light on the diary. Tentatively, guiltily, his fingers moved across the binding. He felt like an eavesdropper, a spy, and yet the book was in plain view in the library for anyone to see. Perhaps the old earl would have been flattered that anyone was interested in his daily thoughts, the private musings he recorded in this musty book.

What kind of man was he? What kind of man had Evelyn spent five years of her life with? Why kind of man had spawned Percival, the third earl, for that matter?

Had he not been so desperate for distraction from the faro tables and from the demons struggling in his head, Sir Hugo might not have cared a whit.

But, what better way to occupy his time? He opened the book, and started reading.

By the time he closed the second diary, his candles guttered and sputtered, threatening to douse him in blackness. His body ached from lack of sleep. But Hugo's discoveries were worth his sore limbs and scratchy eyes. Amazed, he returned the diaries to their place beneath a stack of books. He doubted anyone, least of all Percival, would find them there.

Climbing the stairs to his bedchamber, he thought ruefully that the puzzle surrounding Evelyn and her stepson had just grown more complicated.

And more dangerous.

For if Henry Dethman's secrets were ever revealed, Percival, the third Earl of Goreham, would be completely disinherited.

* * *

By midmorning the following day, the storm had slackened. The snows abated, and the wind no longer howled and keened like a forlorn animal.

Mrs. Shipton had supervised the drawing and heating of several buckets of water which were lugged to Evelyn's bedchamber. The tub was dragged from behind the screen and placed in the center of the room. Stepping into it, Evelyn felt delicious relief as steaming water lapped against her skin. She lowered herself slowly, finally slipping beneath the surface of the water, then bobbing upright, sputtering and smoothing her wet hair behind her ears.

A scrabbling at her door gave her a start. Despite having turned the latch after Shipton's departure, Evelyn instinctively covered her breasts with her hands, and gasped.

Her pulse raced as she watched a small folded sheet of vellum slip beneath her bedroom door. It lay in stark contrast to the deep, rich blues and reds of the Oriental carpet. Footsteps, heavy and masculine, retreated down the corridor outside.

Evelyn leapt from the tub, raced naked across the room and snatched up the paper. The fire in the hearth did little to warm her, and by the time she climbed into the tub again, her teeth were clattering.

There was no envelope, no distinctive seal to identify the note's sender. Just a single fold in a sheet of heavy writing paper, the type of paper one bought at any stationer's store in London. Evelyn quickly scanned the carefully printed note; written in black ink in thick block letters, it was short and succinct.

Dearest Evelyn,

When can we be alone? Eyes and ears surround us; these castle walls close in upon us, keeping us apart, restricting the expression of my true love for you.

Meet me this night in the library, after the castle guests are asleep, at midnight.

Yours always, H.

The note trembled in her fingers. A surge of emotion rose like a flood tide in Evelyn's breast. Was it so hard to believe that Sir Hugo's passion for her had become so unbearable that he simply had to see her? Was he in his chambers, even now, aching to talk to her, touch her, press his lips against hers?

Leaning her head against the edge of the tub, she closed her eyes. The note, its ink blurring beneath the imprint of her wet fingers, fluttered to the carpet. Sir Hugo's voice sounded in her head, repeating the words she'd read, commanding her to come to him.

She wanted to go, wanted to flee to him, and escape the dreadful loneliness that had threatened to crush her spirit these last five years. Her heart beat fast at the prospect of spending a few hours alone with Sir Hugo, wrapped in his arms, snuggled in his embrace.

They'd had so little time together. They hardly knew one another. So far, their time together had been fraught with tension, overlaid with the fear of discovery at any moment. Even their public conversations—especially the one at dinner table last evening—subjected them to a scrutiny which was both dangerous and agitating to Evelyn. She felt a deep privation, a need to be alone with the barrister who had yesterday claimed he "needed her, and wanted her."

She needed him, too. Why, she couldn't wholly understand. He'd disappointed her five years earlier, practically encouraged her to marry the elderly earl. He hadn't wanted to offer her assistance then. What made her believe his motivation was honorable, now?

Indeed, what was it about Sir Hugo that tempted Evelyn to risk her inheritance by accepting an invitation to meet him privately, at midnight? If discovered, such an assignation could only be construed as a romantic rendezvous. With Lord Goreham's embellishing the story, all of London society would soon think she'd been caught *in flagrante delicto* with a handsome barrister.

Why, then, was Sir Hugo willing to hazard her reputation? Was he such a gambler that he thought himself invincible, invulnerable to the whims and vagaries of the London gossipmongers? The hypocrisy of the ton was monumental; Evelyn knew of cases where lords and ladies were caught practically naked in one another's arms, and not an ounce of harm was done to their reputations. In fact, their escapades were recounted in titilated whispers at fancy-dress balls, and they became more in demand for tea parties and court functions than before.

In other instances, little greenies caught behind a potted fern holding hands with a notorious rake had been cruelly castigated. Engagements were broken, and fortunes had been lost, just because an unsophisticated lass allowed a renowned cad to steal a kiss from her. The caprice with which reputations were made or broken by a single utterance from an Almack's patroness was legendary.

In Evelyn's case, there was no doubt that any small indiscretion, the slightest of improprieties, would be enlarged upon until Percival, her stepson, would have the ammunition he required to rob her of her inheritance.

No, she simply could not risk depriving Celeste of her dowry, and her future inheritance.

But, how could she resist the barrister's invitation?

For five years, Evelyn had thought about their brief encounter, the way he'd gazed at her when she lay on Widow Philpott's bed, the way he spoke to her in that soft, gentle, throaty murmur. Even now, the recollection of his voice sent chill-bumps up her spine.

She slid deeper into the warm water, allowing it to lap her chin. There was so much she wanted to ask Sir Hugo. Why had he stepped back when Henry Dethman, the second Earl of Goreham, proposed marriage to her? Why had he so clearly stepped aside, refusing at that point to offer her any assistance, other than his tepid advice to walk out of Widow Philpott's faro house, and take her chances with the London authorities?

Surely, he hadn't thought his suggestion viable. After five years, Evelyn had had plenty of time to contemplate her options that night. Though she wasn't the type to dwell on what was in the past, she often played out different endings to the scenario in Widow Philpott's gambling establishment.

Suppose she had walked out, owing the old tabby money.

Evelyn was fairly certain she wouldn't have got round the block before the widow's bouncers tracked her down, and exacted some unspeakable payment in kind from her.

Suppose she had managed to escape that night, only to return to the hideous, flea-ridden hovel where she'd left Celeste, shivering with a fever, racked with a cough?

The widow might not have found her, but Evelyn would still have been penniless. She'd wagered all her funds, and had no money in her pockets when the last shoe of faro was dealt. Without a farthing, she'd have been forced to find some sort of employment. And since she'd spent her entire lifetime taking care of Celeste, she had no skills with which to find a job. A suitable job, that is.

She could have been hired as a scullery wench, or an abigail, and obtained living quarters along with her meager wages. But, where would Celeste have lived?

The only sort of employment that would have afforded Evelyn sufficient funds to support herself and Celeste was prostitution. And wasn't marriage to the old earl preferable to that? After all, he'd never touched her, never made a single physical demand of her. He'd been generous, if not companionable, and never stinted a penny on Celeste's welfare.

Indeed, though the old man had rarely uttered a pleas-ant word to either female, he'd seen to it that their every need was met, their every whim catered to. His largesse had even made it possible for Evelyn to pursue her academic interests. Five years ago, she'd never thought it possible that she'd be admitted to the prestigious Society for the Study of the Tudor Monarchy. Soon, she would be delivering a speech there, and revealing the premise of her manuscript. Once her book was published, she would earn the respect of her esteemed, scholarly colleagues. All the money in the world couldn't compensate her for the gratification she received for having achieved that respect.

Confused, Evelyn turned on her side, gripping the edge of the tub. Her bath water was lukewarm, but the heat suffusing her limbs intensified. So many emotions she never expected to experience had roiled through her these past few days: desire for a man had overtaken her. Her fantasies had become reality. The man she'd obsessively spied upon every morning for the past five years had materialized before her very eyes.

Was he all that she'd dreamed he would be? Or was she fooling herself? Was he selfish and stingy, too absorbed in his career and his own welfare to help a chit who'd lost her fortunes at a faro table? Or, was he the kind-spirited man she sensed—she *hoped*—he was?

In one anguished moment, Evelyn thought perhaps she'd created an image discordant with the true Sir Hugo.

Then she remembered when he touched her face, kissed her lips, whispered that he wanted her. Her imagination seized on the moment when he turned his dark, brooding gaze on her at dinner. She'd felt an awareness between them that couldn't have been fantasy. Their shared attraction was real. It had affected him as deeply as it had her.

And she loved talking with him. Her fascination with Sir Hugo wasn't purely physical. No, his mind fascinated her, too. His conversation was stimulating, his wit quick. His cleverness, the breadth of his historical knowledge, impressed her. Evelyn and Hugo spoke a language full of idioms and colloquialisms all their own. When he started a sentence, she found herself finishing it. When she spoke, his eyes sparkled with understanding. When they'd held court with one another, everyone around them faded into the cracks of the castle walls.

So, how could she refuse to meet him if he needed her?

Her gaze fell to the faded missive lying crumpled on the floor.

If she stole below stairs at midnight to meet Sir Hugo, who would know? She would take off her slippers—to hell with the freezing floors—and glide like a wraith past Lord Goreham's door. He'd never be the wiser, and her inheritance would never truly be in jeopardy.

But what of the guests who would be coming from the party in the parlor? For the past two nights, the gambling had carried on well into the night; there was no reason to doubt that on this night, the revelers would be retiring to their beds any earlier. If she wasn't careful, she might encounter someone on the stairs.

Evelyn bit her lower lip, debating whether her chosen course of action was imprudent. Of course, it wasn't! She was being reckless, following her heart, doing what she wanted to rather than was right, or dutiful. For once in her life, she was allowing her passions—not her responsibilities—to guide her.

Mind made up, Evelyn turned on her back and slid beneath the surface of the water again. This time, she held her breath a full minute, feeling the tightening of her lungs, the tight ache in her chest. When her need to draw air into her lungs was painfully urgent, she surfaced. Gasping she sat up, her skin tingling, heart pounding. She'd been underwater for five years, struggling to reach the surface of her most deeply suppressed desires. Tonight, she was going to swim free, liberated from the suffocating restraints of her duties, her inhibitions, her fears.

* * *

She sat on the side of the bed in her muslin rail, pulling on a woolen stocking when someone pounded on her door.

Celeste's voice, an excited whisper, penetrated the mahogany panel. "Sister, open the door! Quickly!"

Evelyn rushed to the door, unlatched it, and admitted Celeste. "What is it, for heaven's sake? I'm not dressed."

"Hurry, then. I have something to show you. You'd better wear your half-boots and your warmest gown. We're going somewhere very cold."

"Everywhere is cold," grumbled Evelyn, stepping into a black woolen gown. Her sister fastened the row of buttons up the back, then helped her comb her still damp hair.

"You'd better wear a scarf over your head," Celeste said. "With wet hair, you'll catch your death of cold if you're not careful."

Before they left the room, the girls tucked gloves into their apron pockets, and wrapped shawls around their shoulders. Evelyn, curious as to what mischief her sister was up to, acquiesced in what she considered a bit of harmless fun. Perhaps a litter of kittens had been born in the barn, and Celeste was eager to show them. Or an injured bird had fallen from the sky, and was healing its broken wing beside the hearth in the kitchen.

At any rate, Celeste refused to divulge where she was taking her sister, and Evelyn, caught up in her sister's infectious excitement, allowed herself to be dragged out of her bedchamber by the hand.

"At least there was a fire going in my room, Celeste. What could be so interesting you'd be willing to forego the scant warmth my hearth could provide?"

"You'll see, you'll see." Celeste pulled her sister through the long corridor, past Sir Hugo's room, and down the staircase.

At the bottom landing, Celeste turned right toward the

screen of doors that led into the ancient medieval kitchens. The cavernous room was still the site of all food preparation, but now it boasted modern ovens as well as the hand-cranked rotisseries in the fireplace. The smell of bread baking and beef roasting permeated the room, while smoke exited through a vent in the ceiling.

But, Celeste did not slow down. Evelyn looked about for a new litter of kittens, but met only the curious gazes of the servants and cooks.

The young women crossed the kitchen, and exited through a side door that led to a small herb garden enclosed by a high brick wall.

Cold wind slapped Evelyn in the face. "Celeste, it is freezing out here."

Her sister led her across a flagstone path that fringed the kitchen wall. At the end of the path was a wooden door, and through that door, a stone staircase leading into a cellar. Evelyn was surprised to see, as she crept down the steps behind her sister, a glow of light emanating from within the underground chamber.

She hugged the wall, her hands running over rough, mossy stones. The damp chill in the cellar penetrated her bones, inducing a shiver that rattled her teeth.

"This place is like a dungeon," she whispered to Celeste. "I want to get out of here!"

"Stay!" Her sister, at the bottom of the steps, turned an imploring look on Evelyn. "This is what I want to show you."

As Evelyn's eyes adjusted to the semi-darkness, she made out a candelabra sitting on the center of a crudely constructed wood-plank table. On either side of the candle were two cages made of wire mesh, and inside each cage were at least four . . . little brown mice!

"Oh, Celeste, how dare you!" Evelyn's skin rippled like the surface of a windswept moat. Turning, she made to flee up the steps, toward the warm safety of the castle. But her sister quickly grabbed her elbow, holding her captive.

"They are experiments, Evelyn. Sir Hugo is conducting experiments with these mice."

That curious statement was sufficient to delay Evelyn's exodus. Slowly turning, she surveyed the four mouse cages with renewed interest, and rising revulsion. "What kind of experiments?" she asked quietly, her breath frosting the air.

" 'Tis very odd," Celeste said, moving around the table. From the opposite bench, she picked up a vase, the blue and white Imari vase that had been atop Evelyn's bedroom mantelpiece. "There was some liquid in this vase. I don't know where Sir Hugo got the vase. It looks familiar, but I cannot recall where it came from. At any rate, I had come into the kitchen looking for hot chocolate when I saw Sir Hugo enter from the garden door."

"And your irrepressible curiosity was aroused," Evelyn said drily.

"Quite so. I asked cook what the barrister was doing in the garden, and she said she hadn't a clue. So, I did some snooping until I found the cellar door ajar. Just slightly. I would have been afraid to come down here, but he'd left the candles burning."

"That means he will return shortly, Celeste. We should leave before he catches us here."

The younger girl's eyes rounded innocently. "What if he does? We haven't done anything wrong."

"Whatever he is doing here, I'm afraid it isn't for our eyes."

"Are you frightened of him, Sister? He is rather brooding and mysterious, isn't he?"

Evelyn's patience was thinning. She was far more frightened of Sir Hugo Mansfield than Celeste could ever know, but the child was too young to understand such things. Besides, she would never want her sister to know the temptation she was presently facing. If Celeste realized the true extent of Evelyn's attraction toward Sir Hugo, she'd have good reason to be concerned about her dowry, and her entire future.

Celeste prattled on, oblivious to Evelyn's growing agitation. "It seems he has given one set of the mice a dish filled with the liquid that was poured from this vase. The other mice are drinking water."

A low, masculine voice sounded from the stairwell. "How clever of you, Celeste."

Evelyn whirled, her heart pounding. Facing Sir Hugo, she felt the earthen walls close in on her.

"Sir! You nearly frightened me out of my mind. I pray you do not sneak up on us like that again!" Evelyn's voice was brusquer than she intended.

"I beg your pardon, my lady." But, the barrister's contrition was insincere. A twinkle of sly amusement shone in his gaze. Crossing the dirt-packed floor, he stood beside the table and leaned over the mouse cages. "So, how are the little fellows faring?"

Celeste put her head next to his, all curiosity and innocence. "These two are sick. In fact, I'm afraid that little one there is dead. He hasn't moved in the past few hours."

Sir Hugo straightened. "Have you been down here more than once?" he asked Celeste.

"A couple of times. I stole halfway down the steps once, and watched you pour the liquid from the vase. Earthen steps don't creak, you know."

He laughed easily. "Yes, I know. I do apologize for frightening you both. But I hadn't meant to disclose the existence of my experiments. Not so soon, anyway."

Evelyn pulled her shawl tightly around her shoulders, more out of nervousness than the need for warmth. "Do you mind telling me what the nature of these experiments is?"

His expression sobered. For a moment, Hugo stared at his mice. At length, he faced Evelyn, but when he spoke, his voice was hoarse with emotion—anger, perhaps? "Someone poisoned you, Evelyn."

Celeste's jaw fell slack.

Evelyn's heart skipped a beat. She felt a dizzying sense of unreality. But the barrister's words were clear and unequivocal. "Do you mean to say that when I was ill three days ago, it was because someone poisoned me?"

"I have not quite figured out how the poison was administered to you, but I suspect it went something like this. You arrived at the castle after an arduous trip, and retired to your bedchamber."

Evelyn nodded.

"Some time thereafter, you ordered some tea from the kitchen," Sir Hugo continued.

"Miss Louisa Freemantle and I lay on my bed and drank tea that afternoon. We ate some biscuits and cookies, too. But Lou didn't get sick."

The barrister's brow furrowed. "She drank tea from the same pot? You're certain?"

"Quite." Evelyn glanced at the mice and shivered. "I didn't drink any more tea, until I awoke from my nap. I believe it was around four o'clock. Lou had been gone for some time. At any rate, the wind was howling so outside my window that I couldn't sleep. By then, Shipton had produced another pot of tea. I remember thinking that it was still warm when I poured it."

"Was there anything odd about the way it tasted?"

"There is always something odd about the way Shipton's tea tastes."

Celeste giggled. "She makes the most dreadful witch's brew."

"And how long after you drank the tea did you become ill, my lady?" The barrister's voice was low and coaxing. Evelyn thought it was no wonder he was such an expert trial lawyer. Mesmerized by his eyes, hypnotized by his voice, she might have confessed to murder had he suggested she might unburden her soul by doing so.

"I—I don't know. An hour, perhaps a half hour. I started

feeling nauseated, and, well— it isn't a very delicate subject, sir.''

"I am a lawyer," Sir Hugo answered. "And I am trying to get to the bottom of the strange goings-on that have occurred since this house party convened. Pray, do not be embarrassed.''

"The illness came over me in waves," Evelyn explained, as euphemistically as she could. "After I suffered one bout, and had given up all that I ate in the previous day, I thought I would be all right. I lay down, and attempted to sleep. But the nausea would not leave me. After an hour, I was so weak, I could hardly sit up. Thank goodness Shipton stepped into my room when she did. That was about five o'clock, as I recall. I might have choked to death had she not arrived then, I'm afraid.''

Sir Hugo stepped closer to her. Celeste's eyes widened as the barrister gently grasped Evelyn's arms, chafing them to warm some life back into her body.

"No one is happier than I that Shipton arrived in the nick of time." He held her at arm's length a moment, studying her. Then, almost abruptly, he kissed her on the forehead and set her away from him. He became businesslike, and strode back to the end of the table, staring at the mouse cage.

Evelyn broke the silence. "Come Celeste. We must go now, and I must ask that Sir Hugo not allow you to come down here again. I am quite put out that the kitchen help didn't stop you when you traipsed out the door. You could have caught your death of cold.''

Celeste smiled at Sir Hugo, a brilliant, guileless smile. "She is still so protective of me, regardless that I haven't been sick a day in three years.''

Sir Hugo returned her warm smile. It was obvious that since he'd questioned her after her attack the day before, Celeste had great admiration and trust for the man. Watching her, Evelyn thought she stared at him with a sort of hero worship. It both amused her and frightened her a little that her sister would be forming an attachment with this dangerous man. An innocent attachment on both sides, that was certain, but a bond nevertheless.

The last thing Evelyn wanted was to form a bond with Sir Hugo.

Suddenly, and silently, she wavered on the issue of whether she would meet Sir Hugo in the library. Watching Celeste and Sir Hugo scared her half out of her mind. He was telling the young girl now about the care and feeding of mice, about the scientific principles behind setting up a test group of mice, and something he called a "control" group. It was all very novel and interesting, and Celeste was hanging on every word the man said.

Her sister's innocence, the child's dependence on her, suddenly came back to Evelyn. Good heavens, the child was a total greenie! After a sickly childhood, she'd blossomed beneath Lord Goreham's roof, and evolved into a well-mannered, effervescent young lady. She had a future, one so unlike Evelyn's.

Evelyn so hoped Celeste would never know another day's privation, never face the kind of dilemma she'd faced five years ago. The thought of Celeste having to marry a man she didn't love brought a spasm of pain to Evelyn's chest!

And if Evelyn were foolish enough to forfeit their respective portions of the old earl's estate, simply by allowing herself an indiscreet folly with Sir Hugo, Celeste would have no dowry. She might very well be forced to marry whatever penniless cad would have her. The child would have no say at all in her own marriage, but would be lucky to find a man who would support her, provide for her meanest needs.

No, Evelyn had worked too hard, and come too far, to throw everything away for a moment of passion. Without warning, she changed her mind, realizing that she simply could not meet Sir Hugo in the library that night.

And the more she thought on the subject, the angrier she was at the man who had the audacity to suggest such an indiscretion. True, he didn't know the details of the earl's will, and the significance of her getting caught in a compromising situation with him, but he certainly understood the importance of a woman's maintaining her reputation. Surely, he understood that since she was in mourning, she could not be seen, or even be suspected, of carrying on a torrid affair.

"Come, Celeste!" Evelyn's voice took on a sharp edge. Both her sister and the barrister looked at her quizzically. "I said I do not want you in this damp cellar anymore, and I meant it! Pray, sir, do not tempt my sister down here with your scintillating discourses on science and mice! I've had quite enough excitement for one weekend. The last thing I need is to see Celeste felled by a nasty cough or cold. Perhaps she doesn't remember how sick she used to be, but I do!"

Dutifully, Celeste scampered up the steps. Evelyn followed, but when she was halfway up, Sir Hugo's voice stopped her.

"I am sorry if I offended you or your sister, Evelyn."

She paused, her hand flat against the cold, earthen wall. She felt the very coldness of the ground creep into her bones, as if she'd been buried in a grave and covered with dirt. Her life flashed before her eyes, and that old fear returned to her, so quickly she wondered how she could ever have forgotten it.

Fear replaced all else, barging into her heart and shoving aside any tender feelings she might have had for Sir Hugo. Her memories of Celeste as a young child, shivering beneath mounds of cheap, dirty, moth-eaten blankets, assailed her. She smelled the oily filth of the hovels they'd lived in, tasted the stale bread and the moldy cheese they'd eaten. The smell and taste of her fear was more acrid in her mouth than Mrs. Shipton's witch's brew, as Celeste had aptly named it.

An unbearable weight settled on Evelyn's shoulders as she trudged up the steps, with Celeste's feather-light foot-

steps ahead of her. It wasn't her deceased husband's will
that kept her from giving herself, heart and body, to the
barrister. It was something inside her, something less tangible but just as draconian in its restrictions on her ability
to love.

Unmarried, unattached and untouched. The words haunted
her.

Yet the earl couldn't have been more prescient in predicting Evelyn's inability to love. After five years of a sham
marriage, and many more before that, when her energies
had been spent scrabbling for food and shelter and medical care for Celeste, Evelyn had no illusions about the
harshness of life. She knew the seamy side of it, had felt
the brunt of man's inhumanity to man.

She knew, for example, that romantic love existed only in
books, in romance novels intended to titillate the prurient
interests of silly women. She knew that without social ranking and respectability, a woman was less than nothing in
this world. She knew that strangers could not be counted
on for charity, generosity, even the slightest show of kindness, that if a person could not pay her way in the world,
she was at the mercy of a host of villains. Such as the Widow
Philpott. Such as her stepson, Percival Dethman.

Evelyn knew, too, that a man's affections were not always
constant, that he might love her one day and detest her
the next. Or worse, a woman might love a man, investing
all her hopes and dreams in him . . . only to lose him to
death's cold clutches. Her father hadn't meant to abandon
her and Celeste, but he'd left them alone in the world,
with very little to survive on. Even her deceased husband,
the earl, for all the promises he'd made her, and despite
her having lived up to her end of their marriage bargain,
managed to cheat her in the end.

Racing through the garden on Celeste's heels, Evelyn
welcomed the icy bite of the cold air. In the eleven months
since the earl's death, she had pondered many times why
her husband would have put conditions on her inheri-

tance, and Celeste's. Till now, she'd never given a moment's consideration to failing those conditions. There had been no man who interested her, and she hadn't thought there ever would be one.

Now she felt an immense sadness that the earl had seen fit to restrict her inheritance. It was an insult, a final slap in the face, delivered from the grave. It was another of life's messages, a lesson meant to teach her that romantic love was not to be hers, that financial security for herself and for Celeste was the very best that she would ever achieve, and that her future would always be circumscribed by forces beyond her control.

"Evelyn, whatever is the matter?" Celeste asked her sister as they marched through the kitchens.

Taking Evelyn's arm, the younger girl drew to a halt beside a huge butcher's table where a white-aproned cook stood, poised with a sinister-looking cleaver, ready to hack away at a denuded bird.

Evelyn stared at her sister's upturned face. "Oh, Celeste, you are so innocent. I hope you remain that way, always."

It seemed to her that her baby sister had forgotten all the hardships life had served up to them before the earl offered Evelyn a devil's bargain. Having accepted that bargain, Evelyn knew that her choice had blackened her soul, robbed her of her own innocence.

But, Celeste still had hers.

And as long as Evelyn was alive, she'd do nothing to jeopardize her sister's security, comfort, and peace of mind.

If Sir Hugo thought she was going to meet him in the library at midnight, he was dead wrong.

Chapter Seven

They stood before the fire in the Great Hall, warming their hands, turning their backs and hitching up their gowns to warm their legs and behinds. Evelyn took Celeste's hands between her own, and roughly rubbed the warmth back into them.

"That is enough," Celeste cried, pulling her hands from her sister's, and tucking them beneath her arms. "You are going to rub the skin off my hands!"

"You got much too cold out there," Evelyn scolded. "I won't have you traipsing around outside and exploring that damp basement like some unmannered little hoyden!"

Celeste frowned, a tear glistening in her eyes. "What have I done to anger you, Sister? Or has the experiment overset you?"

"The mouse experiment?" Evelyn faced the fire, but even as the warmth of the flames permeated her skin, a chill crept through her bones. She hadn't given much thought to Sir Hugo's explanations regarding the mice, but now the implication of what he'd told her settled in like a hard winter.

Her voice emerged as a scratchy whisper. "Someone tried to poison me."

"Who would do such a thing?"

"The same person who bound and gagged you, and searched your room."

Celeste lowered her voice, even though there was no one else present in the Great Hall. "Do you think it was Percival?"

"Who else would detest me so much that he would attempt to poison me?"

"And I suppose he could have been looking for the Dethman diaries in my room," Celeste replied, biting her lower lip.

"Yes, although it is odd that he hasn't been in my room looking for them."

"Perhaps he has, and you don't know it."

Evelyn nodded. "You will sleep with me in my room tonight, and we will make a pallet for Mrs. Shipton on the floor. No, no! I'll brook no objection from you, young lady. If Percival is determined to find those diaries, he will stop at nothing short of murder to get them. Now, come, we'll have some tea above stairs. Do you think we should have the mice taste it first?"

Celeste giggled. "I always knew Shipton's witch's brew was deadly."

The two women crossed the hall arm in arm. Evelyn's agitation was mitigated by her confident knowledge of the diaries' whereabouts. Percival would never find them in Celeste's belongings, or hers. They weren't even in the castle, for Evelyn's publisher had given her strict instructions to rent a small metal box at the Bank of London, and deposit the diaries there. Only Evelyn's banker, Mr. Howard Fitzhaven, had a key, and, pursuant to her contractual agreement with the bank, he would not open it without her express permission.

But Percival's objective was more far-reaching than a simple effort to find the diaries and discredit Evelyn's manuscript. He would like very much to see her inheritance forfeited, and he had less than a month in which to accomplish that ambitious goal.

She knew, then, that Percival had invited Sir Hugo to the castle house party for the sole reason of tempting her to make an assignation with him. That was the only explanation for the barrister's presence in the house.

But, how had her stepson learned that she cherished a secret *tendre* for Sir Hugo Mansfield? Had he discovered that she watched him from the window every morning? And did the earl suspect that Evelyn thought about Sir Hugo constantly, that she had done so since the night she met him?

She knew the old earl hadn't told Percival the circumstances of his marriage to Evelyn. The old earl, for all his faults, had never derided or demeaned Evelyn for the manner in which they'd met. He'd promised her that he would never tell anyone—not even Percival—where, when and how he met Evelyn. Not once in five years had he thrown up to her how desperate she'd been that night. Many men would have, Evelyn knew. And she'd been grateful for the earl's generosity in never mentioning the subject.

Once, two years earlier, she broached the subject herself, over supper, on a rare occasion when Celeste wasn't at table.

She had broken the silence with a simple question. "Have you ever told anyone why you married me?"

The old Earl of Goreham cupped his hand to his ear, and yelled harshly, "Eh?"

Biting back her impatience, Evelyn repeated her question. She hated talking in front of the servants; she was not so well-bred as to believe that they were invisible and mute. She knew they watched, and listened, and gossiped among themselves in the kitchens. It was natural that they would, so she hated having to shout her conversation with the earl. Everybody in the house would know what they were discussing.

The earl had tossed down a half-glass of wine before he answered. When he spoke, bits of food fell from his mouth. "Have I ever told anyone why you agreed to marry me? Is that the question?"

"Yes," she answered softly.

"Good God, no! What the devil do you take me for, a fool? Do you think I don't know what those loose-tongued tabbies and eagle-eyed dandies say about us behind our backs?"

"What *do* they say?"

The earl speared the air with his fork. It had been Evelyn's observation that the very wealthy and the very poor had equally casual table manners. Somewhere in between the two extremes of social class and affluence was a middle echelon, which in its aspiration to distinguish itself from those below, and connect itself with those above, had infinitely better manners than either.

"They say you married me for my money!" the old man cried.

For a long moment, Evelyn simply stared at the earl. She hadn't known what to say.

"What do you think about that?" he'd finally demanded, fine particles of his masticated dinner spewing forth from his lips.

Did he want total honesty? Or did he want her to tell him she loved him? Evelyn took a fortifying drink of wine, and stared at her plate. Lord and Lady Goreham had never feigned affection for one another, much less true love. The earl had never made overtures of any physical nature toward his young wife, nor had he ever verbally mistreated her. Their marriage had been conducted on the most businesslike of terms, politely and without rancor, but also without emotion.

Yet Evelyn had proved herself worthy of the title, Countess of Goreham. She maintained her dignity, eschewed extramarital flirtations, and, in public, made it a point not to act repulsed by her husband. She was civil to his son Percival, even when, after she'd become the only female member of the Society for the Study of Tudor Monarchy, the young man exhibited clear signs of hating her.

But there was no question of her having loved Henry Dethman, the second Earl of Goreham.

What did she think about the ton's *conclusions regarding her marriage?*

She'd met the earl's flinty gaze, and replied, "The prattle-pates are entitled to their opinions, my lord. You have been fair in your dealings with me. I have no complaints against you."

He'd stared at her a moment longer, before resuming his repast. The subject had never been mentioned again, but Evelyn always regretted that she couldn't find it in her heart to tell the old man she loved him.

Perhaps in a strange way, she had loved him.

But, not in the romantic sense, nor in the physical.

She thought that something inside her died during her five-year marriage to the earl, something innocent had withered away

Then, Sir Hugo had materialized, in the flesh. It was as if he'd stepped out of her dreams, and into her reality. So, why wasn't she thrilled about it? In less than one month, Evelyn would be free to see as much of him as she pleased, decorum permitting. Why did the very thought of being pursued, wanted, even loved by that man, feel like a shower of pinpricks raining down upon her?

Ascending the staircase to her bedchamber, she felt Celeste's gaze upon her. Her thoughts had become muddled, and if her sister had been talking to her, Evelyn hadn't heard a word the girl said.

When Celeste broke off and headed for her own room, Evelyn caught her arm.

"You are staying with me, Sister. I do not intend to let you out of my sight."

"All afternoon?" Celeste looked crestfallen. "Don't you think that is taking your fears a bit to the extreme?"

"Get a book, if you are bored, or your needlepoint. But you shall remain under my watch from now until the time we return to London. You've been attacked once; it won't happen again!"

Celeste stepped into her room, quickly chose a book, then trudged beside her sister to the end of the hallway.

With her hand on the doorknob of her bedchamber, Evelyn went completely still. Celeste stepped on her heels, colliding into her.

"Listen!" From inside the room came the sound of heavy footsteps, then a heavy grating sound as if a heavy piece of furniture were being shoved across the floor. Evelyn whispered, "Stand back, Celeste, and be ready to run and fetch help."

The younger girl inhaled sharply, but retreated an inch. Evelyn turned the knob, and pushed the door open. It swung wide, hitting the wall, affording a full view of Evelyn's room, its huge four-poster bed, small nightstand and the tole screen behind which her bathing tub was situated.

The room was in shambles, counterpane and sheets pulled off the bed, drawers opened, and clothes strewn round the floor. Pictures hung on the walls at skewed angles, while several tapers and an ormolu candelabra lay tipped on their sides.

Someone had been in her room. *Where was the interloper?*

With Celeste, Evelyn crossed the threshold. Standing in the midst of her ransacked room, Evelyn's blood ran cold. Quietly, she moved about the room, peering behind the bath screen, getting on her hands and knees to look beneath the bed. No one was present in the room except her and Celeste.

"I heard someone," she said, taking her younger sister's arm.

"But there is no one in here now," Celeste replied in a small voice.

The sisters held each other tightly, their hearts thumping wildly. Someone had indeed been in Evelyn's room—looking for the Dethman diaries, no doubt. But, how did that person escape these four walls?

Was there a ghost in Goreham Castle who could walk through walls, or simply vanish into thin air?

After assuring one another that there was no one hiding in Evelyn's bedchamber, the sisters began the arduous task of straightening a room that looked as if it had been torn apart by thieves.

Folding her undergarments and nightrails, Evelyn thought of the note slipped beneath her door by Sir Hugo.

Her emotions were in an uproar. Sir Hugo's appeal alternatingly soothed and terrified her. One moment she thought she couldn't live without him, regardless of the effect an ill-timed connection with him would have on her and her sister's future inheritance. After all, if he loved her, wouldn't he take care of her, provide for her and her sister? And wouldn't the proceeds from the sale of her book be sufficient to launch Celeste into London society?

The next moment, she resented Sir Hugo's intrusion into her life. Rolling a pair of stockings into tight bundles, she reflected that her life had been at sixes and sevens since he'd appeared at the castle. Evelyn's normally boring routine had been viciously upset. Now, she had to deal with emotions and urges that she'd spent years suppressing. She had to face fears and desires that she'd spent years avoiding. Everything she'd bargained for—a secure life versus romantic love—would be overturned were she to allow the barrister to insinuate himself into her heart.

"Evelyn, are you all right?"

She started at her sister's voice, turning to see Celeste's mouth twisted in a grudging half-smile. Following her sister's gaze, she realized that she'd placed the chamber pot on her nightstand and slid the teapot beneath the bed.

Perhaps she had gone a little mad, because Evelyn couldn't cease thinking about Sir Hugo and the decision she faced.

How many times had she altered her mind regarding the barrister's invitation to a clandestine rendezvous? Half a dozen, at least. And now, after this latest debacle—finding her room ransacked, her belongings tossed about like flotsam—she found herself leaning heavily, if not reluctantly, on the strength and support the barrister's presence in the castle offered her. His nearness supplied her with a reservoir of strength, an extra reserve of character and mettle that she alone did not possess.

Was it true that two people in love were stronger together than they were apart? Was it true that the very act of loving made a person stronger?

Why then did she resent the vulnerability that loving Sir Hugo instilled in her?

And she did resent it, deeply. She hadn't worked this hard to suppress her weak emotions only to have a handsome barrister come along and destroy her carefully constructed little world. It was a safe world, a world where she was cloistered in a fine house, with fine food to eat, and fine clothing to wear. She was safe, and Celeste was safe. There was no danger of getting her heart broken because her heart was not on display to be mishandled or broken. When she married the earl, she sold her innocence in exchange for an ivory tower. She had become comfortably sequestered there, with her books and her studies.

Her ivory tower was impregnable.

Or was it?

Evelyn spent the next few hours in miserable silence, glad to have something to do with her hands. But, folding clothes and rolling stockings was scant diversion from the confusion and heartache that were swiftly closing in on her.

* * *

The sounds of the gambling hall filtered through the narrow passageway leading from the parlor, then glided across the hall and wafted up the staircase. Sir Hugo lay on his bed, fully clothed, hands folded across his chest.

He stared at the plaster medallion in the center of the ceiling above his head. Once again, he was vaguely struck by the incongruity of the room's contemporary furnishings and late eighteenth-century architectural details. Parisian wallpaper, painted with nightingales met a pale-green dado, below which were panels of moiré silk. A writing desk with ormolu edges, a Chippendale chair and a chaise-longue with crocodile-shaped feet were some of the room's more ostentatious ornaments. But the most glaring anachronism in the medieval castle was the gilt-framed mirror opposite Sir Hugo's bed.

He hated that mirror. It taunted him with his own reflection, and for the life of him, he couldn't figure out how it also reflected the sound of the gambling hall, below stairs in a separate wing of the castle. Noise couldn't travel that far, and yet that mirror seemed to soak it up and spit it back out at Sir Hugo. It was as if his own image stared back at him with deep loathing, and a mockery to match his misery. He hated that mirror because it was he who lived there. He hated himself and the demons who choked his soul.

It was exhausting, living each day in fear that his feet would take him to St. James's, or some other more seedy establishment in the surrounding environs. It was draining, emotionally and physically, to resist the seduction of the gambling halls.

Sometimes a voice in his head whispered, *"Just one hand of whist. What would it signify?"* Or, *"A few hours of faro, and then you'll be satisfied."*

Another voice—sometimes so faint Sir Hugo could barely hear it—whispered back, *"If you play one hand, you'll play another. And another. Until you've lost every guinea you own."*

Some men lacked the ability to drink without drinking till they fell down. Some men couldn't leave the ladies alone. And some men liked speed, danger and daring, racing their fancy carriages and phaetons at break-neck speed, risking their own and their horses' lives, just for the thrill of the wind in their faces.

For Sir Hugo, it was the thrill of the win, the snap of the cards, and the excitement of the game of chance. It was the blood-pumping, spine-tingling headiness that he experienced each time he wagered deep and won. The smell of money, liquor and cheap women. The feel of the green baize beneath his fingertips, the clink of the chits in his hands, the thrum of his heart when a cheer went up around the faro table.

He loved to gamble, loved to win, loved to set his mind to figuring odds, counting cards, calculating the risks of any bet. Loved it with a passion that terrified him.

Just as his father had done, he supposed.

It was in his blood.

And he despised himself for it. Hated the disillusionment of losing, the sickening drop of his stomach that accompanied each unwelcome turn of a card. Hated the penuriousness that resulted from his inevitable losses, for no matter how much he won, he always lost more. Hated the obsession that drove him to the faro table, the whist table, and roulette wheel. Hated the person he was when he gambled.

So he didn't. Or, rather, he hadn't made a single bet since the night he left Widow Philpott's five years ago. His inability to rescue Evelyn had devastated him, shocked him into reality, shamed him into rehabilitation.

But, was he truly cured of his obsession, his need to gamble?

That was his dark secret, for he struggled each day with the need to make a bet. Sometimes, he made imaginary bets with himself, wagering five pounds on whether it would rain, or a guinea on whether a verdict in one of his cases would be favorable. Even that was dangerous, he knew, because if he won in his imagination, that demonic voice that lived in his head would tempt him to take his acumen to Brooks's or Watier's.

Resisting the tables was the hardest thing he'd ever done. Until he met Evelyn, the Dowager Countess of Goreham. And now, he couldn't resist her either. He couldn't cease thinking about her. It took every ounce of strength he possessed to keep from descending the stairs and heading for the parlor where Lord Goreham's guests were happily playing cards, drinking and laughing raucously. It took even more strength than that to resist heading down the hallway toward Evelyn's room.

He knew she was there. At dinner, Miss Louisa Freemantle had explained that Evelyn was feeling weary and that the sisters were dining in their room.

Folding his arms behind his head, Sir Hugo sighed restlessly. His frown was so deeply embedded that his facial muscles actually ached when he yawned, and stretched them. The exhaustion of fighting his own inner urges, of arguing with his inner voices, overwhelmed him. As the clock in the Great Hall below struck midnight, Sir Hugo dozed off.

He awoke to the sound of something scrabbling at his door. Still fully dressed, he swung his booted feet to the floor. In his depression, the barrister had stretched out on his bed without disrobing. Quickly lighting a taper, he moved across to the mantelpiece in his bedchamber, and studied the face of the glass-enclosed clock. It was well after three o'clock in the morning, a time when everyone in the castle, including the guests who'd indulged their gambling fever in the parlor, should have been in bed.

The candle cast vague, gloomy shadows over the room's furnishings. A scrap of white gleamed beneath the door, drawing Sir Hugo across the room. With each step he took, the floorboards squeaked. Though the storm had abated, nocturnal sounds from outside still buffeted the castle walls. A chill swept over Sir Hugo's shoulders as he bent to retrieve the paper on the floor.

It was a single sheet of cream-colored vellum, heavy and expensive. A monogram—EGW—was engraved in gold at the top of the card. The script was a soft flowing hand that spoke of intelligence and elegance. *Evelyn's writing.* The thought that he was holding a message from her in his hands sent a shocking, magnetic thrill through the barrister's veins.

Wax dripped from the candle and splattered the note as he read.

> *Darling. Come to me. I am alone in my room, awaiting you. Please don't make me beg you, Hugo. I love you above all things.—E.*

He turned the paper over in his hands, tested its texture, held it to his nose. The words lilted from the vellum and wrapped seductively around his heart. She wanted him. She needed him. How could he refuse her?

His blood warmed. The need to see her, touch her, hear her voice, held more appeal than any faro table or whist game ever could. He would have walked miles to get to her, but he didn't have to. Evelyn, the Countess of Goreham, was but a few steps down the corridor.

So near, he felt her pulse reverberate through the castle like thunder. The walls seemed to vibrate with her presence. The air hung thick and fragrant with her essence.

Tucking the note in the waist of his breeches, the barrister quietly opened his bedchamber door. Not a creak or groan of floorboards sounded. Stealthily, he moved down the hallway until he stood before Evelyn's door. He laid his fingertips on the mahogany slab that separated them. He held his breath, listening, hungry for the merest sound of her breathing, her light footsteps, the crackle of a horsehair brush through her long blond hair.

A knock would wake the other guests. He tried the door

knob, and found the latch removed. Slowly, Sir Hugo pushed open the door and stepped into Evelyn's bed-chamber.

Moonlight spilled through the window, washing the room in shades of silver. Sir Hugo was surprised that Evelyn was in her bed, obviously asleep. Hadn't she just pushed the note beneath his door? Wasn't she awaiting him?

Perhaps she'd crawled back into bed because it was cold, frightfully so, in her room. Glancing at the fire dwindled now to twinkling sparks, Sir Hugo thought it was no wonder she'd returned to the warm cocoon of her blankets. With a small smile on his face, he crossed the room and stood beside the huge four-postered bed.

He held his candle aloft.

"Evelyn?" He whispered, bending over her, his fingers hovering above her head.

She didn't stir. How could she have fallen asleep so quickly after slipping her invitation beneath his door?

He bent lower and fingered the cotton mob cap that covered her curls. "Evelyn, darling, I am here." He breathed deeply, inhaling the scent of . . .

Liquor? Snuff? Unwashed flesh?

With a jolt, Sir Hugo straightened. As he did, the figure in the bed rolled over. Beneath the lacy fringe of the cap, Percival Dethman's sharp features split into a cadaverous grin. His sharp little teeth gleamed in the candlelight. A bone-chilling cackle escaped his lips.

The fear and anger that surged through Sir Hugo's body drove him to the brink of violence.

Chapter Eight

"Expecting someone else, Sir Hugo?"

"Where in the devil is Evelyn?" The barrister spoke through clenched teeth, his blood roaring in his ears.

The third earl tossed off the covers, and sprang off the bed. Standing at his full height, his head, as he ripped off the mob cap, met Sir Hugo's shoulders. But the barrister didn't dare kill him with his bare hands—not yet. Not until he learned where Evelyn had been secreted, or what had become of her.

The room, bathed in semi-darkness, closed in on the two men. Their animosity for one another thickened the air with the smell of decay, evil, hatred. Lord Goreham's eyes shone brightly, as if he savored every second of the tension that surrounded them. Sir Hugo, in that moment, had never felt such blinding rage. Purple spots danced before his eyes. His fingers itched to close themselves around Percival's throat. Silently, he relished the notion of crushing his thumbs into the man's Adam's apple, squeezing the life out of him, leaving him like a crumpled rag doll for dead.

But he had to find Evelyn first.

"Where is she?" the barrister breathed.

"Would you be referring to my *stepmother*?" The earl's mustache twitched mischievously.

Sir Hugo's fury exploded. He leapt toward the smaller man, and, grabbing him by the lapels, lifted him off the floor. A gratifying look of terror flashed in the earl's eyes, and his mouth fell open. His booted feet kicked ineffectively at the barrister's shins as he dangled in midair.

"Put me down this instant!" Percival's entreaties were sputtered out in frantic gasps.

"Not until you tell me where Evelyn is!"

"Yes, all right!" The earl's complexion had gone ashen, and his voice was as squeaky as the rusty under-carriage of an old phaeton. "Put me down, I beg you!"

Sir Hugo gave the smaller man another rough shake for good measure. Then, without releasing the earl's lapels, he lowered him to the floor. The instant Percival's feet touched the carpet, a more natural color swept his face.

After a fit of coughing and gulping in air, the earl met the barrister's expectant gaze. "Come, sir, I will take you to her."

"First, you will tell me where she is," Sir Hugo said, tightening his hold on the earl's coat.

A faint smile lifted the corner of the earl's lips. It was just enough to flame the fire of anger still smouldering in Sir Hugo's gut. Drawing back one fist, he prepared to pound the little man's face to pulp.

A voice in the doorway halted his action. Arm drawn like a bow, Sir Hugo froze at the sound of Sir Cuthbert's admonition.

"Don't do it, Hugo."

Maintaining his hold on the Earl of Goreham, Hugo turned to stare in amazement at his friend Cubby and the small black pistol gripped in his hand. Advancing toward the center of the room, the solicitor gestured with the snout of the gun.

"Release him."

Hugo's stomach twisted in a knot. Releasing the earl meant surrendering whatever tenuous control he had over the situation. Refusing to accede to Cubby's demand, however, might earn him a bullet hole in his temple. While his mind whirled with possibilities, searching for avenues of escape and alternatives, he struggled to project an outward calm. It wouldn't do to let these scoundrels realize he was terrified for Evelyn's sake. Hugo had every intention of rescuing her, even if he didn't quite know how he was going to accomplish that at the moment.

Slowly, he released his hold on Percival's coat. The earl inhaled deeply, crooked one finger beneath his cravat and twisted his neck.

"You could make this easy for yourself and for Evelyn," Sir Cuthbert said.

"In what way?" Sir Hugo stared at the two men, standing shoulder to shoulder, their eyes hard and glinting.

"Tell us where the Dethman diaries are," the earl replied.

"How the hell should I know?" The barrister was truly confounded. Did these buffleheads think that Evelyn had confided such a profound secret in him? And if he did know, why would he betray her by telling them?

"The earl will make it worth your while," Sir Cuthbert said.

"You're that desperate to retrieve the diaries?" Puzzled, Sir Hugo tried to remember all that he'd heard about Evelyn's manuscript and the diaries she'd based her research on. "What is in those diaries that you are so afraid to have made public, Lord Goreham?"

"The Dethman family name does not deserve the ignominy that Evelyn Waring's silly little manuscript is bound to reap. If anyone is entitled to reveal family secrets concerning the Dethman influence in King Henry VIII's court, it is a Dethman by blood."

"Not by marriage," murmured the barrister.

"Quite so." The earl drew himself up to full height, lifting his chin in a childish display of injured pride. "I take great umbrage at Evelyn's presuming to write a history of the Tudor court, details of which were obtained from private family diaries belonging by all rights to me, not to her."

Sir Hugo turned to the solicitor, Sir Cuthbert. "I am quite confused by all this. Tell me, Cubby, did Evelyn not have the permission of the old earl to use the diaries for purposes of researching her biography of the Tudor king?"

Cubby cast an uneasy glance at the earl. "I'm quite certain the old man had no inkling what Evelyn planned to do. She was . . . shall we say, capable of using her charms when she wanted something from the old man. There is no way to know precisely what she told the earl, but she surely didn't explain that she intended to publish a manuscript relying almost exclusively on the Dethman diaries."

"But she did obtain his legal permission to use the documents?" Sir Hugo persisted. "And permission to keep them in her custody?"

Cubby's color deepened. "Legally. Technically. Yes."

Silence prevailed for a long moment. At length, Sir Hugo, his eyes flickering off the nose of the gun which remained pointed at his heart, said, "It appears that the countess is well within her rights in refusing to relinquish control of the diaries, Percival. Why are you so adamant that she do so?"

"I told you," said the earl. "The Dethman diaries belong to me!"

"Professional jealousy, perhaps?" The barrister rose on his tiptoes in mockery of the diminutive earl. Clasping his hands behind his back, he flashed a beaming smile at Percival. "I suppose it is embarrassing that after all these years, you have failed to take the trouble to peruse the musty volumes in your father's library. Just think of the treasures you could have unearthed yourself had you taken the time to do so."

"Watch yourself," Sir Cuthbert warned, his eyes sliding from the barrister to the earl.

Sir Hugo continued. "Will you be humiliated before the London Society for the Study of the Tudor Monarchy? Will you be a laughingstock, having sponsored Evelyn for membership at your father's request, and unwittingly allowed the admittance of the one person—a female, no less—who recognized the wealth of historical documents hidden at Goreham Castle, waiting to be dusted off and studied?"

"Shut your mouth, sir!" Percival's black eyes snapped.

"Or are you afraid that the diaries might contain some spicy tidbit of salacious historical gossip that will actually tarnish the Dethman family name?"

The earl, despite his recent encounter with the barrister, and perhaps emboldened by the presence of Sir Cuthbert brandishing a pistol in Hugo's direction, leapt forward.

Eager to give the little man a thorough beating, Sir Hugo's fists rose to meet him and he leaned his weight forward. Before the men could engage in fisticuffs, however, Sir Cuthbert shoved himself between them. For his troubles, Cuthbert received a blow to his kidneys from a wild-punching Percival, and a split upper lip from the well-aimed blow thrown by Sir Hugo.

A single gunshot cracked the air, its deafening report instantly followed by a shattering explosion of glass. As panes of leaden window glass showered the floor, the three men loosened their grips on one another, stumbling back in shocked realization of how closely someone had come to being killed.

Aware that Sir Cuthbert's double-barreled gun was now pointed at his chest again, Sir Hugo was impressed by the danger inherent in the escalating altercation, and the odds which were rapidly stacking ceiling-high against him.

The gunshot had badly frightened the other men, as well. Sir Cuthbert's hand shook violently, adding to the danger of the situation. His tousled hair hung over his brow, and his eyes were round as saucers as he retreated toward the open door.

"I told you I didn't want any part of this, Percival! Someone is going to get killed, and we'll all be sharing an apartment in the Tower before those stinking diaries are recovered."

"Don't be a fool," the young earl snarled, rounding on his partner in crime. "You're in too deep to suddenly sprout morals and ethics. It's to the dungeon, now, and be quick about it. You know what to do."

"I don't like it," Sir Cuthbert repeated, the tip of his gun quavering in Sir Hugo's general direction. But the earl's vicious expression apparently persuaded the solicitor that he should continue with the agreed-upon plan. Swallowing hard, Sir Cuthbert reluctantly met Sir Hugo's gaze. "Hurry up man, there behind the bookcase."

Lord Goreham crossed to the side of the room opposite the tole screen and bathtub. On the far wall was a bookcase that stretched from floor to ceiling. Had Sir Hugo inspected it more closely, he would have earlier noticed the odd way in which the dark mahogany framework of the case clashed with the painted pale blue dado, or chair-rail, that ornamented the room's walls. With amazement, he watched as Lord Goreham gave one side of the bookcase a hearty shove.

A grating noise accompanied the secret door's movement. The entire bookcase swung on a hinge, exposing a dark passageway behind the wall.

He should have known. Gritting his teeth, Sir Hugo cursed himself silently. Built during the days of religious persecution, this castle was probably riddled with secret passageways, hiding places, even chapels, where, during the Reformation, loyal Catholics continued their clandestine worship.

"Damn you, Percival," Sir Hugo muttered, with barely suppressed violence.

"Go on, then." Sir Cuthbert waved his gun, gesturing

toward the bookcase. "Don't make me force you, Hugo. I am truly sorry for all this."

"Oh, shut your yammering!" Lord Goreham had lost his patience with his less determined accomplice. Jerking his thumb in Sir Hugo's direction, he said, "You first. The rush lights are burning, but watch your step. The stairs are slippery, I'm afraid. And don't try anything courageous, Hugo. Evelyn's life now depends on you."

Percival's remark struck fear in Hugo's heart. Suddenly, the earl's plot came into focus. One way or another, he intended to obtain the Dethman diaries and prevent Evelyn from publishing her biography of King Henry VIII. It remained unclear to Hugo why the biography was such a thorn in Percival's side. But it was apparent that the earl would stop at nothing to halt publication of the manuscript.

Hugo's weakness—his affection for Evelyn—was now the earl's ammunition.

His feet felt like lead blocks as he made his way down the narrow staircase. Behind him, Sir Cuthbert and Lord Goreham followed, pulling the bookcase shut behind them. Dark and damp, the passageway wound its way toward the bowels of the earth. The further Sir Hugo descended, the colder and more silent the atmosphere grew, until he reached a landing, lit dimly by burning wall torches, its stone floor covered in straw rushes.

Water dripped through the cracks in the stone walls, and echoed mournfully through the antechamber where the three men stood. Squinting in the semi-darkness, Sir Hugo saw several doors, heavy wooden panels with iron studs and old-fashioned lock mechanisms. The blackness and desolation of this underground warren of torture chambers closed in on him. He feared for Evelyn. Imagining her fright, he burned with anger. Sir Cuthbert and Lord Goreham would pay for their mistreatment of her. Hugo would see to it, if it was the last thing he ever did.

"This way," Lord Goreham said, removing a huge iron

ring of keys from a nail driven into the crevices of the stone wall. He fumbled with the lock of the door on Sir Hugo's immediate left. With a grunt, he pushed it open and led the way down another long passageway.

"Go!" Sir Cuthbert pressed his gun to the small of Hugo's back.

He had no choice but to follow the earl. His boots scraped the damp stonework, and his gaze, adjusting itself to the darkness, searched the empty cells for some sign of Evelyn.

At the end of the narrow passageway, the earl stopped. On his right was a small cell, a hole carved out of the earth. A small door, to which Lord Goreham held the key, was set in iron bars. And huddling in the darkness, on the ground beneath the flickering light of a torch, was Evelyn, the Countess of Goreham.

Sir Hugo threw himself at the bars, his arms reaching through to touch her.

"You'll get to her soon enough," the earl said, laughing. He placed the proper key in the lock, turned it and opened the door. Hugo nearly knocked him down to get inside the cell.

"Evelyn!" He fell beside her, wrapping her in his arms, pressing his cheek to her hair, still fragrant despite the stink of the underground dungeon. "Are you all right?"

Between sobs, she said, "I am unhurt. They have provided me with a blanket, so that I am not too, too cold. And I have eaten hot porridge and drunk chocolate in the past hour. But, Hugo, I am so frightened!"

The heavy iron door clanged shut. Sir Cuthbert and Lord Goreham peered in through the other side.

While Cubby wore a weary, contrite expression, the earl was positively gloating. "Would you care to tell me now where the Dethman diaries are?" he asked.

"Never!" Evelyn, clutching Hugo's arms, lifted her chin a notch, and scowled at her captor.

"Little fool!" To show his disgust, the earl spat, then turned on his heel and marched down the passageway.

Cuthbert, after throwing Hugo a rueful half-smile, followed his leader. After a moment, their bootsteps faded, and the heavy door at the end of the corridor banged shut.

The harsh finality of that door slamming shut caused Evelyn's heart to skip a beat.

She turned her face to Hugo, surprised by the relief and comfort she absorbed from his presence.

"He must have sneaked into your room and snatched you from your bed while you were sleeping," the barrister said, with disgust in his voice.

"Yes. When the bookcase moved, I almost died from fright. It woke Celeste, too, and there was just enough time to send her to hide behind the bathtub screen. I pray that she is safe!"

His arms around her were like bands of iron, not the cold bars that separated her from liberation. In such dread circumstances, decorum hardly entered Evelyn's mind. She didn't care if it was wrong to allow this man to hold her snug against his chest. She didn't care if their limbs were tangled, their fingers intertwined, their faces pressed together.

She cared for nothing but that Hugo was near to her. That he'd come to rescue her. It hadn't yet occurred to her that he might not be able to rescue her.

"Oh, Hugo! What shall we do?" Tears streamed down her face, and she shook uncontrollably.

For a long while, he merely held her close. They huddled together on the cold, damp floor, their backs to the wall. Hugo's whispered assurances slowly crept into her bloodstream, strengthening her, emboldening her. When he shifted his body, and framed her face with his palms, Evelyn met his dark, soulful gaze without fear.

"Don't be afraid," he whispered, tipping up her chin.

She wasn't. Tingles exploded in places Evelyn would have blushed to acknowledge, but she wasn't the least bit afraid. Not of Lord Goreham, anyway. Or of Sir Cuthbert's pistol. Or even of being locked in this dismal torture chamber for the rest of her life.

Truth be known, she thought if the earl threw away the key to her cell, she might die happily in Sir Hugo's arms. All thoughts of her predicament faded to nothing when the barrister lowered his head and kissed her.

It was a hungry kiss, full of need and urgency. Sir Hugo, his half-lidded gaze gleaming in the shadows of the rushlight, made a noise deep in his throat, a guttural sound that ricocheted through Evelyn's body like loose cannonfire. His need, his desire, were branded on her lips. The heat from his palms suffused her face, and radiated through her body. Hot liquid pooled in her loins. She ached to be possessed. She ached to be taken and claimed by this man who held her in his thrall.

Their breath mingled, and their teeth clashed. Sir Hugo's hands slid from her face to her neck. Beneath her heavy woolen robe was nothing but a thin nightrail, and beneath that sheath of muslin Evelyn's skin rippled with goose-bumps.

She felt his fingertips, slightly callused, slip beneath the hem of her neckline. Moaning softly, she captured his fingers in her own and pressed them to her flesh.

Nothing had prepared her for the intensity of the sensations that quaked through her body. Evelyn longed for Hugo's touch, yet the fear that she'd so boldly tamped down, now came roaring back.

It was a fear like she'd never known. Not the fear of hunger or poverty or failure. Not the fear of an uncertain future. It was fear of her own emotions, fear that she wouldn't be able to control them.

Seized by desire, Evelyn drew her lips from Hugo's. Her arousal was so intense, so heated, that her loins throbbed. She wanted him so badly, it was painful.

She was terrified that the feelings she experienced would rob her of her own strength and independence. She had overcome the odds by escaping poverty, and securing for herself and her sister a comfortable life. Not only had she married well when she wed the aging earl, but she'd earned his respect and affection. She'd kept her self-respect by refusing to succumb to the overtures of handsome, virile young bucks who would have gladly provided sexual satisfaction to a young, love-starved countess.

If she gave in to her desires now—if she allowed the barrister to possess her—would she be throwing away all that she'd struggled for? Her intuition told her that once she tasted the barrister's flesh, pressed her lips to his bare chest, ran her fingers through his hair, she'd be lost to him. She'd be one with him. She'd lose something of herself.

Of that she was certain. For, even now, as she drew back and stared into Sir Hugo's dreamy gaze, she felt herself melting, blending with him, body and soul.

That was the last thing she wanted to happen.

She had to maintain her singularity, not just for another few weeks until the conditions of the earl's will were fulfilled, but for always.

She had her career to think of, after all. Loving a man wasn't worth throwing away her future, her sister's dowry and her independence. It was doubtful any man other than the deceased earl would tolerate her spending days with her nose poked in a book, staying up all hours of the night scribbling pages of notes and manuscript. So doubtful, it wasn't even worth discussion. Hers had been an unconventional marriage in many ways, and Evelyn was quite sure she didn't want to be leg-shackled to a man who would expect her to be a mere appendage of him.

Better, then, to call a halt to these fevered grapplings.

Grasping the barrister's hand, she shoved it away. "Don't!"

His eyes widened, but he instantly drew back, releasing her from his embrace. "Evelyn, I would never do anything to hurt you. We will go slowly. I promise I will never hurt you.''

He dipped his head, and drew her knuckles to his lips, kissing them. With his eyes squeezed tightly shut, he put so much passion into that chaste kiss that Evelyn trembled with renewed desire.

Hugo lifted his head. His gaze fell to her lips, and she moved toward him, offering her mouth for plunder.

Drawing her close again, he kissed her, long and deeply. His teeth nipped at her lips, his tongue traced the outline of her mouth.

Evelyn's breathing quickened. With both hands on the barrister's chest, she pushed herself away, bending backwards. But Hugo's head nestled in the crook of her neck, and then a trail of kisses, delightfully abrasive from the scratch of the barrister's beard, rained down upon her tender, white flesh.

Gasping, she managed to murmur, ''No, no. We must not!''

His labored breathing fanned the sensitive skin along her neck. A harsh, animal-like sound, ripped from his soul, echoed off the dank walls of the tiny cell. Hugo's head came up, and his gaze bore into Evelyn's.

She could hardly look at him. Wanting him so badly that her body ached, yet determined to resist him, Evelyn barely managed to control her emotions.

Yet she did, and when she spoke, her voice was amazingly composed. ''I do not wish to make love to you, Hugo.''

His brow furrowed. Releasing her, he swallowed hard. ''The first order of business is to escape these prison walls. How selfish of me, how foolish of me—''

She pressed her fingertips to his lips. ''No, you do not understand. I do not ever want to make love to you.''

The pain marring his expression deepened. ''I would never force myself on a lady. Or any other woman, for that matter.''

Evelyn's heart squeezed. Her rejection had injured him,

yet she was adamant that she'd done the right thing. She refused to risk an emotional entanglement, a relinquishment of her individuality, her independence, everything she'd strived for. Having made that bargain with herself when she married the Earl of Goreham, she wouldn't renege on it now. If she did, she'd invalidate every principle she'd held dear for the past five years.

Admitting that love was more important than financial and emotional security would be tantamount to branding herself a liar, a traitor and a cheat. Evelyn had to hang on to whatever shred of self-respect she could. She had to subjugate her selfish, unrealistic, girlish, romantic desires for the life she'd created. She was far more comfortable with it than with all these roiling emotions Sir Hugo engendered in her.

"I am sorry, sir. Perhaps, I am not like other women."

"You are merely frightened. 'Tis to be expected, given your inexperience." He sighed. "When the time is right, you will let me know. I won't push you before you are ready."

"You don't understand! I will never be ready! I don't want to make love to you, or any other man. I—I find the entire matter unpleasant, even to discuss."

Shock registered on his features. Evelyn thought she sensed a deepening of the cold in the tiny cell, along with a tightening of Sir Hugo's lips. "I know that many women find the act of lovemaking an arduous chore, but I had thought . . . I had sensed that you . . ." His voice trailed off as he scooted backward along the hard floor, putting distance between himself and Evelyn.

She felt as if an arctic wind had blasted her heart. Cringing, she watched Sir Hugo recoil, and withdraw into himself. She was pushing him away, literally as well as emotionally. Pushing him, driving him, forcing him, from her. Which was what she'd intended her cruel words to do. Yet, the realization that Sir Hugo was distancing himself from her was like a sword thrust into her belly.

Hot tears welled in her eyes, but she blinked them back. A wave of resentment bowled over her. She wanted her old, comfortable life back. She wanted her heart back. Not knowing how to react to the irrepressible emotion thundering through her body, she willed it away.

She didn't know how much time passed while the two of them shared that cell in uneasy silence. Sir Hugo stood and paced the floor, his bootsteps heavy and angry. Occasionally, he broke the silence with a muttered curse. The cold isolation of the dungeon was oppressive. Evelyn's hope slipped further away, and her heart ached as she began to think she would die in that cell.

The grating sound of the door opening at the end of the corridor gave her a start. With her back to the wall, arms hugging her knees to her chest, she shuddered at the thought of Sir Cuthbert's or Lord Goreham's return. Surely, one or both of the men had come to torture her, to force her to tell where the Dethman diaries were hidden. She wondered if she would have the strength to resist, or whether at the first sign of pain, she would cave in and tell them the name of her banker, who had safely secured the ancient documents in a vault at the Bank of England.

Her head popped up, and her gaze met the barrister's.

"Don't be afraid, my lady." He stood at the door to the cell, his fists coiled around the iron bars. "I shall die before I let those monsters harm a hair on your head."

She believed him. Gratitude shimmered through her. Gratitude and guilt that she'd injured such a brave and honest man. Yet her ears pricked at the footsteps traipsing down the corridor; they were light and feminine, the sound of slippers on stone, not leather-soled boots.

Celeste's bright yellow nimbus appeared on the other side of the iron bars. When Evelyn had last seen the child, she was lying beside her in bed, clad in nothing but a woolen gown. Now the child was wearing her serviceable grey smock and an old pelisse with huge, apron-like pockets on the front. Her face was smudged with mud, but her eyes were bright as they peered into the shadowy cell.

"Thank God, you are all right!" Evelyn pushed up from the floor, cringing at the stiffness of her limbs. She crossed to the cell door, and pressed her face through the bars. Just being able to touch Celeste, and know that she was safe, set her heart to thudding.

But, instantly, her relief changed to fear. "How did you get here? You must hurry away, before that evil Lord Goreham finds you here."

Sir Hugo said, "Have you got the key to this cell, Celeste?"

She held up a huge iron ring on which half a dozen ancient skeletal shaped keys dangled. "I took it off the peg on the wall, but I don't know which one opens this particular cell door."

Evelyn's pulse skittered. There wouldn't be much time, and it would take Celeste considerable time to try every key on that ring.

Celeste poked a key in the rusty lock, turning it until Evelyn feared it would snap off. She tried another, and another, to no avail. Her hands trembled as the seconds ticked by.

Evelyn's fingers wrapped around the iron bars so tightly that her knuckles were white. She held her breath, keenly aware of the tension radiating off Sir Hugo's body.

Yet, he spoke with perfect calmness to Celeste. "Don't worry, you will find the right one. You're doing superbly."

With each key that she tried, failing to unlock the cell, Celeste's trembling worsened. Her hands shook so that the keys jangled wildly on the iron ring. When there were two keys left, she dropped the entire lot of them on the stone floor.

"Oh, no! Evelyn, I am sorry!" The younger girl bent to retrieve the keys from the sodden rush-strewn floor.

Then, footsteps sounded on the stairwell leading to the dungeon. The angry shouts of Lord Goreham and Sir

Cuthbert could be heard as they made the landing, then crashed through the open door. Celeste had barely straightened when the men were upon her.

Sir Hugo, gripping the iron bars, pressed his head hard against them. His stomach clenched with frustration. So near! A few more moments, and Celeste would have found the key that opened the cell door.

Lord Goreham snatched the keys from the girl's fingers, then shoved her toward Sir Cuthbert. "Ah, you're a wily termagant, aren't you? I should have known you were sleeping in your sister's bed last night, and that you slipped out of her room before I nabbed you, too. I hadn't thought of it when I shoved that love note beneath your sister's door!"

Evelyn's voice betrayed her disappointment. "You mean, you wrote that note? Hugo didn't?"

"If you'd shown up in the library, I'd have abducted you there," Percival snarled. "When you didn't, I wrote a second note, on your stationery, and slipped it beneath Hugo's door. How the devil do you think I lured him to your bedroom?"

"Let's get on with it," muttered Sir Cuthbert, tightly gripping Celeste's forearms.

"Let her go!" Evelyn pleaded.

"If you hurt the girl, I'll tear you apart limb to limb," Sir Hugo warned.

Celeste struggled against Sir Cuthbert's hold on her, but she was outmatched in both size and strength. Still, the solicitor grimaced as she landed a backward kick to his shin.

Laughing softly, Lord Goreham produced a small pistol from the waistband of his trousers, and aimed it at Celeste's squirming body. The girl froze, going limp in Sir Cuthbert's arms.

"What the hell are you doing, Percival?" Sir Cuthbert held the girl's shoulders, but his face registered shock at the earl's suddenly apparent aim to shoot the girl.

Sir Hugo felt Evelyn's sharp inhalation. The fury rising inside him was unquenchable. "Shoot her, and you are a walking dead man," he said to Lord Goreham.

The earl slanted a sly grin in Evelyn's direction, but his arm remained outright, and the snout of his pistol remained pointed squarely at Celeste's heart. "Oh, I had meant to have some fun with this. I had thought to torture you, Hugo, until Evelyn admitted not only that she'd had an affair with you, but confessed where she'd hidden the diaries as well. You see, that would have been killing two birds with one stone."

"Percival, listen to me—" Sir Cuthbert's voice quavered.

"Shut up! I've had enough of your sniveling!" The earl waved his gun wildly, then continued in an oily, malicious drawl. "But this prissy little hoyden ruined everything. Where on earth did you hide when I grabbed your sister from her bed last night, my sweet?"

Celeste's lower lip swelled, and she scowled darkly. Even with a gun pointed at her, she refused to show her fright. "I heard your footsteps behind the wall an instant before Evelyn did. I had only enough time to leap out of bed and hide behind the screen. But, I peeped through the cracks and saw everything, including the secret passageway behind the bookshelf."

"Clever little kitten," said the earl. "But not quite clever enough."

"Drop the gun," Sir Hugo said.

"As your solicitor," inserted Sir Cuthbert, "I must warn you that the penalties for murder—"

"Shut your bloody trap, Cubby!" For a moment, the earl's face turned purple with rage. Everyone held their breath, given the volatility of the madman and the fact he continued waggling his gun in Celeste's general direction. At length, the earl's demeanor calmed, and he faced Evelyn with a demonic smile. "We are wasting precious time. As your sister's intervention has quite altered my plan, I must insist that you tell me now where the Dethman diaries are.''

"How do I know you won't shoot her after I tell you?'' Evelyn asked.

The earl rose on his tiptoes. ''I suppose you'll have to take my word for it.''

"Let the child go,'' Sir Hugo said, ''and Evelyn will tell you where the diaries are.''

The earl drew back the hammer of his gun with his thumb, and squinted down the sights at Evelyn's heart. ''Tell me now,'' he replied evenly.

Evelyn spoke quickly, the words tumbling like dice from her lips. ''My banker, Mr. Howard Fitzhaven, has possession of them. They are secreted in a vault at the Bank of England, Percival. You will need my permission to gain access to them.''

"Then you shall write a letter authorizing me to take possession of the diaries.''

"I am afraid that won't suffice,'' Evelyn said. ''The letter of instruction given Mr. Fitzhaven by my publisher states clearly that unless I give my personal authorization to retrieve the diaries, they are not to be given to anyone else. Regardless of what sort of letter or writing you might have with my signature affixed. Signatures are so easily copied, you see. It was Mr. Murray's precaution, not mine.''

"Damme! Then, I shall simply have to take you with me to London. Immediately!'' The earl poked his gun in his waistband, then stalked to the cell door. He quickly found the correct key, and unlocked the door, but before he opened it, he yanked his gun out again.

"Stand back, Hugo!'' Percival cried. ''We'll make a trade, here. Celeste will keep you company for a while, and Evelyn will go to London with me. The roads are passable now, from what I hear. In fact, I believe most of our guests are preparing to leave above stairs. I shall make your apologies, Hugo, and explain that you had to leave suddenly before daylight.''

"You'll not get away with this," Hugo said. His chest spasmed as Cuthbert shoved Celeste into the cell.

The young girl fell into her sister's embrace, but their reunion was brief. The earl reached in and grabbed Evelyn's arm, pulling her outside the cell. Sir Hugo flung himself at the closing door just as Lord Goreham turned the key and locked it.

Evelyn's expression, as she looked over her shoulder, robbed Sir Hugo of his breath. His arm stretched through the bars, and his fingers grappled with the air that separated them. He'd never felt more powerless and lonely in his life.

Nor had he ever witnessed such strength and heroism. Evelyn's unselfish act, her quick willingness to tell the earl where the diaries were, thus ending any chance that the manuscript she'd labored over for years would ever be published, was an unparalleled demonstration of sisterly love. Hugo loved Evelyn for it. Loved her, but couldn't help her.

Sir Cuthbert stumbled backward, retreating from the cell as if he'd witnessed an unspeakable horror. "I'll be back, Hugo. I'm not going to London right away, and if it is any consolation, I won't allow you to starve."

Hugo stared at his former friend, a stranger to him. "But, if the earl instructs you to kill us, what will you do then, Cubby?"

The man colored, and turned his back. His muttered response was barely audible, but Hugo heard it above the drip-drip of water seeping through the cracks, and the soft whuffling of Celeste as she huddled against him.

"I said I won't let you starve, Hugo. I'm afraid that's all I can promise you, old boy."

Chapter Nine

It took twice as long as normal for Lord Goreham's carriage to make it back to London. By then, it was early evening, long after the doors of the Bank of London had been closed for business. Cursing his luck, and the weather, and making vague promises about what Sir Cuthbert would eventually do to Celeste and Sir Hugo, Percival Dethman entered the Goreham town house like a malevolent storm. He banished Evelyn to her room with dire warnings of what would happen if she breathed a word of what was going on to anyone, or attempted to pass a note to a servant, or send a footman off with a missive to Miss Freemantle. Then, the earl went out.

At the sound of the door slamming behind her, Evelyn threw herself on her bed, dissolving in a fit of tears. Her concern for her sister's safety was so overwhelming that her chest ached, and her head throbbed. She'd failed. She'd failed at the one thing in her life that she'd endeavored to do, and that was protect Celeste from the harsh realities of life. Since Evelyn's father's death, her one reason for living had been to care for Celeste, to do for the child what their parents had been unable to do. The fact that she'd failed to protect her baby sister from the evil clutches of Lord Goreham filled her with rage and grief.

And to make it worse, her own actions had drawn Celeste into this intrigue. Had Evelyn not been determined to have her manuscript published, Lord Goreham would not have been driven to prevent her from doing so. It was her own pride, she concluded, that put Celeste in harm's way. Her foolish pride. Pounding the mattress with her fists, Evelyn loathed herself for the ambition that had compelled her to peruse those dusty diaries in the first place.

Her maid entered the room, and inquired whether she would care for tea. Evelyn had lifted her head, shook it, no. The maid stood uncertainly in the center of the room, hands clasped at her waist. After biting her lip, she chose to hazard a more personal question.

"Are ye all right, then, m'lady? Is there anythin' else I can get for ye? A hot bath, perhaps? Or some chocolate?"

Through a veil of tears, Evelyn stared at the young girl. Could she trust her to take a message to Miss Louisa Free-mantle, or Lady Ramsbottom? Or perhaps she should dash off a note to the Bow Street Runners, and summon them immediately. After all, she wasn't concerned in the least about her manuscript at this point; she only cared that Celeste and Sir Hugo were rescued from that foul torture chamber before a lethal chill crept into their bones, and they died of consumption.

Brushing her tousled hair from her face, Evelyn stared at the maid, weighing the risks of defying Percival's demands. Sniffling, she slowly pushed herself to her elbows, then sat up and dried her tear-stained face with a muslin square. Her hesitation cost her.

The third Earl of Goreham entered the room. Dressed in black satin knee pants, black coat, white stockings and one of the most elaborately folded cravats Evelyn had ever seen, he stood in the center of the room, and with a flourishing gesture, smoothed his thin mustache.

He curtly dismissed the bewildered maid. "You may go. But fetch the countess's abigail, and be quick about it. We are going out."

Left alone with the earl, Evelyn felt her skin crawl. "I'm not going anywhere with you, Percival," she said through clenched teeth.

Smiling broadly, he replied, "I don't see that you have much choice, my lady. You see, I have just returned from my club where I learned from an acquaintance that your admirer, Lady Ramsbottom, is holding a dinner party this evening. It seems the old tabby planned this party ages ago, long before she accepted my invitation to Goreham Castle."

"She just returned to town. There is no possible way that she can be expected to keep her obligation."

"Dear Lady Ramsbottom. Her servants were quite prepared to carry out their employer's instructions even when the inclement weather delayed her return from the country. The dinner party will go on, I hear."

Evelyn eyed her stepson suspiciously. "What has that to do with you?"

"Everything. I have arranged for us to be included in the guest list."

"Impossible! We cannot invite ourselves to Lady Ramsbottom's party! 'Tis unheard of! I won't go!"

Eyes narrowed, the earl drawled, "Oh, you will go, my lady. You have no choice. I have only to send Sir Cuthbert a message, and he will carry out my instructions to punish his prisoners for your disobedience. Really, Evelyn, you shouldn't tempt me."

For a long moment, she stared at the man who stood in her bedchamber, grinning maliciously. At length, she said, "Why is it so important to see Lady Ramsbottom tonight, Percival? What sort of trickery have you contrived this time?"

"You're learning, dear. Certainly, I have no compelling need to solicit any more of Lady Ramsbottom's prattle about what an intelligent and beautiful girl you are. According to my friend at Brooks's, however, she has invited your dear Mr. Fitzhaven—that paragon of discretion—to dinner."

Evelyn's mouth went dry. "You cannot possibly mean to corner the man at a dinner party. As I have told you, Percival, the Dethman diaries are in a vault. Mr. Fitzhaven can only retrieve them for you during normal business hours."

"Perhaps. But you shall tell the man this evening that I will be at the bank first thing in the morning. Why waste precious time, dear? I intend to have those diaries in my possession before nuncheon tomorrow. You see the Society is meeting tomorrow afternoon—had you forgotten? And I want to make sure I am telling the truth when I announce that the publication of your manuscript has been indefinitely delayed."

"You are a monster," Evelyn said softly. Her chest burned with rage, but she was powerless to prevent the earl from carrying out his nefarious scheme. As long as Celeste and Sir Hugo were within the earl's control, she was a pawn in the evil man's game.

Of course, she hadn't forgotten the meeting tomorrow afternoon. She had planned to give a speech, revealing some of the less sensational aspects of her new biography. Now, her dream of being published had slipped away, and with it all the respect she had earned as a scholar among the esteemed members of the Society. When the Earl of Goreham announced that her manuscript was shelved, she would be a laughingstock. The humiliation of her defeat struck her like a boxer's blow.

Percival patted his cravat, and smoothed the front of his wasp-waisted trousers. He was obviously pleased with himself. "Come, then, Evelyn. We mustn't be late. Lady Ramsbottom was relieved to hear that we could stand in for two of her guests who suddenly came down with the ague. She won't appreciate it if we hold up the supper."

Soft footsteps announced the arrival of the abigail, who upon seeing the expression on Evelyn's and the earl's faces, paused in the door.

The earl brushed past the servant girl as he left Evelyn's bedchamber. Crossing the threshold, he said over his shoulder, "Don't try to be a heroine, Evelyn. This is not a silly romance novel."

In their dungeon cell, Sir Hugo and Celeste made the best of a very bad situation. Celeste knew some very silly parlor games, which Hugo persuaded her to teach him. And Hugo regaled the girl with stories taken from his experiences as a barrister. He thought, after explaining to her the intricacies of the criminal judicial system, she had a delightfully quick mind. Her interest in the law, and her unexpected announcement that she would like to study it some day, amused him.

They sat on the floor, their backs against the damp stone wall. Hugo had stripped off his coat, insisting that Celeste cover her shoulders with it. The girl was irrepressibly cheerful, notwithstanding the dismal conditions of her surroundings. Her only concern, which brought on episodic moments of quiet reflection, was that Evelyn's manuscript would never be published.

"It isn't fair," she said to Sir Hugo, her brow furrowed. "My sister worked so hard on that book. She doesn't deserve what is happening to her."

"I couldn't agree more." Sir Hugo wrapped his arm around the girl's shoulder, and drew her close to him. She was so much like his younger sisters, brave and selfless. He would be honored to consider her his own sister. "Tell me something, Celeste. Do you have any idea what stunning revelations are to be made in that manuscript?"

The girl's lips curved in a shy smile. "Only that it's something to do with one of the Dethman ancestors, and the part he played in one of Henry VIII's divorces. Evelyn says it won't change history, not very much, anyway. But, it makes for a good story, and shows how unfairly women were treated during those days, particularly women who had the misfortune to catch the king's roving eye.''

"Your sister has a keen interest in history."

"My sister has a keen interest in many things. She doesn't do needlepoint, you know. Even though she insisted that I learn. Nor does she paint with watercolors or play the pianoforte. Which confounds me, because she has been as strict as a drill sergeant in seeing that I learn the feminine arts.''

"I suppose she wants you to be happy," Sir Hugo mused. "And to be happy in this society, a woman must marry well. And to marry well, a young girl must be practiced in those refined arts.''

"Poppycock!" Celeste exclaimed. She giggled as Hugo looked at her with mock indignation. "Well, not everything you said is poppycock. But, I don't think a woman needs a man to be happy, do you?''

"It helps."

She nodded, her gaze suddenly solemn and older than her years. "Evelyn has also seen to it that my education included literature, science and history. I can speak French and Italian fluently, you know.''

"No, I didn't know. How clever of you!"

"And I know a fair smattering of Spanish. Sister says a woman can never possess too much education. She says education is more important than anything else. And that books are like magic carpets because they can transport you to any place or time in the universe.''

"I think your sister is one of the most intelligent creatures I have ever met," Sir Hugo answered. "But do you think she is truly happy living in her single state?''

Celeste shrugged. "I haven't thought of it. Do you suppose she wants a man in her life?''

Hugo shrugged in response, though his nonchalance was sheer theater. He'd done nothing but contemplate whether Evelyn wanted a man since the moment he arrived at the castle and laid eyes on her. Specifically, he'd contemplated nothing but whether she wanted him.

Pity her if she did, he thought with bitter resignation. All he'd done for her since the day he met her at Widow Philpott's five years ago was disappoint her, and let her down each time she needed him.

"You look sad." Celeste's comment interrupted his unhappy thoughts.

He didn't want the girl to lose heart, or realize how dangerous their predicament was. So, he forced a smile to his lips, and gave her shoulders a squeeze. "Hungry, that is all. But, Cubby said he wouldn't let us starve, so he should be arriving with dinner any time now. Come, let's play another round of Name the Composer before our stomachs growl so loudly we can't hear each other sing."

Halfway through a hummed and badly off-key rendition of a Beethoven sonata, which Hugo was forced to admit he couldn't identify, Celeste's voice was cut off by the sound of the heavy door at the end of the corridor opening. Footsteps made their way toward the cell.

Sir Hugo stood, pulling Celeste to her feet beside him. If he was going to make an attempt at escaping, this was his chance. Perhaps he could lure the man close to the bars, and throttle him . . .

Celeste tugged at his elbow. "I forgot to tell you about this." Reaching into the deep pocket of her pelisse, she extracted a tiny brown bottle with a stoppered top. " 'Tis some of the liquid taken from the dishes in the mouse cages."

"Which of the cages did you take this from?" Sir Hugo whispered as the footsteps neared.

"From the cages in which the mice had died." Celeste slipped the bottle in Hugo's hand, then looked innocent as a lamb when Sir Cuthbert appeared outside the cell door.

Bearing a tray of food, the solicitor swallowed hard, his

eyes flickering from Hugo to Celeste. "I said I wouldn't allow you to starve."

"Good of you to remember us," Hugo agreed. "I hope Cook prepared something substantial for our repast. We're quite hungry."

"Thirsty, too," Celeste added.

"No need to worry," Cubby replied. "I brought some tea, also."

"Perhaps you'll come in and share a cup with us." Hugo gave a wry, throaty chuckle at his own joke.

But his levity seemed to make Sir Cuthbert nervous. Placing the tray on the floor, the blond-headed man fumbled with his keys. "Stand back," he warned Hugo and Celeste as he swung open the door, and shoved the tray inside the cell with the toe of his boot. "I've got a gun, and I won't hesitate to use it if I must."

"We know that, old man." Hugo waited till the door clanged shut before he moved toward it, and bent over the tray.

Celeste crossed the cell and took hold of the bars. With her face pressed through the spaces between them, she said, "Why don't you let us out of here, sir? We'll never tattle on you, we promise, if you'll only let us go!"

Celeste whined and pleaded in a high-pitched voice that bore little resemblance to her own. She also positioned her body to shield Hugo while he discreetly unstopped the brown bottle. From it, he poured a liquid substance into the bottom of one of the tea cups, then emptied the bottle into the top of the pot itself. After tucking the bottle beneath a square of muslin, he poured steaming hot tea into both cups. Then, straightening, he offered the undoctored cup of tea to Celeste, who released her hold on the bars to accept it daintily.

Sir Hugo held the other cup and saucer in his hands. He lifted the cup as if to drink, but never touched the china rim to his lips. Instead, he cast a quizzical look at Sir Cuthbert. "Are you all right, Cubby?"

"Of course, I am all right. Why do you ask such a question?"

"You look a little peaked, is all." Sir Hugo stepped closer to the iron bars. "Your eyes . . . are you certain that you're not ill, old boy?"

Sir Cuthbert ran a palm across his forehead, and gave out a nervous little chuckle. "What's the matter with my eyes?"

"They're all red around the rims, like mine were the time I had the consumption," Celeste said. "I was just a baby, but Evelyn has told me many times how peaked my complexion was. And that my eyes were red as beets around the edges. Dear Lord, I pray that you aren't coming down with—"

"Of course, I'm not!" Sir Cuthbert grabbed two of the iron bars and pushed his face through the spaces. I don't look like I'm consumptive, do I?"

"Look at me, Hugo.

Balancing cup and saucer in one hand, Hugo laid his palm on Cuthbert's forehead. "Why, you're burning with fever!"

"I am not! I felt it myself. My skin feels perfectly normal."

"To you," retorted Hugo, rolling his eyes in Celeste's direction. "But if you have a fever, your hand is warm too, for God's sake. You can't detect your own temperature, everyone knows that."

"Everyone knows that," echoed Celeste.

Hugo's pulse quickened. He could have dropped the cup and saucer, reached through the bars, and grabbed Sir Cuthbert. The notion had its appeal, but as Hugo's eyes quickly scanned the floor on the other side of the cell, he noticed that Cuthbert had dropped the big iron ring of keys among the rushes. Even if Hugo pinned Cubby to the cell door, Celeste would never be able to reach the keys. No, he needed to somehow persuade Cuthbert to hand over the keys. Or better yet, to unlock the cell door and release his prisoners.

"You'd better have cook or Shipton fetch you some tea," Hugo advised his captor. "And I'd go to bed after that, and stay there until that putrid fever gets under control."

"Putrid fever! It is not a putrid fever."

"Not yet," Celeste said sweetly. "For me, that was the next stage of the illness, however. La, but I was so sick, Evelyn thought twice I had died in my sleep."

"How sad," Sir Hugo said, again lifting the cup as if to drink, but never quite touching his lips to it. Lowering the cup, he looked at Cuthbert. "Lucky for you that your sister was around to nurse you back to health."

"Nothing but tea—gallons of it—and rest would do the trick," Celeste said. "Tea and rest, that's what Evelyn used to say."

"Tea and rest." Hugo stared sympathetically at Cuthbert.

"Hand me your tea, Hugo," the solicitor rasped. His arm shot through the bars, and his fingers wrapped around the china cup sitting prettily on its saucer.

Hugo frowned, but said nothing as Cuthbert moved back from the cell door, threw back his head and drained the cup of tea in one long drought. Then the solicitor tossed the cup into the rushes, and sighed as china shattered atop the ring of keys lying at his feet.

"Hand me the pot, Hugo," demanded Cuthbert. "I'll drink all of it, then I'll order Shipton to bring me another pot to my bed chamber. You won't be seeing me anytime soon, after that. I will not succumb to this dread disease, no matter what Lord Goreham has instructed me to do."

"Precisely what has he instructed you to do?" Hugo asked coolly, holding the teapot in his hands.

Sir Cuthbert gave a demonic chuckle as he leaned over and scooped up the iron key ring. His hands trembled as he unlocked the cell door, accepted the pot of tea handed to him by Sir Hugo, then slammed the door shut again.

Tossing the lid of the teapot to the floor, he drank from the top, amber-colored liquid spilling down his chin and staining his cravat. When he'd drunk the entire pot, he dropped the empty container to the floor.

Sir Hugo's eyes flickered from Sir Cuthbert to the keys dangling in the cell door.

"He told me to wait for his message," the solicitor said. "That he would send word to me when he had obtained the diaries, and discredited Evelyn's manuscript. And then, I am to release you, Hugo."

"Release me? What about Celeste?"

"She remains at the castle, as a hostage of sorts. You are to ride to London as fast as you can, where you will admit publicly the affair you have had with Evelyn for the past year. You might even marry her if you wish. I don't think Percival much cares one way or the other. But the long-standing affair will preclude Evelyn and her sister from collecting a penny under the earl's will. Once she has agreed not to petition the courts for her bequest, Celeste will be freed."

"That is a mad scheme, Cubby! You know it will never work. Once Celeste is freed, I will tell the authorities Evelyn was blackmailed. The courts will not deny her inheritance under those circumstances."

"It will be her word—and yours—against mine and Percival's." Cubby's face twisted suddenly. When the spasm passed, he continued, "Who would believe the word of a man who is addicted to the heady rush of gambling, so addicted he cannot enter Brooks's for fear he will wager his entire savings?"

Sir Hugo could barely contain his anger, but managed to do so, only because the solicitor's complexion was quickly turning ashen. "How do you know such a thing?"

"I made it my business to know as much about you as I could, Hugo. I followed you. At Percival's instructions, of course. You see, he discovered about six months ago that Evelyn watched you every morning as you crossed Lincoln's Inn Fields, and he took it in his head that she had developed a crush on you."

The realization that Evelyn had watched him every morning, that she had been aware of him all that time, filled Sir Hugo with a wistful yearning.

"Percival is a swine, and I shall make him pay for his misdeeds," Hugo promised softly.

"Perhaps, but he is very observant. When his own informants told him your name and occupation, he retained me to learn as much about you as I could. I know more about you, Hugo, than your dear old mum could say. For example, I know that you were present the night Evelyn lost her fortune in Widow Philpott's. And that you failed to offer her a shilling. Now, that wasn't very gentleman-like, was it?"

"If you know the whole story," Hugo seethed, "then you know why I was unable to offer Evelyn my assistance."

"You were so deep in dun territory, you couldn't have loaned her the money for a hackney cab." Suddenly, Cuthbert's expression screwed into a grimace of pain. When he spoke, his words seemed to be wrung out of him with tremendous pain. "You see, I do know the whole story, old boy, all of it."

Not all of it, Sir Hugo thought. There was no way Cuthbert could know how much Hugo loved Evelyn. There was no way anyone could comprehend the enormity of Hugo's guilt at not being able to assist her five years earlier when she was forced to make her Faustian bargain with the Earl of Goreham.

Sir Cuthbert bent double, and experienced an episode of unpleasant retching.

Celeste covered her mouth with her hand, and turned a shade paler. She looked away as the solicitor fell to his knees amid the rushes, and his symptoms became more violent.

Hugo's voice contained a trace of amusement. "Feeling poorly, are we, Cubby?"

The solicitor removed a muslin square from his pocket and wiped his mouth. Beads of sweat dotted his upper lip, and his eyes were glazed and wild-looking. On his hands and knees, he lifted his face to Hugo. It was a pitiful sight, the tow-haired man reduced to crawling on the floor, pain contorting his features and robbing him of dignity.

Sir Hugo felt no sympathy for the man.

"Hugo, what is happening to me?" Cuthbert rasped.

"You've been poisoned."

Cuthbert's face froze in a rictus of horror. "Dear God! The tea! You've murdered me!"

"Not precisely. Not yet, anyway," Hugo drawled. "There is an antidote. Would you like me to tell you the antidote, Cubby? The key to survival, as it were? Or shall Celeste and I remain locked in this dungeon cell forever while your dead body rots on the floor beside us?"

"Tell me the antidote!" Cuthbert scuttled toward the cell door, but was halted by another episode of sickness.

"Can you reach the keys, Cubby?" Hugo asked. "If you will unlock this cell door, I will gladly furnish you with the antidote to the poison you have consumed."

"I think so," replied the man, breathlessly. He scrambled toward the cell door, his trembling hand reaching for the keys. Half-standing, the solicitor just managed to unlock the door before he collapsed again.

Hugo took Celeste by the hand, and together they slipped through the open cell door, careful to avoid the disgusting remnants of all that Cuthbert had consumed in the last day or so. Pinching the tip of her nose, Celeste said, "Pray, tell him the antidote, sir. I don't think I can bear to leave him in this condition."

"You are a kind young girl," Hugo replied. "After all that Sir Cuthbert has done to damage your future security and ruin your sister's reputation, you still have the heart to be concerned about his health. Truly, I am amazed!"

"Help me," whispered Cubby, his forehead pressed to the floor as he clutched his belly.

Sir Hugo sighed. Bending over Cubby, he grasped the man's arm and helped him to his feet. Haltingly, the two men made their way down the corridor and up the stairs, following Celeste as she emerged in Evelyn's bedroom.

"Pack your portmanteau, Celeste," Hugo told her. "And meet me below stairs as quickly as possible. We must get to London right away."

"What about him?" Celeste asked, looking over her shoulder.

The three made their way down the hallway, Hugo pausing at Cuthbert's guest bedroom door. "I shall see that he is tucked into bed, and furnished with all that he needs to overcome this malady. The sickness will last another twelve hours or so, and as long as he continues to down sufficient liquids, he will recover completely."

"So that is the antidote?" Celeste asked, standing at her own bedroom door.

"On the contrary," Hugo replied. "There is no antidote, except rest and liquids. And I shall instruct cook to fetch some fresh ginger for him to nibble on. We are only treating the symptoms of the poisoning, but it will pass from Cuthbert's system soon enough. I'm afraid he won't be very comfortable for the next day or so."

As if in response, Sir Cuthbert let out a mournful groan, prompting Hugo to kick open his door, and rush him into his room.

Celeste closed the door behind her, shivering at the sounds of Cuthbert's distress. But, she lost no time in carrying out Hugo's instructions. After throwing as many clothes as she could in one small suitcase, she hurried to the Great Hall and waited by the front door. When Hugo descended the stairs, calling servants, summoning stable boys and ostlers, she watched with growing admiration.

The handsome barrister, with his sad, intelligent eyes, and his broad, furrowed forehead sent the Goreham Castle staff into an immediate flurry of activity. Food was packed for the trip to London, blankets gathered and stacked to stave off the cold. A carriage was drawn up outside, and a driver was quickly installed on the high bench. Before a half hour was up, Sir Hugo and Celeste were prepared to embark on their arduous journey to London. Weather permitting, they would arrive before the third Earl of Goreham had time to carry out his dastardly plan to ruin Evelyn's professional reputation, and rob her of her inheritance.

Hugo's heart pounded like a hammer as the carriage lurched and the horses gained momentum crossing the bridge that spanned the moat. Catching Celeste's bright-eyed gaze, he recognized with some embarrassment, the look of hero worship on her face. It was obvious the young girl imagined him her and her sister's savior.

That she should pin her hopes on such a worthless man as he felt himself to be, startled Sir Hugo. And embarrassed him. He couldn't shake the feeling that had he not failed Evelyn five years ago, she wouldn't be in this precarious situation now.

He wondered if he could live up to Celeste's expectations. Could he be the man that the young, idealistic girl saw when she gazed at him?

For that matter, could he be the man that Evelyn saw when she looked at him?

Loving Evelyn, he realized, instilled in him the need to be worthy. For her, he could find the strength necessary to overcome the demons that had possessed him for years. For her—he would do anything.

But the question remained, would Evelyn Waring, the Dowager Countess of Goreham, want him if she knew the terrible secret that he harbored? Would a woman who'd been willing to gamble everything she had in exchange for her sister's security be able to love a man who couldn't wager a farthing without losing himself to his addiction for gambling?

Sir Hugo shuddered as he watched the frost-covered landscape slide past outside the carriage window. A coldness gripped his heart. Never knowing when his affliction would overwhelm him, he'd lived for years in constant fear of succumbing to his weakness. The constant battle that raged within him had left him cynical, full of self-deprecation, and convinced that he was unlovable. In some ways, he supposed, his self-absorption had rendered him incapable of loving. His focus was on himself, on winning the war against his own private demons.

He never had believed that a woman could love him. Nor had he wanted that responsibility, because it demanded a candor that his gambling addiction wouldn't allow. The self-examination that loving Evelyn required was painful to Sir Hugo. Looking deep into his heart, he saw many things about himself he didn't admire. Yet he saw that his heart had the capacity to love another person. He recognized his need for love. And he admitted to himself that he wanted Evelyn to love him in return.

He would prove himself worthy of that love if it was the last thing he did.

On the leather squabs opposite him, Celeste fell asleep and snored gently. Sir Hugo reached over and tucked the blanket more snugly around her body. Then he settled back in his seat, and watched her.

She was so young and innocent. He envied her for a multitude of reasons, but mainly because she had grown up knowing the unconditional love of the bravest, kindest woman he'd ever met.

Chapter Ten

Lady Ramsbottom's Drury Lane town house was, under ordinary circumstances, one of Evelyn's favorite salons. The older woman, who'd married off three daughters to wealthy aristocrats, had taken Evelyn under her wing the instant she met her. Plump, outspoken, and widely reputed to be a conversational bore, Adelaide, Lady Ramsbottom, remained a doyenne of Mayfair society. Her late husband's social ranking was of the highest order, her girls had married sensibly and well, and there wasn't a soul among the *ton* whose lineage wasn't well-known to Lady Ramsbottom. The breadth of her knowledge concerning everyone's pedigree was astonishing; her generosity was equally prodigious.

She greeted her young friend Evelyn with a mixture of surprise and delight. "I was so pleased to hear from Percival that the two of you made it back from Kent. The roads were quite treacherous, don't you agree?"

"Ghastly," replied Percival, grasping his stepmother's arm.

They stood in Lady Ramsbottom's parlor, surrounded

by dinner guests dressed in their finest garb. At Lady Ramsbottom's request, her guests dressed as if they were on their way to Almack's, the men in black satin knee pants and stiff, white cravats, the women in low-cut evening dresses.

"Are you all right?" the older woman asked, oblivious to her guests milling around her. Her gaze shot to Percival's hand on Evelyn's arm, and her lips formed a straight line.

"Quite," Evelyn said, fighting the urge to grimace as Percival's grasp tightened. She wanted to bury her head on Lady Ramsbottom's shoulder and cry her eyes out. But, as long as Percival controlled the fates of Celeste and Sir Hugo, she had no choice but to participate in this charade. "I am a little tired from the trip, that is all."

"So good of you to extend last-minute invitations to us," Percival inserted, smiling unctuously at the hostess.

She arched her brows. "When you discovered that I would have two empty seats at my table, Percival, and were conscientious enough to offer to fill them, how could I refuse you?" Looking back at Evelyn, she added wryly, "It isn't every day that you witness such thoughtful behavior from an uninvited guest."

Evelyn dared to twist her lips. "Thank you for having us."

"You are welcome at my home any time," assured Lady Ramsbottom, her gaze firmly pinned on Evelyn. "Come now, I see the butler is about to announce dinner. You shall sit next to me, dear. And Percival, you are seated at the opposite end of the table, I believe."

Percival held out both elbows, and gallantly led Lady Ramsbottom and his stepmother to the dining room. Once inside, as guests circled about the table looking for their place cards, Percival seated the ladies, and headed for the opposite end of the table. Evelyn noted with horror that he actually plucked a couple of name cards from beside their respective place settings, and rearranged them.

Lady Ramsbottom saw him, too. "Percival Dethman!

Whatever are you doing? You know better than to rearrange the place cards.''

Some of the ladies who were seated looked from their hostess to Lord Goreham. He laughed off any suggestion that he'd done something impolite, and placed his card next to Howard Fitzhaven's. As the men seated themselves, Lady Ramsbottom glared at her impertinent guest. But one look at Evelyn's pleading expression halted any further objections. Clearly chagrinned, she fixed a counterfeit smile on her face and picked up her soup spoon.

The meal progressed with interminable agony for Evelyn. She hardly touched the pheasant consommé, nor the cold fish course served afterward. A succulent main course of roast duckling accompanied by sweet peas and braised turnips was nearly untouched when the footmen cleared her plates. Dessert, bowls of sweet cream studded with clouds of billowy meringue, brought the acrid taste of bile to the back of her throat.

Evelyn was relieved when Lady Ramsbottom announced that the meal was finished. Breaking with protocol, she added, ''And we shall all adjourn to the drawing room for port.''

Reassembled in the cheerful room, warmed not only by a crackling fire, but also by its deep gold painted walls, Evelyn perched on the edge of a Sheraton chair. She held a glass of port to her lips with trembling hands. While a young lady that she didn't know—but who was obviously aspiring to catch the eye of another of Lady Ramsbottom's eligible guests—murdered Mozart on the pianoforte, Evelyn watched Percival.

He stood beside the mantelpiece, rising on his toes as he engaged Mr. Fitzhaven in conversation. The banker with whom Evelyn had entrusted custody of the Dethman diaries wore a look of grave concern on his face. At intervals, he turned and glanced at Evelyn, whose heart pounded like a drum. What on earth was Percival saying?

What sort of slanderous remarks was he peddling to the banker in order to induce him to release the diaries?

At last, after Percival had warmly clapped the banker on his back, Mr. Fitzhaven ventured toward Evelyn. "May I sit beside you for a moment, Lady Goreham?"

She nodded, acutely aware of Percival's scrutiny. She had to be careful what she said; she would say nothing to endanger the welfare of her sister and Sir Hugo.

The little banker, with his round nose and balding pate, spoke with a pronounced lisp. For all that he appeared like a bumbling man, however, he was one of the most well-respected financial advisors in all of London.

It was widely reputed that he'd made a fortune on the Exchange, and that despite his mercantile lineage, he could have bought and sold half of the men who lived in Mayfair. As such, his favor was curried by the fashionable set, and he was treated like a duke. It was only behind his back that titled men mocked his lisp and laughed uproariously at the artlessness with which the little man folded his cravat.

"Dear girl, I hope you are faring well," he said, perched on a creaking cane-bottomed Grecian-style chair. "Your stepson has informed me of your . . . ah, indisposition."

"My indisposition?" Evelyn cut her eyes at Percival, who stood beside the pianoforte, pretending to listen to the young girl who was so intently pounding the ivories.

From across the room, the young earl tilted his head, met Evelyn's gaze and held it.

Through gritted teeth, she said, "Whatever are you talking about, Mr. Fitzhaven?"

The man's face reddened. " 'Tis a terrible humiliation for you, I'm sure, to admit that your manuscript is a forgery, a fraud, a plagiarism, as it were. I understand you're wanting to keep the whole affair a secret, and believe me, you are fortunate that your stepson is willing to sweep the matter under the carpet."

Evelyn's blood ran cold. She steeled her nerves, just as

she schooled her expression into a mask of equanimity. "A plagiarism, Mr. Fitzhaven? Is that what Lord Goreham told you?"

"You were overset at the death of the old earl. That is understandable. Unlike a man, a woman is controlled by her emotions, which are often so extreme and volatile at times of crisis."

"Crisis?" Evelyn repeated dully.

The banker nodded. "Percival explained to me the conditions of your deceased husband's will. I suppose a beautiful young woman such as yourself can't be blamed entirely for succumbing to the charms of a young buck. Especially after years of living with such an older man."

Here, the banker's gaze took on an avidity that bristled the wispy hairs beneath the bun at Evelyn's nape. Instinctively, she hugged herself despite the warmth of the nearby fire.

Her mouth fell open, her lips rounding in silent indignation. "Percival told you . . ."

Mr. Fitzhaven leaned so close that his brandy-laden breath assaulted Evelyn's nose. "About the barrister . . ."

She drew in a sharp breath. Her life—and that of her sister—flashed before her eyes. So, her stepson had done what he'd threatened to do, besmirched her reputation by bruiting it about that she was having an affair with Sir Hugo Mansfield. Which was the farthest thing from the truth. *Except in the privacy of her own thoughts.*

"Mr. Fitzhaven, you mustn't believe everything that Percival—"

Her protest was cut off by her stepson's materialization beside her chair. The young man bent stiffly at the waist, and offered his hand to Evelyn. "Come, my lady. Mr. Fitzhaven has kindly agreed to turn over the diaries to me in the morning. First thing. You needn't trouble yourself with going to the bank; after all, it isn't a proper place for ladies, and your reputation has suffered enough as it is."

As Evelyn stood on shaky knees, the diminutive banker

rose alongside her. "You should be grateful to your stepson, Lady Goreham. He has informed me that despite your having failed to live up to the conditions of your husband's will, he will be agreeable to allowing you and your sister to continue on at the Lincoln's Inn Fields town house."

Lord Goreham gave her an avuncular smile that sent chills up Evelyn's spine. "I wouldn't cast my stepmother into the streets, dear me, no. And poor Celeste . . . she hasn't done anything wrong. Why should she suffer?"

"Then you shall furnish her a dowry, and see to it that she has a proper Season?" Evelyn said. If her sister was well taken care of, that was all that really mattered, wasn't it? Her own hopes and dreams were shattered, along with any opportunity she might have had to form a more intimate or lasting friendship with Sir Hugo. He certainly wouldn't have anything to do with her now that she was disgraced and disinherited.

And when he learned his own name had been dragged into this scandal—that Percival had accused him of seducing her—then he would be furious. His own reputation was at stake. In the end, he would revile Evelyn for the trouble she had caused him.

But, none of that mattered if Celeste made her coming-out, and was furnished a dowry. Then, the girl could find a proper husband, a man who cherished her and who would take care of her. She wouldn't wind up like Evelyn, having made bad decision after bad decision, having gambled everything she had, only to find herself, years later, broke, cast out of polite society—an event which was sure to happen when Percival's fabricated scandal broke—and totally unloved.

Blinking back tears, Evelyn allowed her stepson to lead her across the drawing room. There was a hollow feeling in the pit of her stomach, and a gaping hole in her heart. Fighting to maintain an air of composure, she said goodnight to Lady Ramsbottom, feigning the megrims to excuse her early departure.

The older woman looked at her skeptically, then said to Percival, "Take care of her, then. I shall inquire of her health tomorrow."

Evelyn nodded absently, hardly aware of her actions as she left Lady Ramsbottom's house and clambered into Percival's waiting carriage. When her stepson pulled down the window shades, drenching the interior of the equipage in darkness, she was glad for the respite from his amused gaze. Sighing, she leaned her head back, and wondered where she would acquire the strength to survive until Celeste was delivered safely back to her.

If she could only talk to Sir Hugo. If she could only see him, touch him, hear the sound of his soothing voice. The quiet strength he exuded, which she had come to depend upon in the short time since he'd re-entered her life, eluded her now. She needed him.

But, with her reputation in tatters, her financial security forfeit, and her name linked to his by scandal, she was certain he would never speak to her again. *Why would he?* She was the cause of his being tossed in a dungeon cell, after all. Percival had described to her in excruciating detail the dank and dangerous conditions of the medieval torture chamber beneath Goreham Castle. Every time Evelyn pictured her sister and the barrister imprisoned there, her skin crawled.

And it was all her fault. Her ambition had imperiled Sir Hugo's life, and jeopardized Celeste's future.

As much as Evelyn loathed herself, there was no way that she could envision Sir Hugo failing to feel the same way.

The next morning passed in a blur of pain and humiliation. Evelyn's depression weighed her down, reminding her of the medieval torture that called for pressing the accused beneath boards and rocks until life was extinguished. Getting out of bed was a monumental struggle.

She sat at the breakfast table, staring vacantly at the empty seat ordinarily occupied by Celeste. "Is the earl at home?" she asked a maidservant who poured hot tea in her cup.

"No, m'lady," the young woman replied. "I heard the others say Lord Goreham went out first thing this morning. Told his valet he wouldn't be back until late this afternoon."

Evelyn poked a piece of dry toast in her mouth, and forced herself to chew. The thought of Percival Dethman obtaining possession of the Dethman diaries made her stomach hurt. Unable to vent her rage, Evelyn felt her throat constricted into painful cords. Sipping her tea, she nearly choked. Wasn't there anything she could do to prevent her stepson from halting the publication of her novel?

Not without putting Celeste and Sir Hugo at risk, she reminded herself.

Balling her hands into fists, she pounded the table, upsetting her teacup and rattling the china saucer. The maid came scurrying into the breakfast room, crying, "Is everything all right, m'lady?"

Rising, Evelyn cast the young girl a bleak look. "Yes. Go away, now. I want to be alone."

Passing into the front drawing room, Evelyn stood at the window overlooking Lincoln's Inn Fields. There for the past five years, she'd watched Sir Hugo Mansfield stride down the street, passing in front of the Goreham town house each morning, his schedule as regular as the night crier's.

In her imagination, she pictured his intense gaze, his somber expression. What thoughts brought furrows to that broad forehead? What pain brought such sadness to that hazel eyes?

For years, Evelyn had played a sort of game with herself, imagining what Sir Hugo's life was like, what sort of entertainment kept him amused, what kind of friends heard his confidences. In her mind's eye, she saw him in court, clad in his barrister's robe and full-bottomed wig. His voice, deep and clear, resounded off the paneled walls, commanding the entire court's attention, judge and jury, spectators and litigants alike.

He was a well-respected man, a brilliant jurist, she'd heard it said of him. But, so serious. So private. And his introspection, his refusal to allow the world to know what he was thinking and feeling, fueled Evelyn's imagination. What motivated Sir Hugo? Who was he—really?

Her fist slammed into her open palm. Evelyn stifled a sob, gulping convulsively until her composure returned. Sir Hugo would forever be a mystery to her now. Her own ambition had cost her the opportunity to ever know him.

A niggling thought reared its head. *The opportunity to know him . . .* Had Sir Hugo never been invited to Goreham Castle in Kent, she would never have said a word to him. Why had Percival invited him in the first place?

It was crystal clear Percival had invited Sir Hugo to the castle with every intent of throwing him together with Evelyn, forcing a compromising situation on them, then declaring that Evelyn had forfeited her inheritance by failing to live up to the conditions of the second earl's will.

How had Percival known that Evelyn had, for the past five years, nurtured a tender spot in her heart for Sir Hugo?

Brushing away tears, staring at the grassy square that was Lincoln's Inn Fields, and the stone buildings of the law school and courts behind it, Evelyn drew a sharp breath. She'd stood at this window every morning at the same time for five years. Of course, Percival had watched her. How many times had he sneaked up behind her, peering over her shoulder, his fetid breath ruffling the hairs on her nape?

More times than she cared to count!

And how many times had he stood beside her, stroking his mustache and tracing the trajectory of her gaze?

With a certainty, Lord Goreham had been aware of her

obsession with the man who walked past the town house each morning. Undoubtedly, he'd taken pains to discover who that man was. Between Goreham and Sir Cuthbert—who had obviously been Percival's accomplice from the beginning—it hadn't been difficult to do.

They'd delved deep into Sir Hugo's background, Evelyn deduced. Deep enough to learn that he'd been present the night the old earl offered marriage to Evelyn.

Had her deceased husband divulged the details of that horrid night to his son? Evelyn didn't think so. There were other ways Sir Cuthbert and Lord Goreham could have discovered what happened that night. Lady Philpott could easily have spilled the beans.

Shuddering, Evelyn half-turned from the window. As the clock on the mantelpiece chimed the hour, servants quietly cleared the breakfast table, occasionally glancing nervously at their mistress, whose usual good nature had suddenly soured. Evelyn noted the time, eleven o'clock. The London Society for the Study of the Tudor Monarchy would be meeting in an hour. Percival would be there, the diaries in his possession, and he would publicly denounce Evelyn's manuscript.

She wondered if he would tell the esteemed members of the Society that she'd plagiarized his work. Perhaps he would simply substitute his name for hers, and allow publication of her biography of the Tudor king to proceed. It would be like Percival to take credit for her work, without bothering to read the diaries and discover what was really in them.

It suddenly occurred to Evelyn that poetic justice might prevail if Percival did publish the book under his name. Allowing herself a wry chuckle, Evelyn pictured Percival's surprise when, after claiming authorship of the scholarly treatise on Henry VIII, he learned he'd besmirched the reputation of his Dethman ancestors.

Most likely, he would flip through the diaries before he consented to the publication of her biography, even under his own name. But, the letters—having been written in the 16th century, when ink was scarce, paper was flimsy— were so elaborately penned the modern readers could barely transcribe them, Evelyn doubted seriously he would quickly glean the revelations contained therein.

An inspiration hit her like a bolt of lightning. If Percival intended to publicly denounce her at the Society meeting, perhaps she should be present. She might not be able to dissuade Percival from decrying her as a fraud, but perhaps she could goad him into publishing her book . . .

If she could only assure that the book was published *before* Percival discovered what was in the diaries, and absent his actually examining the manuscript which was at the publishers ready to be printed . . .

Hurriedly, Evelyn raced up the curving steps, calling to the servants as she made the landing. "Send my abigail, quickly! And have a footman hail a hackney cab. We haven't much time, and I must be at Lord Hardy's town house on Park Lane within the hour."

In her room, Evelyn sat at her mirrored vanity, and hastily scrawled a message to Miss Louisa Freemantle. "Take this below stairs, and instruct a footman to deliver it to Miss Freemantle's home. Be quick now, and hurry back. I believe I shall wear my pale green walking dress today. No need to fade into the background for my purposes!"

"Oh, Evie!" Louisa Freemantle sat on the leather squabs opposite Evelyn. Having heard her best friend's story, she reached across, and squeezed her gloved hands. "I wouldn't blame you for never speaking to me again! And to think I was developing a *tendre* for that loathsome Sir Cuthbert . . ."

" 'Tis not your fault, Lou." A deep rut jolted the rented post chaise, fanning the ostrich plume that ornamented Evelyn's yeoman's hat. Grasping a brass handle on the compartment's side, Evelyn offered Louisa a forced smile. "Truly, I believe Cuthbert was drawn into this sordid affair by his client, Lord Goreham."

"But Cubby was too weak to resist Percival's demands," Louisa said, her expression one of disappointment. "The earl must have offered him a princely sum to dig up the dirt on Sir Hugo. Oh! When I think of all those questions Cubby asked me about your manuscript. When he learned I had assisted you in editing portions of the book, he took such an interest in me. I thought it was because he admired my intellect."

Evelyn shook her head. "We would all like to think it was our intelligence and wit that attracted men, wouldn't we?"

Sniffing, Louisa drew a handkerchief from her reticule. Blinking rapidly, she said nothing until the carriage drew to a stop before Lord Hardy's Park Lane residence.

"You know the plan, Louisa? If anyone questions your attendance at this function, you are to tell them you edited part of the manuscript. With those credentials, no one will object to your accompanying me to a single meeting."

Louisa, who'd dressed as hastily as Evelyn had, wore a white muslin gown with a dark blue spencer jacket. Military epaulets at the shoulder contrasted sharply with the demure femininity of her nearly sheer dress. Waiting for the tiger to open their door and assist them to the street, Evelyn said, "Aren't you cold, Lou?"

"Certainly." Belatedly, Miss Freemantle studied Evelyn's walking dress. "Evie. . . you're not in black!"

Lady Goreham wrapped her dark green sarcenet pelisse more tightly around her middle. The carriage door swung open, and she paused at the threshold, her hand in the tiger's firm grip. Over her shoulder, she said, "Dear girl, I am no longer in mourning. It is official."

The two women descended to the street, then walked arm in arm to Lord Hardy's front door.

"Tell me again," Louisa said. "What are we to do when

Lord Goreham takes the floor and denounces you as a fraud, and tells the Society that the manuscript was written by him?''

Evelyn reiterated the speech she'd composed for Miss Louisa Freemantle. The taller woman nodded, silently committing her role to memory. When the front door opened, both women greeted the butler with wide smiles, then swept across the threshold.

An hour after Evelyn departed Lincoln's Inn Fields, Sir Hugo's carriage, borrowed from the Goreham stables in Kent, ground to a halt in front of the Goreham town house.

He was barely able to restrain Celeste from leaping out of the carriage before it stopped.

"Let me go! I want to see Evelyn!" The young girl hit the street running, and raced to the front door.

Sir Hugo followed her inside, his pulse galloping. He wanted to see Evelyn, too. More than he'd ever wanted anything in his life. Yet the thought of confronting her when he felt he'd failed her—again—filled him with terror.

Evelyn's abigail ran down the steps, her features smeared in a moue of bewilderment. Skirts clutched in her hands, she met Celeste in the entry hall. "Miss Waring, whatever are ye doin' back? The earl, he done said ye was stayin' on at Goreham Castle another fortnight, at least!"

"Where is she?" Celeste brushed past the servant, and took three steps in one giant leap.

"She's gone!" the maid said, staring at Sir Hugo in utter confusion.

Celeste pounded back down the steps and stood in front of her. "Where has Evelyn gone?"

"I don't rightly know, I just dressed her is all!"

A footman appeared on the landing, a small boy dressed in knee-breeches and woolen waistcoat that had seen better days. Staring down at Celeste and the abigail, he seemed reluctant to enter the conversation.

Sir Hugo caught the child's glance, and said, "Do you know where the lady of the house went?"

Shrugging, the boy descended the steps in boyish hops. He landed on the bottom step with an insouciant glance at the abigail. "I knows what I heard, is all. I delivered a letter to Miss Louisa Freemantle at just after eleven o'clock. When I returned, a hackney cab was waitin' for m'lady. I heard her tell the driver to take her to Curzon Street, see, that's where Miss Freemantle lives."

"What about the earl?" Sir Hugo asked, laying a coin in the boy's open palm.

"He left out early this morning, before he'd even 'ad his breakfast. As he was gettin' in his carriage, I heard him tell the driver to take him to the Bank of England by way of Chancery Lane, then Fleet Street past St. Paul's."

Sir Hugo ran his hand through his hair, pondering the footman's information. Then, he turned to Celeste. "Stay here. I'm going to Louisa Freemantle's house. When I find Evelyn, I will return—"

"I'm going with you." Her eyes flashed brilliantly, and her chin lifted a notch.

This time, Sir Hugo had no intention of putting Evelyn's younger sister in harm's way. If there was one thing he knew about Lady Goreham, it was that she was a lioness when it came to protecting her flaxen-haired cub. Grasping the young girl's shoulders, he met her cornflower gaze. "Your sister would be furious with both of us if I were to permit you to accompany me. Sorry, Celeste, but I must insist that you remain here."

She started to protest, but Sir Hugo's expression was implacable. Celeste clamped her lips shut, her eyes shimmering with unshed tears. Then she rose on her toes, and threw her arms about Sir Hugo's neck.

"Please bring her back!"

The barrister froze, startled by this display of emotion.

It had been a long time since a young girl had thrown her arms about him; he was reminded of his younger sister, Anabelle, who as a child had once clung to Hugo as he left the house.

"Don't go, Hugo. Father is bound to return home any minute, and he'll be in his cups and growling like a bear."

Hugo was a young buck by then, quickly following in his father's infamous footsteps, eager to get out of the house so that he could haunt the St. James's gaming hells himself. Considering what little he'd had to wager then, he'd played deep enough to experience the heady rush of winning, and to know the frustrating rage of losing.

He'd held his sister at arm's length, then, and laughed at her.

Regret—bitter and heartfelt—washed over him. Slowly, his arms encircled Celeste's delicate frame and he laid his cheek on the top of her head. She sobbed, her body trembling in his embrace. Dear God, he thought, how could anyone dare to disappoint this child? How could his father have been so cruel to his own mother and sisters?

How could he have, for that matter?

Gently, he set Celeste at arm's length. "There, now. Dry your tears. Then, go to your room, take a long hot bath and crawl into bed. When you awaken from your nap, Evelyn will be home, I promise you."

Between hiccoughs, Celeste eked out, "Promise?"

He kissed her forehead, nodded, then turned on his heel and raced out of the house.

"Curzon Street," he called to the driver as he leapt into the carriage.

His heart squeezed at the realization he'd promised Celeste what might very well be impossible. Hugo didn't take promises lightly. Since the night in Widow Philpott's when he was unable to help Evelyn, he'd scrupulously avoided making promises he couldn't keep.

Which was precisely why he had never promised a

woman that he would love her forever, that he would be a worthy husband, or a loving father.

Knowing that his days were consumed with battling the desire to gamble, Sir Hugo had never believed he could promise his love to any woman. He was bound to disappoint her, bound to succumb to the temptation of the gaming tables eventually. And even if he didn't, there would always be something inside him that gnawed at him like a ravenous wolf. Between his law practice and his determination to avoid winding up like his father, there simply wasn't enough left over for a woman.

He didn't have it in him to love a woman, so why lie to himself—or her?

Still, with each breath he took, with each rotation of the wheels that drew his carriage, he grew more anxious, more desperate to hold Evelyn, the Countess of Goreham, in his arms. He'd held her once, had felt as if her goodness had poured right into his bones. He had thought, then, that he was unworthy of a woman who'd risked all she had for her sister.

A man who'd left his own mother and sisters to cope with their drunken father—a man who for years had followed in the footsteps of that poor excuse for a husband—was foolish to think he deserved the countess's love.

But he hadn't been in a gambling hell for five years!

Seizing on that fact, Sir Hugo clung to it like a drowning man. Was he cured of his affliction? Was five years' abstinence long enough to constitute a *cure?*

Only when the ceiling hatch opened, and the driver called down for further instructions, did Sir Hugo's thoughts refocus. He looked out the window, unsure where Miss Freemantle resided.

A chimney sweep and his two climbing boys walked alongside the street, carefully avoiding the neatly manicured patches of grass that bordered Curzon Street's town houses. Sir Hugo signaled the driver to a stop. Then, he opened the carriage door, and asked the soot-covered man where Miss Freemantle lived.

"Two houses down on the left, guv'nor," the man said.

After tossing a coin at the man, and two more at the boys, Sir Hugo jumped to the street, and ran. The maid who opened the shiny white door reluctantly informed him that Miss Freemantle had left the house nearly half an hour earlier.

"With her friend, the countess," the woman added.

"Do you know where they went?" Sir Hugo asked, resisting the urge to grab the servant, and shake the information out of her.

"As a matter of fact, I do."

Sir Hugo was glad he'd filled his pocket with coins; every bit of intelligence he squeezed out of his domestic informants cost him a shilling.

Slipping her coin in her apron pocket, the maid smiled. "I heard 'em talking. They was headin' for Park Lane, where Lord Hardy lives. Some sort of society meetin', I believe."

"The London Society for the Study of the Tudor Monarchy?" Sir Hugo had turned his back on the woman before she could answer.

Back in the carriage, he directed the driver to Park Lane. Speeding down Piccadilly, as fast as the traffic would allow, he tapped his foot impatiently. At Park Lane, the driver turned north, slowing in front of a cream-colored brick town house. Eschewing the assistance of the tiger, Sir Hugo opened the door, and landed on the ground running. He pushed through the unlatched door of an elaborate iron gate topped with gilded finials, and raced up the flagstone walk to the glossy black-painted front door ornamented with Coade stone.

He lifted the heavy leonine brass knocker, and pounded violently. Footsteps sounded quickly; the door opened to a glimpse of highly polished parquet floor and a sparkling chandelier.

"Come in, sir. You are late." There was an air of weary resignation surrounding the aging butler, dressed in formal black knee pants and holding a small tray on which several glasses of champagne were balanced.

Without explaining that he couldn't be late because he hadn't been invited to the Society's meeting, Sir Hugo crossed the threshold. From above stairs, wafted the sounds of much talk, deep-throated laughter, and the clinking of glasses. *The sounds of masculine revelry, without a single female voice to soften the din.*

Aware that Evelyn was the only woman member of the Society, Sir Hugo wondered if she felt out of place. A wry smile came to his lips. No, she wouldn't, he thought. Evelyn Waring, the Dowager Countess of Goreham, had earned her right to be here. There was no reason for her to feel ill at ease among these men. For her intelligence and scholarship, she was as highly esteemed as they were.

The butler led him upstairs to a drawing room handsomely decorated with mahogany paneling, richly textured Axminster rugs and wall-to-wall shelves filled with books. Men wearing elegantly cut waistcoats and snow white cravats thronged the room, obscuring any sign of Lady Goreham or Miss Freemantle. Hugo's heart pounded as he wound his way around clusters of men, all talking about King Henry VIII from what he could ascertain.

A loud but faltering voice quelled the buzz of conversation. Sir Hugo saw that the speaker, standing at a podium at the far end of the room, was a rather greasy-looking man with a shock of unruly brown curls. The man—Sir Hugo assumed he was Lord Hardy—looked affable enough, even if he bore not the slightest resemblance to a scholar.

"Gentleman—oh, and Lady Goreham—we are about to commence. Our first order of business is an unusual one. It seems that Lord Percival Goreham has a word or two to say about the countess's manuscript. We have all been eagerly awaiting its publication, so perhaps Lord

Goreham has some news regarding the publication date of the book.''

"Thank you, Lord Hardy.'' Percival disengaged himself from the crowd, stood behind the podium, and paused dramatically.

While silence settled over the crowded room, Sir Hugo scanned the faces surrounding him. His gaze locked with Evelyn's. She sat on a small divan on the opposite side of the room, her back to a wall filled with books. Beside her was Miss Louisa Freemantle, whose hands were intertwined with Evelyn's.

It seemed to Sir Hugo that Percival's voice faded to nothing. Only Evelyn existed for him at that instant, and only the awareness that shimmered between them signified. A warmth stirred in Hugo's chest; his heart skipped a beat, then raced erratically. The urge to cross the room and sweep Evelyn into his arms was compelling, but he froze, uncertain what his next move should be. Percival's demented determination to ruin Evelyn's reputation brought danger to this otherwise serene setting. He dare not act in haste until he knew what Lord Goreham was about.

He turned his attention to Percival's speech. An uneasy rumbling had erupted among the scholars, and many of them cast furtive glances in Lady Goreham's direction.

"I am deeply distressed to announce,'' the third earl said, rising on his tiptoes behind the podium, "that my stepmother Evelyn Waring, the Dowager Countess of Goreham, stole the Dethman diaries from me, along with my manuscript, which she then wrote out and copied in her own hand. It was that manuscript which she submitted to her publisher Mr. Murray, and passed off as her own work. Not wishing to embarrass my deceased father's wife, I held my tongue publicly, while beseeching Lady Goreham to confess her misdeed.''

"I don't believe it!'' shouted Lord Hardy, standing at the front of the room. He peered over his shoulder at

Lady Goreham, as if entreating her to deny the charges made by her stepson.

But, to Sir Hugo's infinite surprise, Evelyn uncoiled her fingers from Miss Freemantle's clasp, rose slowly, and said in a clear, mellifluous voice, "I am afraid everything Lord Goreham has said is true. My manuscript is a forgery, and everything I have written was stolen directly from Percival Dethman."

Chapter Eleven

When Evelyn stood, she felt that her stomach remained on the divan. Her knees wobbled beneath her gown, and without Louisa's firm grasp on her elbow, might well have buckled. She didn't know how she mustered the strength to walk toward the podium, chin lifted, gaze pinned firmly on an invisible spot straight ahead of her.

Whispers trailed in her wake, like the rustle of grass when a snake slithers past. She tightened her hold on Louisa's fingers, grateful for her friend's support. Her face felt hot and clammy as she stood at the front of the room before a sea of skeptical, bewildered gazes.

"It is true," she repeated. "The manuscript I touted as my own, a biography of Henry VIII based partly on the Dethman diaries, is actually a forgery. I simply copied what Percival had already written. The book is his, should he choose to allow publication of it to go forth."

Lord Hardy's voice cracked with disbelief. "Then why hasn't Percival spoken up before now? It's been nearly six months since you announced your plans to publish a new biography, Lady Goreham. It is simply inconceivable that the earl would have refrained from exposing you as a fraud before now."

Sir Hugo quietly threaded his way to the front of the room. Standing beside Lord Hardy, who smelled as if he'd taken his last bath six months previous, and then in a tub of brandy, he stared in amazement at Evelyn. Flanked by Miss Freemantle and Percival, she was the picture of equanimity. Her features were composed serenely, her posture erect yet relaxed.

Their eyes met, and a shock of poignant empathy connected them. Sir Hugo's breast ached for her. *Her pain was his.*

Miss Freemantle interrupted the thrum of whispered speculation. "I edited Lady Goreham's manuscript, and therefore I am aware of the fraud which was perpetrated. It is true; the book belongs to Percival Dethman, Earl of Goreham. I should only hope that he allows the manuscript to be published—under his name, of course."

The women turned to Percival whose expression registered surprise and uncertainty. He seemed tentative about agreeing to the publication of the biography, but Sir Hugo had no notion why, unless the book contained information that would put the Dethman reputation in disrepair.

He thought he saw a twinkle in Lady Goreham's eyes as she stared at her stepson.

Percival cleared his throat. "I do not know—"

Suddenly enlightened, Sir Hugo stepped forward. "Surely you want your work to be published, Lord Goreham."

The earl's face turned into an ugly scowl. He certainly couldn't admit that he didn't know what the manuscript contained, or what the Dethman diaries revealed, not after announcing to the Society that Evelyn was a fraud, and that he was the true author of the book in question.

"Stay out of this, Sir Hugo," the earl snarled.

"I'm afraid that's impossible, Percival," the barrister replied smoothly. "You see, Sir Cuthbert told me all about your evil scheme to discredit the countess, and your plan to deprive her of her inheritance."

"I have contrived no such scheme to deprive the countess of anything! 'Tis her own indecorous behavior that has resulted in her forfeiting my father's bequests."

Through a clenched jaw, the barrister spoke in a low, threatening tone. "You are a liar, my lord."

A collective gasp was drawn by the group of scholars crowding the front of the room to get a better view of the main actors in this drama. Miss Freemantle wrapped her arms protectively around the countess's shoulders, and gaped at the two men verbally squaring off with one another.

Evelyn drew in a sharp breath, and said, "Hugo," on a soft exhale.

Lord Hardy muttered, "Someone bring me a strong drink."

Percival's beady eyes bulged; his face turned purple with rage as he clutched the lapels of his own coat, and rocked upward on his toes. "I had intended to spare my step-mother the embarrassment of announcing this publicly, Hugo. But, since you are determined to make a spectacle out of yourself, I shall have no choice but to meet your challenge. The truth of the matter is . . . are you sure you want me to go on, Hugo?"

"If you dare." The barrister stepped forward, fists clenched at his sides.

Donning a smug smile, Percival looked out at the curious faces turned toward him. "My father's will specified that Lady Goreham and her young sister Celeste would receive their inheritances, if, and only if, the countess remained unmarried, unattached and untouched during her period of mourning. That period has not yet ended."

Lady Goreham's eyes snapped, as she spoke. "Two more weeks, Percival!"

The earl replied in an oily manner, "Two weeks or two months, my lady—it doesn't make any difference at all.

The fact remains that you have been caught in a compromising situation with Sir Hugo Mansfield, and therefore you are ineligible to inherit under the conditions of my father's will.'

Whispers and gasps rippled through the crowd behind Sir Hugo. Lord Hardy shifted his weight from one foot to the other, nervously dabbing at the sweat on his forehead with a pocket square. The earl folded his arms across his chest and smirked, clearly pleased with himself for having finally ruined Lady Goreham's reputation, both as a scholar and as a woman.

She opened her mouth to defend herself, to protest the earl's slanderous accusation, then hesitated. Guilt assailed her, clutched at her heart and robbed her of the ability to speak. She hadn't met the barrister in the library, but she had allowed him to hold her in his arms, to kiss her, to whisper intimacies in her ear. Had someone overheard them? Had someone seen them?

And even if Percival hadn't any hard evidence of her fleeting encounter with Sir Hugo, wasn't she guilty enough in her thoughts? She'd certainly wanted the barrister to kiss her . . . truth be known, she'd wanted much more.

Watching Sir Hugo's face alter to an expression of sheer hatred, Evelyn felt the moment spin into eternity. A dizzying sense of unreality washed over her. Embarrassment and apprehension tied her stomach in knots as she realized the enormity of her situation: Percival had now publicly accused her of plagiarizing his manuscript, and he'd challenged her right to her inheritance, to boot.

She'd gambled everything, and lost.

And there was nothing anyone—least of all Sir Hugo—could do to help her.

Sir Hugo took a step forward. "I shall not allow you to cast aspersions on Lady Goreham's character. She has done nothing to deserve this calumny. Retract your slanderous remark, my lord, or I shall—"

"You shall do what, sir?" Percival spoke boldly, but his fluttering hands betrayed his fear.

Sir Hugo's calm demeanor and icy stare bespoke no such hesitation. "Or I shall be forced to call you out, Lord Goreham."

"Call me out?" Percival gulped, but under the scrutiny of his peers, seemed determined to meet the barrister's challenge. "Will you be my second, Hardy?"

The curly-headed man threw back his head, and drained his snifter of brandy. Thereby fortified, he exhaled and shuddered. "Frankly, I would rather dine well and drink some good wine, Percy. I would rather do almost anything than second you at a duel, as I have precious little experience in such matters."

Percival sputtered, "Don't be missish, Hardy! You can spare a few hours away from the gaming tables to lend me a hand."

"I shall have to sober up first." With that, Lord Hardy handed his empty glass to a servant.

"As for the terms of our duel," said Sir Hugo, "If I remain standing, Lord Goreham, then your objections to the countess's inheritance are to be withdrawn, and you must return the Dethman diaries to her possession."

"*If* you remain standing." Percival stroked his mustache. "Agreed."

"One shot only, my lord," Hugo suggested.

"Agreed," said the earl.

"I prefer swords," Sir Hugo said.

" 'Tis my prerogative as challenged to name the weapons. I prefer pistols," countered Percival.

Hugo nodded. Pistols it would be.

Evelyn's heart thundered. Now, what had she done? In addition to putting Sir Hugo and Celeste in harm's way, depriving her sister of a dowry and bringing scandal down on her own head, she was the cause of two men dueling. Should either die, and most likely one would, she would never forgive herself. As much as she hated Percival, she didn't want to see him with a bullet lodged in his brain.

As for Sir Hugo, the very thought of his being injured filled her with terror.

"No!" She wrested herself from Miss Freemantle's embrace, and stepped forward. "I will not allow it. See here, Percival, I shall relinquish my rights to the Dethman diaries. They are all yours, you already have possession of them. As for my inheritance, all I ask is that you give Celeste her dowry. Nothing for myself! God knows I have survived on my own wits before; I can do it again!"

"Hear, hear!" said Lord Hardy. When Percival shot him a malevolent look, the man cleared his throat and turned to his servant. "I'll have another. No use in sobering up too soon."

"Tomorrow morning at dawn." Sir Hugo named the place, an open field between Goswell and City Road.

In a voice reeking with bravado, Lord Goreham said, "I will be there."

"Christ on a raft!" Lord Hardy turned to the gawking onlookers, and said, "This meeting is over. Everyone, please clear out."

Tears welled up behind Evelyn's eyes, but her anger forestalled the shedding of them. Anger at herself for having caused such a debacle; anger at the two men whose masculine pride promised to kill one or both of them.

The Society dispersed, with Percival fleeing to another part of the house. The room had nearly emptied when she confronted Hugo.

"What sort of nonsense is this? A duel? You'll get yourself killed, Hugo. And for what?"

"For your honor, my lady," he replied softly.

"Don't you understand that my honor is not worth your risking your life?" she asked him, in a tone more brittle than she'd intended.

As his slate gaze scanned her gown, taking note no doubt of the fact she'd given up her widow's weeds, Evelyn's limbs tingled. The effect of his stare on her was more palpable than it had ever been; heat erupted in her most intimate places at the slightest demonstration of Sir Hugo's physical hunger for her. When his eyelids dropped, and his expression tightened, Evelyn experienced a spasm of discomfort in her chest. A gush of liquid fire in her loins. A need for which there was no antidote.

Miss Freemantle and Lord Hardy stood on the far side of the room, their heads together, talking in low tones.

Sir Hugo closed the distance between himself and Evelyn. For a moment, she thought he was going to sweep her into his arms, but he drew up short and took her hands in his. They stood toe to toe, their gazes locked. The air surrounding them thickened and crackled with tension.

"I love you, Evelyn." Sir Hugo's voice was hoarse, as if it had been clawed from his soul.

"Then do not engage Percival in a duel. I couldn't bear it if you were killed."

He grasped her arms, so tightly she winced. "Don't you understand, Evelyn? The blackguard had called you a fraud, and accused you of conducting yourself in an unseemly manner. Were I to turn my back on such effrontery, what kind of man would I be?"

"A live one."

A rueful grin twisted the corners of Sir Hugo's lips. "Celeste is at home, safe. She will be so happy to see you."

Evelyn nearly collapsed with relief. "Thank God!"

"And poor Sir Cuthbert . . . well, I will tell you all about that later. In the meantime, I must prepare for tomorrow's duel. I've no second, so I must attend to some business matters."

"You would concern yourself with business the night before a duel?"

"If I should die, my lady, everything I own will belong to you and Celeste. I shall prepare my will tonight so that there is no question of your being provided for."

Her head fell forward on his chest, and sobs racked

Evelyn's body. Sir Hugo's arms encircled her, drawing her near. She cried until there were no more tears, then she blew into the muslin square he held to her nose.

His chuckle warmed her heart. "There now. Don't cry. Your Celeste will be taken care of no matter what happens. And so shall you."

She could barely speak over the lump in her throat. "I've made such a mess of things!"

"No, you have not." She was surprised at the vehemence in his voice. "And I will not tolerate your flagellating yourself, Evelyn. You're a good woman, with a heart of gold and a limitless capacity to love. Why, you're the finest person I have ever met."

Then why was her soul so desolate? Why was her safe, ordered little world bursting apart at the seams?

He brushed tears from her upturned face, his fingers warming her flesh.

"I love you, Hugo. Please call off the duel."

"I cannot retract my gage."

"You would if you loved me."

He froze, his features hardening. Setting Evelyn at arm's length, he said, "I am not like you, Evelyn. There are limitations to my ability to love. You know so little about me, I wonder if you would not be horrified if you really knew me."

"Nothing you could say would frighten me away, Hugo."

He looked away, but held his tongue. A tense silence spun out while Evelyn stared at him, at the emotions boiling beneath the surface of his expression. At length, he looked at her, but his gaze was hooded, his tone remote. "Good night, Evelyn. I shall see you on the morrow."

With that, he pivoted on his boot and marched from the room, past Miss Louisa Freemantle who stood at the sideboard clinking her brandy glass to Lord Hardy's.

Bereft, Evelyn watched Hugo's retreating back. Then, she joined her friends at the sideboard.

"Care for a drink?" Hardy asked her.

With a dismissive gesture, she declined the snifter he offered her, reaching for the crystal decanter instead. Tipping it to her lips, she took a long drought. She set it down with a shudder, then met the frankly amazed gazes of both Louisa and the inebriated lordling.

"Come, Louisa," she said as the liquor burned her throat. "Celeste is at home, awaiting my return. And I must retire early this night. Because I fully intend to attend that duel in the morning."

"Oh, dear, you mustn't!" Hardy hiccupped violently, then clapped his hand over his mouth.

But, Evelyn had made up her mind. She was dragging Louisa out of the room by the hand even as Lord Hardy refilled his brandy glass.

The next morning dawned cold and gray. An icy drizzle dampened Evelyn's sour mood as she greeted Miss Freemantle.

"We're fit for Bedlam, both of us," Louisa muttered, as she closed the door of the rented post chaise behind her. Seated on the squabs opposite Evelyn, she frowned her displeasure and pulled her woolen coat more tightly about her. "What does one wear to a duel, anyway?"

"Grey wool is appropriate for us both, dear," replied Evelyn, after knocking on the ceiling to signal the driver to depart. She'd already told him that after picking up Miss Freemantle, they were heading toward the grassy field between City and Goswell Streets. Tossing a lap blanket to her friend, she added, "I am grateful you didn't wear black. I've had enough of mourning clothes myself, and I wouldn't want to give poor Hugo the impression we were skeptical about the outcome of this event."

Half an hour later, the carriage slowed to a halt at the intersection of two dirt roads. Light traffic at such an ungodly hour of the morning ensured that the Bow Street Runners would not be summoned to intervene in the duel—not until it was over, at least. If all went according to schedule, the encounter would be concluded before most of fashionable London was out of bed. Evelyn shuddered as she stepped from the carriage, convinced that in mere minutes, one or both of the duelists could be dead.

Louisa leapt from the equipage, and the two women walked the short distance to the two carriages parked just ahead. One was the Goreham rig which Sir Hugo borrowed when he departed Kent. The shiny black one, with four magnificent matching grays at the lead, and a blue and red family crest enameled on the door, belonged to Percival, the earl.

A strong northeasterly wind battered the ladies' woolen caps and whipped their gowns around their half-booted ankles. They walked past Percival's carriage, and paused at the door of Sir Hugo's. Evelyn had lifted her fist and was just about to rap her knuckles on shiny wood when the door opened.

Head ducked, he stood in the threshold. Evelyn's pulse skittered as their gazes locked. The solemn determination in Hugo's gaze frightened her. She'd never held any man in such high esteem. No man had ever risked his neck for her honor, or put himself out to help her. Her deceased husband's generosity had been no hardship to him, and had come with a multitude of conditions and contingencies. Sir Hugo's regard for her, his willingness to stand up for her, seemed unconditional.

Her heart leapt as his booted feet touched the ground. In snug buff-colored breeches, white lawn shirt and black coat, he was the epitome of masculine elegance. The cold, grey landscape faded to the background at the sight of him. Miss Freemantle's presence was suddenly insignificant. Wordlessly, Sir Hugo took Evelyn's gloved hands and held them in his own.

He drew her into his arms, and she pressed her cheek to his shoulder. She felt the thundering of his heart, the hard muscles of his chest, the strength of his tall, lean body. Then, he lifted her chin, brushing a callused thumb along her bottom lip. Evelyn clasped his wrist, pressing her face to his palm, allowing her tears to score his flesh.

They stood on the desolate roadside, mist swirling around them. Fortified by Hugo's silent strength, Evelyn lifted her gaze to his. His eyes were clear and shining, his broad forehead unlined. Evelyn cupped his clenched jaw, saw a muscle flinch beneath his clean-shaven skin. She knew his body was as tightly coiled as a cobra waiting to strike, yet he seemed calm and collected.

"Hugo." Her words were whispered on a breath. "Please, don't!"

"I must." He bent his head and kissed her gently on the cheek. "It is as much for me as it is for you, dear. If you cannot understand that, please forgive me."

"Forgive you? Oh, God—" Evelyn's voice broke. At length, through tortured efforts to fill her lungs, she managed, "I love you, Hugo."

For a moment, his body tensed. Then, Hugo grasped her shoulders, pressed his lips to hers and kissed her. Deeply. Urgently. His hunger suffused Evelyn with heat and passion. She wrapped her arms about his neck, and clung to him.

Their moment was shattered by Percival's emergence from his carriage. The earl's demeanor, when he leapt to the ground, was in sharp contrast to Hugo's serenity. As he snapped off his gloves, his hands fluttered like a ship's pennant. With mincing strides, he approached Sir Hugo.

Miss Freemantle appeared at Evelyn's side. Taking her arm, the dark-headed woman said, "Come, stand with me at the edge of the field."

Lord Hardy stumbled from Percival's carriage, a gleaming mahogany box in his arms. "Damned queer business this is," he muttered.

"Hardy couldn't walk a straight line if his life depended on it," remarked Evelyn, out of hearing from the men. "What kind of second is that?"

"Well, he isn't Hugo's second, so I wouldn't concern myself," was Miss Freemantle's arch reply.

"But he hasn't even retained the services of a barber or a surgeon. One of the men is bound to require medical care."

"Pray it isn't Hugo," Miss Freemantle said tightly.

The three men walked abreast to the center of the open field. Tucked in the intersection of two dirt roads, the dueling site was a square of trodden grass, a grazing area for cows and sheep, weather permitting. Now, framed on two sides by stands of white birch and maple, the field was a sloppy mess, muddy as a pigsty in places, slick with ice in others. By the time the men reached the center of the field, their knee-high boots were sloshed with mud, the heels caked with manure.

Arms linked, the ladies watched Lord Hardy open the box. Even from a distance, they could see the box's purple velvet lining, and the gleam of two matching Manton pistols made of rosewood and inlaid with silver. As Hardy was failing miserably in his duties as second, Sir Hugo and Lord Goreham each took a gun, and turned it over to test the weight in their hands.

Evelyn's agitation increased during the interminable time it took the men to measure and pour powder down the muzzles of their pistols, then insert balls and wadding, and tamp the ammunition down with ramrods.

Among the men, there was some discussion, most of which Evelyn and Louisa could not discern, concerning the rules of the duel. Hardy swayed precariously, and at one point, Sir Hugo grabbed his elbow to steady him. Then, Percival and Hugo stood back to back, aiming their pistols heavenward.

Lord Hardy backed away, his face toward the ladies. Evelyn thought he was as discomfited by the duel as she, but he had the benefit of alcohol to numb him to the horror of it. When he was a good ten paces away from the men, Hardy stood stock-still, and called out, "Twelve paces, men, then at my signal, you may turn and fire. God bless you both!''

He counted loudly as the two men paced toward opposite sides of the field. When they'd each taken twelve long strides, Hardy yelled, ''Fire!''

Both men pivoted, turning their bodies expertly so as to present the slenderest target to their opponent. Their arms swung up, their pistols leveled. A deafening volley of gunfire erupted, and powder blasts tainted the morning air with twin puffs of sooty clouds. Two thundering booms were answered by startled cries of birds in the forests surrounding the field . . .

As quickly as that, the duel was over.

Lord Goreham was spun around by the ball that grazed his shoulder.

Sir Hugo's breeches were no longer buff-colored, but stained bright with crimson. But he remained standing. Cursing, he tossed his pistol to the ground, and clutched at the wound in his thigh. Blood spurted through his fingers as he doubled over.

Evelyn raced toward him, skating on patches of ice, her arms windmilling. Miss Freemantle ran behind. Lord Goreham passed them both, running in the opposite direction and toward his carriage.

Lord Hardy shrieked. ''Percival, come back! You are breaking all codes of conduct by fleeing the dueling field!''

Lord Goreham screamed over his shoulder, as he scrambled into his rig. ''To hell with the rules, Hardy! Look what he's done—he's put a bullet in my shoulder!''

''The diaries!'' Hugo roared like a baited bull. ''Come back, Percival, you lying son of a—''

Evelyn flung herself at Hugo. White-faced, the barrister caught her in his arms, and kissed her roughly on the lips. She clung to his shoulders, begging him to let Percival escape. ''Leave him, Hugo! You are alive, that is all that matters!''

But, Hugo put her aside, and, half-limping, half-running,

made for the road. Just as he reached the edge of the dueling field, Goreham's carriage lurched forward. After executing a somewhat risky turn that set the rig headed straight for London, the driver whipped the mares mercilessly, and yelled, "Get up!" Ears laid flat, nostrils flared, the horses achieved a galloping pace in mere seconds.

Hardy came from behind panting, face mottled, beaver hat askew. "Damme! Where's he going? Ain't he forgetting about the terms of the duel? Who ever heard of leaving one's second on the field?"

"He hasn't forgotten," ground out Hugo, grimacing against the pain lancing his right thigh. Blood seeped through his fingers as he grasped his wound. He needed medical attention, urgently. But, something about his expression told Evelyn his own welfare was the last thing on his mind.

Blood stained her skirts as she walked beside Hugo, holding his arm. Walking stiffly to his rig, he leaned heavily on her shoulder. He pulled himself into the carriage with a sharp inhalation. Then, he threw himself on the leather squabs, leaned his head back, and yanked off his cravat. Lord Hardy and the ladies clambered in, and sat opposite. Evelyn and Miss Freemantle tied the cravat around Hugo's wound and knotted it tightly.

As the carriage jolted toward London, Hugo's face paled. He licked his lips, as if they were parched, and continually ran his hand over his perspiring forehead. Evelyn watched him, her concern growing. He needed a doctor; he needed to go to bed and stay there until his leg healed.

"Louisa, would it be an imposition—"

Her friend cut her off with a lifted hand. "Of course not. You cannot take him to Lincoln's Inn Fields, after all. Percival will return there eventually, and kill you both if he finds his enemy in the house, recovering from his wounds."

Lord Hardy, removing a silver flask from his waistcoat, interjected. "Excuse me, ladies. But, as a single man living alone in a house outfitted with enough servants to keep Prinny and *all* his women comfortable, I suggest you take Sir Hugo to my abode. There will be no embarrassing questions asked by your parents, Miss Freemantle. It is Miss Freemantle, isn't it?''

"You know it is," replied Louisa, blushing. "But, what about your obligation as a second to Lord Goreham?''

"I am quite sure my engagement as second is at an end. My duty as a gentleman now takes precedence. I never had any grudge against Sir Hugo anyway. Thought the whole thing insupportable, if you want the truth, and tried my best last night to persuade Percival to issue an apology.''

But when Evelyn knocked on the ceiling and told the driver to head toward Park Lane, Sir Hugo lifted his head. Cuffing her arm with a steel grip, he spoke in a raspy voice. "No! I don't intend to permit Percival to wriggle out of our bargain.''

"You're in no position to go chasing after that madman," Hardy argued, amazingly sensible considering his inebriation.

"If you try to force me into a sickbed, Hardy, I'll put a bullet in your shoulder, too!" After a moment, Sir Hugo added, "Where the devil do you think the little fiend has scuttled off to?''

Hardy hesitated. "I wish you hadn't asked me that. But, since you did, I'll tell you. He is going to the last place in the world he thinks you will follow! There, he will be safe to hide the diaries, or peruse them at his leisure. He explained it all to me as we rode out from London this morning.''

"Fine," Evelyn countered. "Then let him go.''

"Instruct the driver to go to Lincoln's Inn Fields first," Hugo told Hardy. "You and the ladies shall get out there, and wait for me.''

"And where are you intending to go, pray tell?" Evelyn asked.

"Where is he, Hardy?" Hugo asked, pinning a dark gaze on his friend.

The other man took a quick swig of brandy before answering. "He has gone to Widow Philpott's faro house. He boasted of what he knew about your . . . ah, past life. And he doesn't believe for a moment that you have the courage to pursue him there."

Did he have the courage?

Hugo took a long drink from the flask Hardy handed to him. The throbbing ache in his leg was nothing compared to the sharp pain in his chest. Lord Goreham's challenge immersed him in self-doubt. The earl knew Hugo had an addiction to gambling. Given his past proclivities for gambling hells and faro houses, it wasn't surprising that with a little detective work the earl had discovered Hugo's weakness.

And that was precisely why the successor earl had invited the barrister to Goreham Castle for a weekend of gambling. He'd meant to tempt Hugo into falling back into his old patterns. Perhaps he'd thought Hugo would be more likely to throw caution to the wind completely. If Hugo could be lured out of the self-imposed isolation he'd exiled himself to five years ago, he might not hesitate to act on his attraction to the countess.

Brandy scalded his throat; but Hugo's heart burned hotter. Percival had set the stage for both Evelyn's and Hugo's downfall. And now, the earl was tweaking his nose again. He'd taken refuge in the one place Hugo wouldn't dare to go, the one place that could truly be the ruin of him.

Lady Goreham sat beside him, her hand on his arm. Even with pain pulsating through his thigh, Hugo's body responded to the warmth of her leg pressed against his. He covered her hand with his, and turned his head to look at her.

"Why does Lord Goreham think you won't go to Widow Philpott's?" she asked. "I don't understand."

He wasn't certain he could explain it. He didn't dare try, not with Miss Freemantle and Lord Hardy staring curiously at him. When the carriage drew up to Lincoln's Inn Fields, Hugo and Lady Goreham remained in their seats while Miss Freemantle and Lord Hardy disembarked.

Louisa turned and peered into the compartment. "Aren't you coming, Evie?"

Lord Hardy said, "He needs a barber, for God's sake. Come on, Hugo, get out of there!"

"You two go inside. We'll be there in a moment," the countess said, reaching for the door. Slamming it in her friends' faces, she turned to Hugo, and pinned him with a leveling gaze.

"What the devil is going on here?" Her voice was low and throaty, raising the hairs on the back of Hugo's neck.

"That's no kind of talk for a lady," he replied, attempting a smile. Succeeding only in a wince, he took her hand in his.

For a long time, the two sat in silence, Evelyn's tension radiating around them. She wasn't going to get out of the carriage until he told her the truth, that much was certain. The countess wasn't the sort of lady who avoided unpleasant topics of conversation. On the contrary, judging from what he knew of her, Hugo deduced she was a very commanding woman. Capable and strong. His own weakness was bound to repulse her.

"Go inside, Evelyn," he implored quietly. "Just go inside and leave me alone."

Just as he feared, she said, "I will not." At length, she added, "Talk to me, Hugo."

His throat tightened. Words formed in his mind, but died on his lips. Avoiding the countess's gaze, Hugo clutched his hands in fists. He couldn't tell her, he wouldn't! What kind of fool told the woman he loved that he was unworthy of her? What kind of paper-skulled man divulged his greatest weakness to the one woman in all the world he wanted to hold him in high regard?

Her opinion meant more to him than anyone's. And if he told her why Percival had retreated to Widow Philpott's, her image of him would be shattered.

He'd rather push her away then expose his affliction. He'd rather reject her, than be rejected by her.

He looked her square in the eye. "Get out of this carriage, Evelyn. Get out, now! I don't want you here!"

She flinched. Slowly, she slid away from him on the squabs, then turned and reached for the door handle.

If he let her go, he'd never see her again. Their lives were crossroads that had finally intersected. If Evelyn stepped out of that carriage, they'd never meet again.

Her fingers grasped the handle, but her body froze.

Emotion welled up in Hugo's throat, choking him. There was so much he wanted to say, yet words failed him. And the fear of repulsing Evelyn panicked him.

She pushed down on the handle, shoving the door open. A cold chill snaked into the compartment as she bent her head. The driver's leather-gloved hand was visible through the crack in the open door. He reached up to assist the lady disembarking his rig.

"No! Don't go!" Half rising from his seat, Hugo reached out for Evelyn, clasping her elbow. Then, with a grunt, he released her and fell back onto the squabs. Hot searing pain shot through him. Lord Hardy was right, he needed a barber to dig out that bullet and suture his wound. Though the bleeding had abated, he felt weak and lightheaded.

She turned, and the door clicked shut behind her. Sliding on the leather cushion, she wrapped her arms around his chest, and pressed her body to his.

"I won't go, Hugo. But you must tell me why Percival went to Widow Philpott's. What secret are you hiding from me?"

Telling her was almost as painful as getting shot in the

thigh. "I haven't been there in five years. You see, I cannot go there. Nor can I set foot in any other gaming establishment, not without risking abject poverty, that is."

Her fingers traced a line bracketing his mouth. She waited in patient silence as he struggled to find the right words.

It was too late to dissemble, he thought, sighing. "My father was a gambler, and at a young age, I followed in his footsteps. As a youth, I squandered every farthing I earned, playing deep at faro and whist. I made it through Eton, studied law, then was called to the bar at Lincoln's Inn for one reason: I had an uncle who felt sorry for me and insisted on paying for my education. He knew better than to hand me the money directly, for I would have wagered every shilling of it. But, by the time I got my robes, I was spending every spare moment away from the courts in gambling hells."

"What about your father? Is he still alive?"

"Oh, no, drank himself to death and died a pauper. Afterwards, my uncle was generous to Mother and to my sisters. Lucky for them a male relation existed who didn't have the gambling fever." The memory of Hugo's failures renewed his self-doubt. Swallowing hard, he forced himself to keep talking. Now that he had begun, talking seemed to fill the emptiness gutting his soul. "I couldn't have supported them, not until I gave up the gambling."

"When was that?" Evelyn leaned closer to him, her perfume surrounding her like a fragrant halo.

"Five years ago," he replied dully. "I'd hit bottom, no doubt about it. I was a successful barrister, earning more than enough to maintain quite a luxurious style of living. But, I resided in a small apartment behind my office— still live there, as a matter of fact. But at least I have a sizeable amount of savings put away. I'm no longer in impecunious circumstances. That's one thing to be grateful for."

"Five years ago," Evelyn repeated. "Did your decision to cease gambling have anything to do with—"

He drew her hands to his chest, half-turning to face her. He needed to look into her eyes as he explained the rest. "Everything. I fell in love with you, Evelyn, that night at Widow Philpott's. I didn't know then that you'd gambled everything in order to win enough to support Celeste—"

"She was so sick," murmured Evelyn, clearly troubled by the memory of that fateful night.

"I only knew that you were courageous, and beautiful. That you were a woman unafraid to risk everything."

Her lips parted, and her breathing caught. "I made a bargain with an old man. An agreement to marry him in exchange for financial security. You must have been repulsed."

"I couldn't help you, Evelyn. Oh, God, how I wanted to! My pockets were let, and there wasn't a single living soul who'd have loaned me a pound. Not with my penchant for gambling, and my track record for losing. I was so far in dun territory, I thought I'd never get out. But, I did. After that night, I never returned."

"Never?"

He drew her gloved knuckles to his lips. "Never," he whispered against them. "But, I fight it every day, Evelyn. The urge to go back is strong. It has never gone away. I don't think it ever will."

She looked puzzled. "You've won, Hugo. Five years and you haven't set foot in a gambling hell. Surely, you've conquered your compulsion."

"How I wish it were that simple." Shaking his head, Hugo released her hands. "If I go to Widow Philpott's, I fear I might not be able to resist the compulsion. The smell of it is still in my nostrils, Evelyn. Even now, the thrill of winning—just the thought of it—sets my heart to racing."

"Then don't go!" Evelyn leaned toward him, her chin jutting in determination. "Just don't go, Hugo. The diaries are unimportant. I don't care about getting that manuscript published, not if it means your undoing."

"You've worked too hard to give up that easily, Evelyn. And I love you too much to sit here and refuse to fight for you." Struggling to his feet, Hugo rapped his knuckles on the trap door in the ceiling. When it opened, he instructed the driver to assist Evelyn out of the carriage, then drive him to Widow Philpott's.

As he'd expected, she protested. He practically had to shove her out the door. When she was gone, he fell back against the cushions with a groan. His leg ached, and his heart ached, and the thought of entering Widow Philpott's, with his mind as weak as his body, terrified him.

But, if he failed Evelyn—again—he wouldn't be able to live with himself.

Widow Philpott's house was unusually quiet, but then it wasn't even breakfast time, and any fashionable buck worth his salt was still in bed. Or, at the least, exercising his cattle on the dirt track that ran round Hyde Park.

The butler who took his coat, hat and gloves lifted his brows at the sight of Sir Hugo's bloody leg wound.

"Tell the Earl of Goreham that Sir Hugo Mansfield has requested his appearance."

"I'm sorry, sir. It is against our rules to divulge the identities of our patrons. I cannot say whether Lord Goreham is here, or not."

"Then tell Widow Philpott I am here. And if she doesn't see me now, I shall leave. But, I will return with a dozen Bow Street Runners who will, no doubt, be more interested than I in the identities of her clientele. Not to mention the validity of her license to operate a gaming establishment. I wonder if she will stand behind her perverted sense of ethics, then."

The butler's expression tightened as he turned and marched up the staircase, his bootsteps grating on the

marble. Within minutes, the ample figure of Widow Philpott materialized on the landing. She propped her fists
on her hips, and stared down at Sir Hugo.

"La! I never thought to see your face again. There's a
game of whist going on in the upstairs parlor. Come, Hugo,
you can still get in if you hurry."

"I didn't come here to play whist." But he felt the snap
of the cards in his fingers. Picturing a winning hand, Hugo
took a step forward.

She crooked her finger in a come-hither gesture, and
he ascended the staircase. On the third floor, they stood
in a marbled foyer, classical in style, with alcoves that show-
cased Roman statues and Greek urns on pedestals. There
were two doors leading into parlors opposite one another.
Leaning on the balustrade, Widow Philpott slanted Hugo
a temptress's look.

"Perhaps you'd rather try your luck at faro."

His mouth went dry. He hadn't played in five years.

"You always were a lucky man," the widow added.

He wasn't sure whether he imagined the sounds of dice
rolling, cards snapping, roulette wheels spinning—or
whether his brain was playing tricks on him. But, the desire
to throw his money on green baize, and to rub shoulders
with daring rakes who shared his love of the *thrill* of winning, came back to him in a fevered rush.

"I—I didn't come here to play faro." But, his fingers
itched to touch the markers, the coppers, and the chits. His
money burned in his pocket, while his heart thundered.

"Just one round, lovie." Widow Philpott turned and
headed toward one of the parlor doors. Pausing with her
hand on the knob, she said over her shoulder, "Lord
Goreham is in here, I believe. Weren't you asking about
him?"

He followed, uncertain whether he entered the room
of his own volition, or not. Stepping inside, he felt nostalgia
overwhelm him. Even at this hour, there was one table of

faro going, and one roulette wheel surrounded by gamblers. In London, the action never truly stopped.

At the far end of the room was the faro table. Five men surrounded it, not including the dealer who stood behind the shoe. Percival lifted his head, met Hugo's gaze and smiled.

With great pain, he limped toward the earl. As he crossed the room, Hugo was assaulted by the sounds and smells of the gambling parlor. He craved it, he wanted it. There was still a part of him that needed it, needed that excitement, that heady feeling of living on the edge, the thrill of winning, the excitement of huge risk-taking.

There were men in the room he recognized, who lifted their hands in greeting, or acknowledged his return with a nod. Inhaling deeply, Hugo realized he felt at home in Widow Philpott's house. In this atmosphere of constant excitement, he felt on top of the world. Winning cases was a mild pleasantry compared to the ecstasy of winning at faro.

He stood behind Percival, the pain in his leg diminishing. Strength flowed through his veins. His head cleared. He glanced at the cards showing in the shoe, then at the abacus beside the dealer, and mentally calculated his bet.

The dealer exposed his hidden card. Sir Hugo would have won, had he placed money on the table. The realization was intoxicating.

Percival turned, grinning. "Let's say we forget our differences for a moment. Come on, old boy, where's your blunt?"

Hugo reached beneath his waistcoat, and withdrew his purse.

"And don't be timid, Hugo. Wager tall, man!" Percival's laughter came in uncontrollable spasms.

Unlacing the strings, Hugo withdrew a paper and handed it to the earl. "I didn't come here to play faro," he repeated through clenched teeth.

The earl's features puckered in confusion as he stared

at the paper. It wasn't a pound note as he'd expected; rather, it was a page, yellowed and crinkled, covered in a flowing cursive hand, written in faded ink.

"What is this?" The earl's hands trembled as he read.

Sir Hugo ripped his gaze from the cards displayed on the green baize, and, wiping his hand over his sweat-covered brow, replied, "It is a page from your father's journal. Seems the old man kept a pretty accurate record of his doings when he was a wild roué. Lucky for you that he did. Otherwise, you might never have known who your true mother was."

As he read the words on the page, Percival's eyes widened. Crumpling the paper, he stared at Hugo. "Where in hell did you find that?"

"In the castle library. Pity you never took it upon yourself to investigate what is in there, Lord Goreham. Your family archives hold a myriad of interesting books, diaries, and ledgers. Not many families can boast of such a well-documented history."

"I'll kill you if you ever breathe a word—"

"That is your father's handwriting, is it not?'

Clutching the wadded paper in his hands, Percival held his fist beneath Sir Hugo's nose. "I'll ruin you—"

But the earl's threat was interrupted by Widow Philpott. Placing a hand on his sleeve, she said, "Would you boys like a private place to settle your argument? You're making my other guests nervous."

Percival turned a look of horror on the woman.

Sir Hugo smiled, despite the pain shooting through his leg. "Percival Dethman, Earl of Goreham, meet your mother, the Widow Letitia Philpott. You see, the earl's wife was barren. Don't look so shocked, Percy. You weren't the first son—your father had quite a few by-blows, it seems. But, you were the only child the countess was willing to take in as an infant, and raise as her own."

Tears welled in the widow's eyes. "You weren't ever meant to know," she whispered.

Hugo continued. "I'm sure the two of you have a lot of catching-up to do, and I don't intend to intrude on this poignant moment. However, I do have some business to conduct back at Lincoln's Inn Fields, and I would appreciate it, Percival, if you would hand over the Dethman diaries."

Lord Goreham's gaze swung from Widow Philpott to Hugo, then back again. "Mother?" he said in a squeaky voice. Then, apparently in a attempt to assume an air of nonchalance, he rose on his tiptoes. When he rocked on his heels, however, his knees buckled and he collapsed to the floor in a heap.

"My baby has fainted!" Widow Philpott accused Sir Hugo with a waggling index finger. "What have you done to my baby?"

"I have done him the veriest favor, madam," Hugo replied. "I have united mother and son. I do hope the two of you are happy."

And with that, Sir Hugo bent down, and plucked Percival off the floor by his lapels. Draping the earl's arm over his shoulder, he dragged him out of the room. Widow Philpott waddled nervously alongside, her hands flapping as insistently as her jaw.

Hugo knew the way to the bedroom. As he half-carried, half-dragged the earl down the steps, he was assailed by the memory of Lady Goreham's venture into that room. They'd both been so different then. She was brave, down on her luck and desperate. He was a penniless ne'er-do-well without an ounce of control over the demons that possessed him.

This time, Hugo entered that room without dread of being exposed. A prospering barrister with an iron will, he had nothing to be afraid of and everything to live for. He knew he wasn't cured of his affliction, but he also knew that he could resist the temptation to gamble.

Tossing Percival on the bed, he stood back and stared at the senseless man. Widow Philpott held a piece of harts-

horn beneath her son's nose. Slowly, the man roused.
His eyes blinked convulsively, then focused on Hugo and
widened.

"I have an offer to make to you," the barrister said,
shifting his weight to his uninjured leg. Licking his lips,
he tasted the sweat his fever produced. A wave of dizziness
washed over him, but he fought it off. "An offer which, I
vow, you will not be able to resist."

Chapter Twelve

Evelyn and Celeste had fallen into each other's arms in the entrance hall of the Goreham town house. Then, with Miss Freemantle, they sat at the breakfast table and shared a pot of tea and a plate of cold scones. After informing Celeste about the outcome of the duel, Evelyn listened with a sick stomach as her younger sister described the scene in the dungeon chamber when Sir Hugo tricked Sir Cuthbert into drinking the tainted tea.

Miss Freemantle shuddered. "And to think, I was developing a *tendre* for the man!"

"Better you should find out now what sort of louse he is," sympathized Evelyn. "I do hope that poison tea didn't make him fatally ill."

Celeste spoke around a cookie she'd popped in her mouth. "Sir Hugo said he'll only be sick a day or so. He said the poison was from ground castor seeds, but he didn't overdose Sir Cuthbert when he spilled some in the teapot."

Evelyn smiled at her sister. "And how did Sir Hugo, who is clearly now your hero, learn that Lord Goreham had made poison from castor seeds?"

"Cook told him that Lord Goreham had asked her for the seeds. Of course, she didn't know what Percival had in mind to do with them." Celeste chewed thoughtfully. "Hugo believes he entered your room through the secret passageway that afternoon."

"I would have heard the bookcase grating," Evelyn said.

Celeste shook her head. "Hugo thinks that Percival hid behind the screen before you entered your room that afternoon. He left us in the Great Hall, remember Evie? And he went upstairs before we did."

Louisa spoke up. "And we lay on your bed, drinking tea and laughing. It makes me shudder to think what that worm heard us say."

Evelyn supplied the rest. "Then, when Lou left, I fell asleep. At some point, I rang for Shipton to bring me tea. I drank some, and fell asleep again. Percival could have slipped out from behind the screen and put the poison in my tea then."

"He probably just walked out of the door after that, rather than risk waking you by leaving through the book-case," Louisa said. "No one was above stairs just then; all the guests were in the back parlor when Grumby ran down and said you were sick."

Evelyn shivered. "It gives me a chill to think that Percival had access to my room through that secret passageway. Obviously, it was the earl who ransacked my room, looking for the diaries."

"And tied me up and blindfolded me, when he thought the diaries might be in my room," added Celeste.

Miss Freemantle chuckled. "How foolish of him to think you would travel with the diaries. Did he think they were packed in your *portmanteau*? Or hidden in your hatbox?"

Shaking her head, Evelyn murmured, "I had no idea how much he detested me. Nor the lengths to which he would go in order to seize my inheritance from under me. Well, it doesn't matter now. I don't care if I never get a penny from my deceased husband's estate. And I don't mind at all if my manuscript never gets published."

"We tried our best to trick Percival into publishing it under his own name," inserted Miss Freemantle.

"Yes, but I suppose he has read the diaries by now, and discovered that they contain intelligence not especially flattering to his ancestors." Evelyn sighed. "It doesn't signify; what is important is that Celeste was returned to me, healthy as a horse, judging from the number of sweet cakes she's consumed."

Just then, the brass knocker on the front door sounded. The butler's voice was succeeded by footsteps slowly ascending the steps. Evelyn's heart skipped a beat when Sir Hugo limped into the parlor, his face ashen, his eyes glazed with fever.

In his arms, he carried two large leather-bound books, their pages yellowed, their bindings edged in gilt.

She leapt to her feet, and met him in the center of the room. Miss Freemantle and Celeste followed, taking the dusty volumes from Sir Hugo's arms and placing them on a refectory table.

"Come, sit on the sofa," Evelyn said, guiding Hugo into the front room, the room where she'd watched him from the window for five years as he crossed the grassy field to the Inns of Court. "Celeste, dash off a missive to Dr. Peeps, then send a footman to fetch him immediately. Tell the doctor it is an emergency, to come at once."

Celeste flew out of the room.

"Louisa, tell the maids to prepare the guest room. We'll need fresh towels, and hot water."

Louisa fled.

Watching Sir Hugo lower his body onto the sofa, Evelyn cringed. His injured leg was stiff, the bloody bandages wrapping his wound sorely in need of attention. His features were drawn tight, and a sheen of perspiration coated his broad forehead.

She sank onto the sofa, unable to keep her hands off

him. Running her hands along his shoulders, she felt the heat radiating off his body. "Come to bed, Hugo."

Racked by pain, he still managed to smile. "With you, countess?"

"Of course not. That would be *most unseemly.*" Her face burned. "On the other hand, I have already lost my inheritance because of my scandalous behavior."

His smile widened, then abruptly twisted in a grimace of pain. "On the contrary, your inheritance is secure, dear. And so is Celeste's. In addition, Lord Goreham intends to call a meeting of the London Society for the Study of the Tudor Monarchy, and publicly retract his scurrilous remarks concerning the authorship of the upcoming Henry VIII biography."

Evelyn's mouth fell open. "You must have been holding a pistol to his head, Hugo! What makes you think the earl will admit he is a liar?"

"He has no choice, not if he wants to maintain his title, his wealth and his position among the *ton.* You see, I did some research in the Goreham library of my own. And it seems your deceased husband was a meticulous diarist. Unfortunately, he documented the fact that Percival was his bastard son, not the result of his union with the former countess. Equally unfortunate is the fact that Percival has an older half-brother, also illegitimate, whom he's never met. Till today, he thought he was an only child."

"The older brother is the rightful heir, then, is that it?"

"I agreed that I would forget I'd ever seen the diary in question if Percival would agree to retract his statements and withdraw his opposition to your inheritance."

Evelyn's brow furrowed. "But what about the older brother? By keeping silent, aren't we conspiring to deprive that man of his rightful inheritance?"

"Old man Goreham's diary contained a wealth of information. Percival's brother has been dead ten years. I didn't tell the earl that part of the story. And he didn't ask."

"And who, may I ask, is Percival's mother?"

"Widow Philpott. She gave him up as a child to be raised by the countess. The former Lady Goreham was barren, it seems."

Evelyn gasped. "Oh, poor Percy."

"Now I have a question for you." Hugo's lips twisted.

"We can talk later, Hugo. You must go to bed. The doctor will be here soon."

He spoke in a rasping whisper. "What in the hell is in the famous Dethman diaries? I'm dying of curiosity!"

Evelyn was relieved when she heard the front door crash open. "Nothing that will alter history," she said quickly, as footsteps ascended the steps. "Except that Percival's direct ancestor, a Dethman who'd ingratiated himself to King Henry VIII, indulged in a longstanding affair with Catherine Howard, his fifth and youngest wife."

The doctor entered, while Celeste and Miss Freemantle hovered beneath the curtained partition that separated the breakfast parlor from the front drawing room.

Carrying a black leather bag, the doctor stood beside the sofa, smiling grimly. "I see you've lost a great deal of blood. Can you stand, sir? I want you in bed immediately."

Hugo held up his hand to forestall the man. "A few more moments, doctor. Alone. Please."

The doctor threw Evelyn a look of disapproval, but joined Miss Freemantle and Celeste.

Evelyn spoke quickly, eager to end her story so that Hugo could get to bed and receive the medical attention he needed. "Catherine Howard was Henry's youngest wife. Historians have long said that she played his game, but played too deeply. Her affairs, according to the history books, embarrassed the king, and offended his sense of masculinity."

"Foolish pride," Hugo murmured.

"The history books tell us that she was a loose woman who had liaisons with Culpepper and Denham," Evelyn went on. "But, the Dethman diaries chronicle a man's efforts to seduce her, to lure her into a scandalous affair that would cause her public ruin."

Hugo gazed at her, his eyes clouded. "You mean one of Percival's ancestors attempted to seduce Catherine Howard?"

"At the king's request, apparently," replied Evelyn. "He wanted to get rid of her, you understand. And after the bad publicity associated with his dismissal of his previous wives, he needed a good reason to end his marriage to Catherine."

"He couldn't afford . . . another divorce?"

"Precisely. So, he hired Dethman to seduce her, to trap her into committing treason. For which, of course, she lost her head."

Confusion mingled with the pain on Hugo's face.

Standing, Evelyn took his arm. "Come, sir. You must go to bed. The rest of the story is simple. Dethman wasn't successful in seducing Catherine Howard, but someone else was. Ultimately, the woman was hung for having affairs with Denham and Culpepper. God only knows whether the allegations against her were fabricated; perhaps they were real, perhaps not. At any rate, the Dethman diaries show how badly Henry wanted to be rid of his wife, and the lengths he was prepared to go to in order to see her disgraced.' "

The doctor assisted Hugo in getting to his feet. The barrister leaned heavily on the man's shoulder, then took a halting step. "There is one more thing I have to say to Evelyn before I pass out." His voice was thick, his words garbled.

Evelyn wrapped his other arm around her shoulders. It felt good to feel Hugo's weight against her body. She was strong enough that he could lean a little on her, too.

He dragged his injured leg behind him as he walked. At the staircase, he paused and looked at Evelyn.

"Just a little farther, Hugo. Can you make it?" she asked.

He swallowed hard, his gaze drunk with pain. "I love

you, Evelyn. If you will have me, I want to marry you. Can you love a man who cannot promise he will always be perfect?''

Hugo, Evelyn and the doctor ascended the stairs in laborious steps, while Celeste and Miss Freemantle stood at the landing and hugged one another in joy at Evelyn's good fortune.

At the top of the stairs, Evelyn, breathing hard from the exertion of helping her injured fiancé negotiate the steps, answered Hugo's question. "I will marry you, Hugo. When you are weak, I will be strong for you. And as for perfection, well . . . that sounds rather boring to me. I wouldn't want to change a thing about you.''

The barrister smiled. Life with Evelyn would bring many things, but boredom would never be among them. In his opinion, he had found the perfect woman.

ROMANCE FROM JO BEVERLY

LOOK FOR THESE REGENCY ROMANCES

ROMANCE FROM JANELLE TAYLOR

ANYTHING FOR LOVE   (0-8217-4992-7, $5.99)

DESTINY MINE   (0-8217-5185-9, $5.99)

CHASE THE WIND   (0-8217-4740-1, $5.99)

MIDNIGHT SECRETS   (0-8217-5280-4, $5.99)

MOONBEAMS AND MAGIC   (0-8217-0184-4, $5.99)

SWEET SAVAGE HEART   (0-8217-5276-6, $5.99)